THE BLACK BRICK

AN "INDIAN NATION" MYSTERY

JACK SPITTLER

BALBOA.PRESS
A DIVISION OF HAY HOUSE

Balboa Press books may be ordered through booksellers or by contacting:

Balboa Press
A Division of Hay House
1663 Liberty Drive
Bloomington, IN 47403
www.balboapress.com
844-682-1282

Print information available on the last page.

ISBN: 978-1-9822-7146-6 (sc)
ISBN: 978-1-9822-7147-3 (e)

Balboa Press rev. date: 09/16/2021

ACKNOWLEDGEMENTS

This work is for my anchor, my wife Maureen and for all my kids, grandkids and great grandkids, who inspired this effort and were my editors and sounding boards.

A special thanks to Michael Jecks, U.K. Author, teacher, lecturer and friend, for his initial guidance, encouragement.

CAST OF CHARACTERS – (ALPHABETICAL)

Jane "Candy" Barr – Atoka Casino Prostitute – 15 years old – (Non-Native American)

Richard "Rick" Blackhorse – Operations Mgr. Atoka Casino – Nephew of Sarah Blackhorse – (Comanche)

Sarah Blackhorse – Mac's secretary – cousin of Rachel Coyote – (Comanche)

Jim Coyote – Founder & Owner of Coyote Ice House & Nightclub – (Choctaw)

Rachel Coyote – Black Brick Gang middle person – Co-owner of Coyote Nightclub & Ice House – (Comanche)

Dutch Eagle – Brother of Myra "Honey" – Cousin of Josey Eagle – Owner of The Beer Shack – Uncle of Sgt. Johnnie Wolf – (Part German, part Creek)

Joseph "Josey" Eagle –Wrangler for Broken Bar Ranch – (Part Choctaw, part Cherokee)

Alessandro "Hoss" Fernandez – Professional Hit man – (Mexican)

Chief Mary Grey Eyes – Chief, Sac & Fox Nation – Stroud OK – (Sac & Fox)

Will "Lizard" Grant – Newest B.B.Gang member – (Sac & Fox)

Jack "Tres" Grant III – Officer with Sac & Fox Nation Police – Nephew of Chief Mary Grey Eyes – Friend of Lt. John Two Feathers and Jay Nation – (Sac & Fox)

Alma Butler Hedstrom – Financial Mgr. – Native American Wannabe – Owner of Broken Bar Ranch

Judge Freeman Hunter – Atoka County Judge – Atoka Okla. – (Choctaw)

Mrs. Louise Hunter – Judge Hunter's wife – (Choctaw)

Andrew (Andy) Jernigan – Asst. to the State Governor on Crime and Indian Affairs

James J. "Uncle Jay" Jones – Attorney – Jay's Uncle – Jan's Brother

Leonard (Lonnie) Justice – B.B.Gang member – "Doer" – Lineage unknown

Ona Little Bird & Naya Little Bird – New recruits assigned to Jay. Cousins – (Choctaw)

Major Clarence "Mac" McCall – Director, Okla. State Police, Dept. of Intertribal Affairs – - State & Indian Nation Liaison Force

Kaid Nashoba – Older brother of Luke Nashoba – Ex-Army Ranger – B.B.Gang member – (Chickasaw)

Luke Nashoba – Younger brother of Kaid Nashoba – Ex-Army Ranger – B.B.Gang member – (Chickasaw)

Indian "Jay" Nation – Liaison Officer, Okla. State Police, Dept. of Intertribal Affairs - State & Indian Nation Liaison Force

Jan Jones Nation – Jay's mom

Vito Palmisano – Mafia hit man. New Jersey mob family. – (Italian)

Sheriff Paul Parker – Sheriff Atoka County. (Comanche)

Lt. Ben Pushmataha – Deputy Chief, 2nd in command – Durant Okla. Tribal Police – (Choctaw)

Myra "Honey Smith" Quattlebaum – Good Friend of Victim Walter Washoe – (Part German part Creek)

Brick Storm – Escaped former leader of the B.B.Gang aka Chase Stormcloud – Lineage unknown

Chase Stormcloud – B.B.Gang Leader – aka Brick Storm – lineage unknown

Brittini "Britt" Thorpe – Special Case Investigator, F.B.I., Reporting directly to Dir.of FBI. – (Sac & Fox)

Lt. John Two Feathers – Assistant Director, Okla. State Police, Dept. of Intertribal Affairs - State & Indian Nation Liaison Force – (Choctaw}

Annabelle Washoe – Wife of Walter Washoe

Walter Washoe – Retired – Victim of Black Brick Gang. – (Choctaw) Eddie Whitecloud – F.B.I., Special Asst. to Director of FBI, & to Dir. Of Homeland Security – (Navajo)

Sgt. Johnnie Wolf – Senior Officer, Muscogee Creek Nation Lighthorse Tribal Police Muscogee Okla. – (Creek)

Blossom Wolf – Daughter of Sgt. Johnnie Wolf – (Muscogee/Creek)

Chief Bill Yellow Feather – Chief, Choctaw Nation – Supt. of Tribal Police – Durant, Okla. – (Choctaw)

OKLAHOMA

PROLOGUE

The Black Brick team had a "Mission". Their concept seemed clear and right. Lonnie Justice was the key to both their success and ultimately their downfall.

Born on a reservation to a well-respected family, Lonnie seemed "odd", early on. He ran away just before his 11th birthday. He was raised on the streets, sleeping under bridges, owning nothing but the clothes on his back and what he could steal. He had been in and out of jail, both juvenile and adult, since he was 10 years old. It was a matter of survival. It was the only life he knew. What probably kept him alive, was the good luck of being tall, muscular and mean. That and the fact that he had feelings for nothing or no one, except himself. At 12 years old, he stood nearly 6 feet tall. He looked 18.

He had taken his licks when he was that age, but no more. Now he had reached 6 foot 5. He took nothing from anybody. Except for the stuff he could take from others through intimidation or violence. The last guy he had beat up, had nearly died. With his long record, the Judge had given him an option. Prison or military enlistment. The Judge was convinced that a little military discipline might turn his life around. Lonnie chose Navy enlistment.

The story behind his forced enlistment, preceded him. Because of his record, his basic training was strictly supervised. They watched him like a hawk. He didn't mind. That was their problem. As long as nobody abused him or threatened him, he chose to leave all of them alone. In fact, being left completely alone, by everyone, was exactly what he preferred. All went well. He didn't have to worry about stealing or fighting for his food. He was provided free food, lodging and clothing. They even let him train in the one thing he enjoyed, Diesel mechanics.

He was assigned to a small supply ship. It was old and in constant need of repair. He liked spending all day in the dimly lit belly of the ship, working on the engines, pumps and various systems. The heat bothered others, but not Lonnie. He was used to it. He had never had any use for air conditioning. He worked alone, slept alone and ate alone. Perfect. Lonnie was "satisfied". Not happy, exactly. Happy was an emotion foreign to him. He was good with being just satisfied. Fate was soon to interrupt in both a vicious and fatal way.

CHAPTER ONE

**It is better to have less thunder in the mouth
and more lightning in the hand.**
(Apache proverb)

Lonnie had been at sea for only a few months. A couple of stops with shore leave had not interested him. He never left the ship. There was an exercise room aboard ship. He was a constant occupant of the weight room. This was the only thing he did when not either on duty or eating or sleeping. In a few months, he had grown into an even more muscular giant. Since he rarely spoke, even when spoken to, he was pretty much left alone. Most of the seamen were young, sociable and in Lonnie's opinion, not worthy of his interest or consideration. The few cases where one of them had tried to either converse or joke with him, were quickly dismissed with a steely-eyed stare, or a growl, or a menacing word or two. His reputation as a loner, spread.

Aboard any ship or probably in most any group of young men involved in any enterprise, there is usually at least one who feels it is his life's assignment to prove to others either how smart, how tough, or how funny he is so that he can gain the goodwill or admiration of others. One such "tough guy" took a personal dislike to Lonnie's demeanor and didn't hesitate to spread that opinion among the others.

Lonnie was aware of it but chose to ignore it. The "tough guy" had developed a buddy who was equally tough and equally obnoxious. There had been stories of how they had bullied their way to the status of "Bosses" who lorded it over the other seamen. Lonnie's history with "Bosses" was long and vicious. Things began to get seriously dangerous when the self-appointed "Bosses" decided that whatever they wanted to do aboard ship was subject to their own choice. In their minds, that meant everything. They never had to wait in line, they always chose to cut in at the head end. This included showers, mail call and food. When they decided to add the weight room to their list of "Us first" protocols, they met Lonnie.

When they walked in, there was immediate quiet. Lonnie was laying on a bench, pumping a three hundred pound barbell. They strolled over to his bench. Lonnie continued pumping iron.

"Hey you, I need this weight rack, right now. You've been on it long enough".

Lonnie kept pumping iron.

"Hey you. You deaf or something?"

Lonnie kept pumping, "The name's Lonnie."

"I don't think so. I think it must be Looney. Move out!"

Lonnie re-racked the bar of weights, got up and stared at Boss#1.

"I said move out. Now, Looney."

Lonnie's first punch caught the man right in the solar plexus, which left him staggered and breathless. At the same time, Lonnie felt a hard blow to his side.

He turned to see Boss #2 aiming a punch at his face. Lonnie caught the fist and with one hand, crushed the man's hand.

This guy didn't have time to howl. Lonnie wrapped his big arm around the man's neck and with a jerk broke his neck. He dropped lifeless to the deck. Lonnie felt a searing pain to his back as Boss #1 had recovered enough to grab a weight bar and slammed it across Lonnie's back. Lonnie grabbed the bar, ripped it from the Boss's hand and hammered it twice into the man's face. He was dead before he hit the deck.

There was a shocked silence in the weight room. The other seamen stood and stared. Then one broke and ran out to alert Security. Lonnie simply returned to the bench and began pumping iron again, as if nothing had happened. As the room emptied, two guards entered with pistols drawn, cuffed Lonnie and took him to a cell in the Brig which normally was only occupied by drunken sailors returning from shore leave, or an occasional fist fight pair. Lonnie was kept in isolation there until they reached home port where he was locked away in the Naval Prison, on base, in San Diego.

He had been appointed a defense council who tried to interview him for his own defense, but Lonnie refused to cooperate. In his mind, he had done nothing wrong. When his trial began, Lonnie would only say that it was just a matter of self-defense. There were several witnesses to the incident. All agreed that Lonnie had been provoked. They also agreed that Lonnie threw the first punch.

Based on Lonnie's clean Navy record, but also noting the circumstance of his forced enlistment and prior legal problems, the Judge ruled that he must undergo a series of psychiatric tests to determine his mental state and the appropriate considerations for his sentencing. After review by three separate psychiatrists, there was no question about his condition. Lonnie was genuinely convinced that his actions were appropriate and under the circumstances, faced with a similar situation, he would likely respond in the same way. He had no remorse for what had happened and no feeling of guilt.

He was ruled a sociopath who should be imprisoned in a facility for the criminally insane, for the rest of his natural life. The sentence was simply shrugged at by Lonnie. Free food, free lodging, free clothing and no need to work. Except to work on some way to escape.

Things move slowly in the military judicial system. First there were appeals, then finally, the date was set for his sentence to be initiated. All who were involved, the jailers, guards, and cell mates, even the defense councils were anxious to get the whole matter behind them. Lonnie had been a dark and silent threat to all concerned.

He spoke to no one after the trial. Not even to the psychiatrists. The most that they could get was either a "yes" or a "no" or occasionally an "I don't know". He ate, slept and continued whatever kind of exercise he could come up with that could be done in his cell. His departure was eagerly anticipated.

On the appointed day, 6 guards, 2 unarmed and 4 armed, were

dispatched to move him to an awaiting prison van where 7 prisoners were already in place, awaiting the final prisoner. It was a typical, breathlessly hot summer day. The guards were sweating profusely. The prisoners were soaked with sweat and complaining. Lonnie only grinned. The heat suited him. It helped him think. His mind was racing. He had thought of nothing else for months, but escape. The launch was at hand.

The plan really wasn't much of a plan. Lonnie understood that. In his mind, whatever he lacked in planning, he more than made up for in strength and determination. He was not going to jail again. Not now. Not ever. It was going to be a long, three day drive to the Federal prison and that was helpful to his plan. He knew there had to be a lot of stops along the way.

The transport van had no toilets, just seats and eyebolts set between their knees to chain prisoners to their seats. The two front seats, for the guards, were screened-off from the prisoners. The back section had four seats down each side with an aisle in the middle. He was seated in the first spot next to the van's back door. There were seven other prisoners similarly chained. No one spoke. No one made eye contact with him. Apparently his reputation had been leaked. That was O.K. He didn't need them anyway.

Security issues had ruled out flying. Driving boiled down to three legs. The plan was, Leg 1 from San Diego to the only Maximum Security facility in New Mexico. This would be the longest day. About 13 hours, plus stops.

Leg 2 was from Santa Fe to Ft. Worth Naval Air Station in Texas, another 10 hour drive plus stops. Special security guards and quarters had been arranged there.

Leg 3, the final one, was from Fort Worth to the U.S. Disciplinary Barracks in Fort Leavenworth Kansas, about an 8 hour drive plus stops. It was the Military's highest maximum security facility. That final leg took Lonnie right through Oklahoma. Home!

The first two days were long and hot, but were accomplished without incident. Day three was "the day".

The first stop was uneventful. Just some breakfast, which was served with them remaining in the van. There was just enough slack in their chains to allow them to eat. He had been working on his eyebolt ever since they left San Diego. He had managed to bend it over and back and had worked hard at bending it back and forth until it was bending easily. Then they stopped for lunch.

The guards never check eyebolts. The bolts were a little over a quarter inch steel. Stupid, he thought to himself.

"Should'a been over a half inch. Prob'ly will be after today".

After lunch, they drove for about an hour and then the guys began to holler for a pit stop. The guards took them, one at a time, according to protocol, into a truck stop to relieve themselves. They took Lonnie last. He had always been a lamb. He even said "yes sir" and "no sir" to the guards, something he had not said to any of his guards up to now. He could see the guards getting more relaxed.

The stench of body odor hung in the air. The Van's air conditioning was not adequate for ten men in such close quarters.

The two guards had vents that let them direct a little cool air directly into their faces and they had windows that opened. The prisoners had nothing except for a few small roof vents which helped very little. The windows were welded shut and barred to prevent opening.

With clear skies, and a temperature in the high nineties and climbing, the prisoner's shirts were already dark with sweat.

"At least it's not raining", thought Lonnie, "hot ain't too bad, but hot and humid sucks."

After lunch, they drove for another hour and then the guys began to holler again for a pit stop. They stopped at another truck stop to repeat the restroom process. The guards were unaware that Lonnie had managed to bend the eyebolt back and forth until it fell victim to metal fatigue and separated. If the other prisoners noticed, they didn't show it.

When the guard climbed in to get the first prisoner, the second guard stood in the doorway to help the prisoners down. In a quick move, Lonnie wrapped his hand shackle chain around the second guard's neck, pulled him into the van just far enough to get a hold on his head and twisted his neck. It made a loud crack and he slid back to the street.

The first guard had turned, in disbelief and froze. Bad mistake. Lonnie could only be called "huge". Well over 6 feet tall and over 250 pounds and quick as a cobra, and as deadly. Lonnie was on him in a flash and after pulling him to the floor, proceeded to hammer him in the face, using his cuffs like a brass knuckle. The guard went limp.

Lonnie searched his pockets and retrieved the cuff key and the van keys. After unlocking himself, he pulled the guard laying outside, back into the aisle.

"Hey man, unlock us. Hurry". One prisoner yelled.

Lonnie thought it was funny and he laughed.

"Sure". Lonnie said. "And have cops and helicopters all over us in a few minutes. No, this is a one-man show."

He stepped out, closed the back door and got into the driver's seat. The prisoners were now screaming, cursing and threatening him with everything they could think of. He only smiled. Next stop, a special place in Oklahoma.

CHAPTER TWO

**It does not require many words
to speak the truth.**
(Chief Joseph   Nez-Perce)

Jay Nation firmly believed that people's names often have an incredible influence on their struggles and their successes in life. At least, it had always seemed so to him. His friends called him Jay. Not because it was his real name nor his nickname. He wished it were the case. No, he named himself Jay to avoid any unpleasantness in his life, like he had during his first year at Spring Street Elementary. That was a long, long time ago. But he remembered it as if it were yesterday.

He went to a shrink for a while to see if his feelings about his name were some sort of mental or emotional aberration. After several months that were draining, both physically and emotionally and seemed to be a tremendous waste of time, he concluded that the shrink was more confused about it than he was. So he quit going. He was not a quitter, normally, but he *was* a hard-headed German/American and he knew when enough was enough.

His name was definitely an aberration. It seems that his parents, being addicted to the Big Screen, wanted to name him something that expressed their devotion to the movies. His parents had decided to name him "Indiana". They had seen the movie Indiana Jones a number of times and there was never any question about the name of their first child. But then, Fate interceded and the hospital forgot the "a" on the end of his name on the Birth Certificate and his parents didn't catch the error. So, he entered life with the name "Indian".

His mom and dad often said that it was destiny, because it indicated their deepest social belief. You see, they spent a lot of years serving as missionaries on an Indian Reservation in Oklahoma. Jay often wondered if they didn't love the people they dedicated all their time to, more than they did him. Make no mistake, his time on the reservation was happy, productive, and he learned more than he probably ever would have in some other location. The people were great. Not wealthy in a monetary sense, but unbelievably wealthy in honor, courage, heritage and resourcefulness. He still visited several of them, whenever time permitted.

But back to his name. His parents loved the Indians they worked with and since his dad's last name was "Nation", Jay became "Indian Nation". No middle initial. His parents said middle initials or middle names were just a waste of time and people didn't use them anyway. Not true!

He was convinced that a person's name mysteriously impacted their life. For example, why is it that so many college professors and bank presidents and others, always focus on their middle names. M. James Barrett, F. James Loprest, J. Paul Getty. How about the Financial Wizard - T. Rowe Price? Of course, he realized that it was their education and expertise that made them what they are, but he'd bet they started life as Mike, Frank, John and Tom! Not him. He started life as "Indian Nation". Now, you wouldn't think that there would be any real confusion involved in that. But you would be wrong. Here is an actual example from Jay's early childhood, dealing with a reporter taking interviews for an article he was writing. Such interviews were a frequent occurrence on the reservation.

"Where do you live son?"

"Here at the Indian Nation."

"What do your parents do here?"

"They serve the Indian Nation."

"What is your name?"

"Indian Nation."

"No son, I said what is *your* name?"

"Indian Nation".

"Son, do you have some sort of hearing problem?"

"No sir, I don't think so."

"Then tell me your name."

"Indian Nation."

… "Perhaps it might be better if I could speak to your parents,"

His parents called him "Indy" while he was living at home. He didn't really care much for it, so by the 6th grade, he was "Jay" to his friends.

He had an Uncle named Jay who he liked a lot. Uncle Jay never called him anything but "Indiana". And after a while, he even got his Uncle to start calling him "Jay". But, his parents? No way. It was always "INDIAN" or "Indy". He left home as soon as he hit 18.

Life after that was exciting. He moved in with his uncle and learned many things about life and he took up farming. When he was 21, Uncle Jay got him a job with the Sac & Fox Reservation Police in Stroud, OK. and he loved it. At the time, he had no idea that police work sometimes involves being inflicted with physical injury, kidnapping, etcetera. But reality soon changed all of that.

CHAPTER THREE

**We will be known forever
by the tracks we leave.**
(Dakota proverb)

"All Points Bulletin. Be on the lookout for a black 10 passenger prison transport van. Last seen heading north toward the Oklahoma/Texas border on Indian Nation Turnpike near Hugo Oklahoma. Suspect is armed and dangerous and has been judged Criminally Insane. Do not apprehend without heavy backup. Following is all information concerning this escaped prisoner."

"Wow, guys, look at this." Said an officer, excitedly.

The bulletin quickly passed around the office in the Muscogee/Creek Tribal Police H.Q. and was an instant motivator. Every officer was thinking about how such an arrest would be a feather in their cap and a great career helper. One officer, in particular, was more than interested. He jumped up and went outside to make a cell phone call to his confidential contact.

"Did you see the stuff on that escaped lunatic?"

"Yes I did," the contact answered.

"What do you think?'

"I think he may be exactly the man I am looking for, if we can get our hands on him before the others do."

"Of course, every mother's son in Oklahoma is going to be pulling out all the stops to be the one making the big pinch."

"Right, but our interest is different. We want the man, not the 'pinch'. I have already started calling in favors that local informants owe me. You do the same."

"No problem."

"I want anything you have on him, as soon as you have it. This guy may be good and he might not."

"I gotcha. But you will never know unless I can find him first."

"Exactly. And I appreciate your heads-up on this one."

"Look, I owe you. I'm just sending you the rap sheets you asked for. I don't know why you want them and I don't want to know. You helped me when I had nowhere else to go. So, I need to do you whatever favors I can. But that's it"!

"How is she doing, by the way?"

"The Chemo seems to be working, but she still has a long way to go. Without your help, she probably would be dead by now."

"She is strong, friend."

"Yeah, but she's only 10. I don't want to lose her like I lost her mom."

"Hang in there guy. And keep me informed on the thing we talked about."

It didn't take long. In less than twenty four hours, the trail began to narrow. Possible hiding places, relatives, former friends or cell mates, all of which made for an interesting web of possibilities. He passed on every bit of information he received, as he had promised. Out of the myriad of possibilities, one became more and more favored. This tip had come straight to him. An informant had it on good authority that there was a relative in Oklahoma, on the Choctaw reservation, that could be the most likely destination. Also, this relative lived alone and she was the only person to visit Lonnie while he was in the Navy holding cell. This last bit he quickly passed on to his contact, as promised.

CHAPTER FOUR

**Humility provides clarity, where
Arrogance makes a cloud. Do not be led by
someone whose judgement and actions are
clouded by arrogance.**
(Lakota saying)

C hase Stormcloud's cell phone buzzed.

"Chase".

"How many times do I have to tell you, no names on these phone calls?"

"Sorry."

"Prove it by making me never have to mention it again."

"Yes, understood."

"Are your guys ready to roll?"

"Always."

"I am having a special weapon delivered to you early this afternoon. Familiarize yourself with it and call me when you can pinpoint a target at 10 to 15 yards. I expect that call this afternoon."

"That's fine. The target and location?"

"You'll get that when I know you're ready."

The package was delivered a short time later. It took Chase an hour to become familiar and accurate with the weapon. It was the first time he had ever handled a tranquilizer gun. He had seen a few of them in his past life in law enforcement, but had never held or fired one.

Chase made his call.

"O.K. Boss, preparation complete. I can hit a two inch circle at 15 yards. Bright sun today, but a night shot shouldn't be any harder at that range."

"O.K. Now listen carefully. The target is a virtual giant. He is tall, muscular and not nearly as smart as he is vicious. You are to take no chances. Find him, don't get too close, hit him with the tranquilizer dart and if he doesn't go down, hard, give him a second shot."

"Wouldn't that kill him?"

"I don't pay you to question my orders. Do it and keep me informed. Once he is knocked out, call me for instructions. And take some heavy logging chains and shackles to lock his hands to his ankles."

"O.K. Where and when?"

"The *when*, is now. The *where* is somewhere around Durant Oklahoma. Call me when you are in the area and I will give you the exact location."

"Got it. On the way."

As they prepared to go, Chase thought to himself, "With two openings on the team, this might be a good opportunity to fill the most critical one. Provided we can catch this guy and get him 'flipped' to the cause."

So far, training and marksmanship had consumed most of his time. It was exciting to think that they were getting very close to being fully operational. The boss said there were already several "missions" lined up. The stand-by pay was O.K., but once operational, the bonuses for a clean job were more than Chase could ever have made on the outside. Plus, they would be getting rid of "bad actors" who made it hard for the good guys to do their jobs. Some jerks had a knack for wiggling out of any consequences for their actions. Pay-offs, legal mumbo-jumbo, holes in the Miranda and search warrant mechanisms, bleeding heart judges and out-and-out political "deals", made it impossible to stop corruption and bribery and made a joke of the judicial system, in his opinion. *They* were the solution. *They* were the true soldiers in the war on crime. *They* were "Vigilantes".

Chase called. "O.K. boss we are in Durant."

"I'm texting you the address. It's just a few miles north of Durant. Stay out of sight until its dark. The owner is an older lady who lives alone. The target is most likely already there."

"If he's there, how do you prefer we take him, crash-in or lure him out?"

"Set the house on fire."

"… Understood."

After locating the address, Chase parked at a distance and then stationed his team behind an old barn on an adjacent property about 100 yards from the targeted house. There was a tractor parked inside with a full gas tank. That saved them having to siphon gas from their vehicle. They began filling buckets.

"O.K. guys, listen up. One bucket all over the back door and surrounding frame. I will handle that one. One bucket full on each side of the house. I didn't see any side doors, but check anyway. If you find one, coat it, if not, coat the side anyway. Then light it up. Leave the front clear. It's starting to get dark. We should be 'Go' in about an hour. Till then, rest, hydrate, pit stop if needed and make sure your lighters work. We only have one shot at this."

The hour passed quickly. There were lights on in the downstairs windows. Dark still on the upper floors. Chase broke the silence.

"I see shadows moving around behind the curtains. More than one. Since she lives alone, he is definitely there. I am going to update the boss and then we will go."

After calling in the update, Chase checked his lighter again, checked his gun and looked at his watch.

"O.K. guys let's go."

The team climbed over a rail fence and quietly approached the rear of the house. With hand signals, Chase split them up. He counted to ten to give them time to get in place, then he sloshed gasoline all over the door and frame, lit it, grabbed his rifle and headed around the house, passing the flaming side and stopping at the front corner. He rested his rifle on the porch railing and pointed it toward the front door and waited.

Nothing was happening. He could hear the fire crackling, the gasoline had done its job, but there was no noise or movement from inside the house. Something was wrong.

Chase was debating what to do next when the front door burst open. Coming out of the light into the dark is temporarily blinding. Chase had counted on that. But in this case, it didn't help the team because the giant standing in the doorway had his arms wrapped around a shorter female who he was using as a shield and his gun was pressed to the back of her head. She was crying. Screaming.

"Help me. Help me."

"Shut up!" Lonnie hollered. "Back off, whoever you are, or I'll put a hole in her head, so help me."

He began to slowly move across the porch.

"Help me, please." She moaned.

"Shut up", he said.

She continued to struggle ineffectively. Chase knew he had only one option. In cases like this, a good cop would always stand down.

"Stand down". Chase shouted.

The giant continued slowly toward the edge of the porch.

"Everybody, stand down." Chase shouted again.

This is what any good cop would do because shooting the guy might cause him to have a reflex that would fire the gun anyway, killing his captive. But Chase was not a good cop. He was a soldier on a mission. The lady would just have to be "collateral damage".

Chase put the dart into the back of the giant's right shoulder. His reflex did make him fire, but it also caused his arm to jerk away and the shot missed. The giant dropped like a rock. A second dart was unnecessary.

The lady collapsed, still sobbing.

"Who are you?" the lady said, still crying.

"C.I.A." Chase lied. "And if you say a word about this to anyone, you will end up in federal prison. You got that?"

"Yes sir."

They shackled and chained the giant. It took all three of them to get him into their vehicle. Chase turned toward the lady who was crying as she watched her home burn.

"Not one word."

Chase called his boss. "Mission accomplished."

"Good man."

"What do you want us to do with him?"

"Is he hurt?"

"No."

"Blind fold him, gag him, and leave him chained. Take him to your place. Let me know when you get there."

"Will do."

He was still asleep, or seemed to be, when they got back to the old barn. They chained him to a 4 inch steel pipe from the well pump. They left him gagged and blindfolded and his hands shackled to his ankles. Chase called in. It was now in the wee hours.

"Is he still asleep?"

"Yes. Or he's playing possum."

"No problem either way. Here is what I want you to do. Oh, and when we're done, tell your guys they did good. I am sending you all a nice bonus."

"Fine. Thanks."

After getting his instructions, Chase told the guys to take turns keeping watch. Then they settled in to get some sleep. Around daylight, they were all up. They had breakfast. No one spoke. They sat waiting, glancing at Chase. When he finished eating he checked his watch and rose from his seat.

"O.K. guys, the boss said 'good job' and that we will be getting a bonus. Here is what we do now. Everybody in the car, we are going for a ride."

"What about the big dude?" Asked the gang member named Kaid.

"We'll just leave him here. I want to spend a couple of hours telling you about him. You'll be glad I did, if it all works out."

As they turned south on the main road, they didn't notice a big four-door sedan turning into the barn road that they had just left.

CHAPTER FIVE

Love your life. Perfect your life.
Beautify all the things in your life.
(Chief Tecumseh   Shawnee)

I t didn't take long for Jay to fit right in to the team at Stroud Police. And he continued his education with night school, financed by Uncle Jay who was a fairly successful attorney working primarily with Native Americans.

Most of his time was just driving around, patrolling. For the first couple of years, the hardest part of his job was usually on Friday nights and Saturday nights. There were several night clubs and just plain "dives" around the borders of the reservation. He couldn't do anything off-reservation, but there were always plenty of speeders, drunk drivers, fist fights and domestic abuse issues to keep him busy.

Liquor was not sold on the reservation, but there was plenty around. Sometimes, the economic hardships on the reservation were so severe that he heard tales of a mother feeding her child newspaper, just to have something on his stomach. He did what he could to help, but he couldn't do much. Most of the families were hard working and decent. "Salt of the Earth" as his Uncle Jay used to say. For the habitual drinkers, he let them sleep it off on a cot in the jailhouse and then turned them out after they sobered up. There were only a few occasional incidents where a drunk husband would take out his frustration on his family. Fortunately, these were not frequent and usually not severe.

He had the respect of many residents and he respected them as well. Sometimes when there is no money and only a little food in the house, a little respect goes a long way.

Jay was 26 years old when he finished night school. He was from German/Scotch-Irish ancestors (yeah, they are Scots and Scotch is a drink, but for over 300 years it has been "Scotch-Irish". Old habits are hard broke). He was not what you would call handsome, but he was told by some friendly females that he looked "Cute". Whatever that means. Babies are cute. Pets are cute. He wasn't sure he wanted to brag about being a 26 year old who was "Cute". Anyway, he stood about 5' 9" with a shock of light brown hair that had always been impossible to control, so he just let it grow however it wanted. His eyes were light green and matched neither his mother's nor his father's eye color. That still was a puzzler to him.

He probably weighed 170 lb. after a big meal, and it was nearly all muscle. High school had toughened him up, early on. When he was about 13, he began to really bloom. He put on weight, grew a few inches and got involved with the school wrestling team. He was school wrestling champ for his last two years and qualified for State in his senior year.

He did extremely well at State and had the State Championship in sight. Then, the coach explained that he would soon see his name in the headlines and that it would also be engraved on the first place trophy for all to see. He said that trophies went to the first three places and Jay would probably be first. Coach was jubilant. He spread his hands in the air and said, "First Place, Indian Nation".

Jay was understandably concerned about that. Most everyone knew him as "Jay". His high school plaques had all said "Jay Nation". He asked his coach if it could just say "Jay Nation". But the response was "No." It had to be his legal name. No way! He could not have that happen. He ended up placing a solid fourth place, right where he planned to be.

He worked hard to keep fit. He didn't lift weights, but he was a jogger and when he was not working or jogging, he worked hard to take care of his mini-ranch/farm and do all of the tending of a few cows, chickens and raising most of the vegetables that he ate. A lot of which he gave to folks who he knew needed the help. You could say that he was "an O.K. guy". He dated, went to church when he was not on Sunday duty, and did his best to live up to Uncle Jay's example.

Uncle Jay had helped him buy his little mini-ranch near Stroud Oklahoma, between Tulsa and Oklahoma City and Jay guessed that Uncle Jay was the closest thing he had to a father, since his dad passed away when he was about 20 years old. Mom, Jan, still lived in the old house. He had tried to get her to move to his house, but she liked her independence and still managed quite well on her own. Jay still mowed her lawn on Sundays whenever it needed it and her Sunday mid-day dinners, were to die for.

Would he ever get married? He didn't know. Maybe. But if he did, it would have to be someone really special.

Not because he was that picky, but he learned a lot about love and marriage and family, from his folks and Uncle Jay. He knew if he could find someone who could tolerate his job, its craziness and sometimes demanding hours and the occasional risks, then he would know at "Hello" that this was the right one for him. Until then, dating was OK. For right now, he figured life didn't get much better than this.

CHAPTER SIX

Inside of me there are two dogs. One is mean and evil and the other is good, and they fight each other all the time. When asked which one wins I answer, The one I feed the most.
(Chief Red Cloud   Lakota)

J ay soon found that his official name could also draw him some *welcome* attention. And *that* resulted in a job offer. He was interviewed and hired by the State to work in a newly created branch of the State Police having to do with liaison between State and the local Indian Nation Police Departments. His title was Liaison Officer, but his actual duties consisted of being a detective to backup both the State and local cops in matters that were unclear about jurisdiction.

They basically wrote their own rules about what they were responsible for. This went on for nearly a year, off and on while they built interagency relationships. You would have to say that they were sorely needed and greatly appreciated by both entities they served. There were about 20 of them, counting detectives, administration, legal and forensics. That doesn't sound like much. However, it was a real culture shock for Jay, having been one of only 5 total on the Stroud force.

One thing that did change, was the quantity and the magnitude of seriousness of the crimes he got involved with. In his years at Stroud he worked on only one murder case and it was a slam-dunk, since the husband immediately admitted to the crime.

With his new job and office in a brand new, state-of-the-art, building in Oklahoma City, the cases were more frequent. Constant, in fact. And it was not uncommon to be working on two or more murder cases or burglaries or car-jackings at the same time. And petty crimes were almost too frequent to be able to do anything about. It was both frustrating and challenging, but the rewards were also satisfying when you knew, just knew, that you were making a difference.

He tried to keep his cubicle straight, clean and orderly. Not the typical detective's desk. It sometimes got some joking mention by his coworkers, but Jay would say,

"Hey, that's just me."

He didn't have a closed office. That was for the top two guys, the Department Director, Major Clarence McCall and his second in command, Lt. John Two Feathers, a full-blooded Choctaw.

Major McCall was a quiet, non-political, pragmatic leader, who was rarely questioned by anyone. Either up the ladder or down. His background and experience were legendary. Jay felt honored to have been picked to serve under him. And that respect grew as time passed.

Lt. Two Feathers was also very quiet. To an extreme! When you said good morning to him, if he grunted, that was a conversation. And grunts were rare. He was much shorter than Major McCall. The Major being at least 6'3" and John being about Jay's height, 5'9' or so. And where the Major was a little paunchy at around 275 pound, John was about 160. Fit and rugged. Olive complexion, black salt and pepper hair and piercing black eyes. Maybe they were dark brown. It was hard to tell, since they stayed almost hidden under his bushy black eyebrows. He was not tall, but square, with wide shoulders and a square jaw. He had a scar that ran from just under his left eye to his chin. Jay was advised, early-on, not to ask about it. So he didn't.

John was about the most intense investigator that Jay had ever seen. It almost seemed like John was a volcano, set to explode at any minute. While the Major was pleasant and wore a smile as if it was surgically implanted, John had never smiled, to anyone's recollection. Not to say he was unpleasant, just focused, intense and down to business. He took his job very seriously. That, Jay liked.

For most of the first year, John had him working on border crossing speeders. That helped Jay to develop a sense for knowing *"who"* he told *"what"* to and how to try to arbitrate jurisdiction disputes. He also developed some great friendships. While there were a few hiccups along the way, he was able to keep the battles polite and professional... Well, most of the time! One very memorable exception was the recent "Walking Eagle" matter.

CHAPTER SEVEN

**When you were born, you cried and the world
rejoiced. Live your life so that when you die,
the world cries and you rejoice.**
(Cherokee proverb)

Joseph "Josey" Eagle was *enormous*. A part Choctaw and part Cherokee ranch hand. If he weighed anything, he weighed well over 300 lb. and at 6'9", he was a muscular "Goliath". He was a wrangler with Broken Bar Ranch.

The new owner of the Broken Bar, was a wealthy but completely obnoxious city dude. A cowboy wannabe, by the name of "A. Butler Hedstrom". He arrived on the ranch as a result of a foreclosure on the once profitable Broken Bar. It had been in the Barr family since the Great Land Rush of 1889. There were a total of 7 "Land Rushes" and Jedediah Barr was luckily in the first one. It was the most famous one, where Oklahoma captured the dubious distinction of being nicknamed "Sooners", because instead of waiting for the U.S. Army-supervised "Shotgun Start" at high-noon, many sneaked ahead "Sooner". It was never quite clear if Jedediah had waited till high noon, or left a little "Sooner".

Hard times had fallen on the current Barr family. Walter Barr, Jedediah's great grandson, who had inherited the property, suffered first, a drought that killed many of his cattle and devastated his crops. Then, the loss of his wife and only child, Walt Jr., to Influenza. This last tragedy drained what spirit he had left. He just gave up. And soon after, he simply dropped dead. Some said he died of a broken heart. With no living relatives, the ranch reverted to the bank and a Mr. A. Butler Hedstrom bought it.

If you asked Jay to say what he thought were A.Butler Hedstrom's most likeable strong points, he would have been lying if he said anything other than "He doesn't have any". However, with that said, he was the source of a hilarious, insider joke around the office. A. Butler Hedstrom was referred to, simply, as "A ButtHead"!

He was barely 5' tall. Fully clothed and dripping wet he may have weighed 115 lb. He looked like a jockey. He had a very narrow face with a big nose. The best description would be that he looked somewhat "Rat-faced". Of course, his unusually large, flap ears didn't do much to change that impression. Duded-up in his embroidered Jeans, Studded belt with a grapefruit-sized buckle, snakeskin boots, cowboy shirt complete with a purple (ugh) string tie, topped off with a cowboy hat the size of a barrel lid, he could get immediate, total silence in a crowded bar, just by walking in.

This all probably would sound to some as rude or disrespectful, but there were few, in fact none that Jay knew of, who had any use at all for A. Butthead. Of course, he was very fair. He insulted everyone equally and to do business with him was an act of self-abuse. But as a cop, you can't let personal feelings influence your obligation to enforce the law, equally. So, Jay bit his tongue and smiled anytime he was in Butthead's presence, which was, thankfully, seldom.

Soon the guys were saying that Butthead must have been a trillionaire, the way he spent money. He fought the drought by irrigating most of his 160 Land Rush acres. Until 4 new wells could be drilled, he had the water hauled in. It took 6 water trucks, making daily deliveries, 7 days per week. Then, new fences, a remodeled main house and bunk house, new tractors and on and on and on. When they heard that he had added an Olympic sized swimming pool and an elaborate entrance gate highlighted in gold leaf, John spoke a huge speech, for him. John would normally only answer questions when asked, but rarely initiated a conversation.

"Must be his daddy's money" he blurted out, one day.

That was 5 whole words, back to back, and most surprisingly, uninvited. They all were stunned.

You would never have predicted that recently a serious, life-threatening matter would occur to A. Butthead that almost brought State and local officers to war. Jay was, regretfully, right in the middle of it.

Apparently, it started innocently enough as a breakfast matter. Then, *Fate* stepped in.

Neither A. Butthead nor Josey Eagle could be described as being diplomatic in how they spoke. To anyone. Including each other. But, they got along. Somehow, they had either worked out their differences or they just tolerated each other. Still, in Jay's mind, it was obviously not your typical boss-employee relationship.

No, it was a ticking time bomb. And the explosion was not an "If". It was a "When".

CHAPTER EIGHT

**Don't be afraid to cry. It will free your
mind of sorrowful thoughts.**
(Hopi proverb)

It was on a Saturday night, police records show, when Jay got a call
from the Creek Nation Police Dispatcher and almost immediately
after that, a call from the State Police H.Q. The subject of each call
was the same. Something had happened that had both departments
claiming jurisdiction over a border incident that had just blown out of
all proportion. It seemed the Creek officers had crossed into the Sac &
Fox Nation in pursuit of a suspect and both the State officers and the
Sac & Fox officers were in such a violent dispute between themselves
and with the Creeks, that it looked like a war was about to happen.

"The last thing we need, an Indian Uprising. I thought those ended
in the late 1800's." Jay muttered out loud, as he jumped in his truck.

When he arrived at the scene, it was total chaos. There was a line
of police cars and a few cars belonging to the State. They were in
a line, back to front and apparently were set up for about the most
forbidding blockade that he had ever witnessed. Two cars were on their
sides and a big black Cadillac sedan was basically sideways against the
two overturned cars. He immediately identified it as belonging to A.
Butthead. About 50 feet beyond the crash scene was a big black Hummer
which was upside down with all the glass apparently broken. The reason
to say "apparently", is because the roof was mashed completely flat

against the body. Like the lid on a cookie jar. It took a few minutes for him to survey the scene and try to make some sense of it. Then he recognized the Hummer as the one owned by Josey Eagle.

As he recovered from what he had been trying to absorb, he became aware of a ruckus going on, just a few feet in front of the crash scene. Several officers in uniform were actually fighting. Blows were being thrown, a crowd of other officers were cheering them on and there was only one person in sight without a uniform. Or at least not an officer's uniform. As the person was being dragged away from the Cadillac, Jay recognized the "uniform". It was unquestionably the get-up worn by A. Butthead. Jay's mind was racing.

He thought to himself,

"I am supposed to be the guy who keeps this sort of thing from happening, but at this point I'm unsure of two things and I am sure of a third thing. First, the scene is surreal and I have no idea how it occurred. Second, why are three different branches involved and are actually fighting with each other? Third, I am sure that it will be up to me to bring order to this chaos, somehow."

Jay tried shouting at them, but either they didn't hear him or they didn't care. He could only think of one thing to do, since his experience didn't cover cop wars or Indian uprisings and all the officers appeared to be either Creek, Sac & Fox or some of his guys, who were mostly Native Americans of various nations. The noise was so loud, he immediately thought of one of his pieces of crowd-control equipment that he had never had the opportunity to use. Jay opened his truck door and pulled out his official Police Dept. electronic megaphone. He scrambled up on top of his vehicle's roof and then pressing the trigger, he began a speech. He had no idea what he was going to say.

"NOW HEAR THIS, NOW HEAR THIS. BY ORDER OF THE GOVERNOR OF THE STATE OF OKLAHOMA, THIS ALTERCATION IS COMMANDED TO STOP. ALL OFFICERS IN THIS STATE ARE ORDERED TO CEASE AND DESIST.

THE SUSPECTS OR PERPETRATORS ARE TO BE BROUGHT TO THE AREA IN FRONT OF THE CADILLAC SEDAN

AND WITH BOTH HANDCUFFS AND ANKLE MANACLES SECURED. THEY ARE TO BE LAID ON THEIR BACKS IN A CLEAR AREA AND PROTECTED AGAINST ANY HARM. THIS BY ORDER OF THE GOVERNOR OF OKLAHOMA. DO IT NOW!"

There was dead silence. He wasn't sure that he had the authority that he just stated, but as a law officer, he had taken an oath to uphold the laws of the state and the law certainly wasn't being upheld right now. Nothing was happening. Everyone was just looking at him.

He felt a shaking of the truck and there beside him, he was relieved to see Major McCall, rising and relieving him of the megaphone.

"NOW" he barked! And the officers began moving.

Jay did see one officer, as he was approaching A. Butthead, "accidentally" kick him right in his rear. Hard enough to lift him off the pavement. Then he grabbed both of his legs and drug Butthead to a clear area some distance from the front of his Cadillac.

"Ouch, you …"(long Bleep). Butthead was yelling. "Oow, I'll have your badges. You stupid bunch of Oooowwww."

Josey Eagle was another matter. It took about 10 guys to flip the Hummer back on its wheels. They had to get the Jaws-of-Life apparatus from one of the State cars and pry the lid off the cookie jar that was formerly Josey's Hummer. He was groggy and his arm was bleeding. It took 6 men to carry him to lay beside A. Butthead.

Major McCall began interviewing the officers involved for the State, Sac & Fox and Creek forces. After a quiet, deep and very lengthy interview, the crowd disbursed. The two suspects were safely in the back of Major McCall's big sedan. Jay heard him tell both of them that if there was any trouble, he would turn them back over to the other officers and they could take their chances. They each moved over against opposite sides of the back seat and it looked like order was restored.

"Great Job, Jay, you handled a tough matter very professionally." Mac said, not smiling, but looking pleased.

"What in hell did I just handle?" Jay said. "I still don't know what happened or why the officers were in a fist fight! The Creeks are one of the five so-called Civilized Tribes. There was nothing civilized going on that I could see!"

"Jay, let me put these two away in jail and then let's you and me grab a cup of coffee and I'll fill you in."

In an hour, they were sitting in the all-night coffee and donut shop near the office. No jokes please. Yes, cops love donuts. They are usually given to cops free, along with coffee because the more cops on hand, the safer it is for all-night cafes. Call it "paid protection".

Major McCall, or "Mac", as he lets his guys address him when they are alone or off duty, was calm and cool as a cucumber. While Jay was still "wired". Mac started by asking Jay how his ranch and farm were going. Jay had to bite his tongue to keep from saying it out loud, but he thought to himself,

"Great Gory Gobs. How can he be talking about my ranch when we just had a major Indian uprising, cops trying to destroy each other and heaps of devastated equipment, belonging to several different entities, including ours."

"Fine." Jay said sourly, with more than a little impatience.

"Look Jay, things happen in our line of work. The adrenaline rush is needed in order to cope with things that have to be decided on the spot, with no advance warning and sometimes with no past experience. You did *'exactly that'* tonight and you did it very well. However, you still have to know when that adrenaline is no longer needed or important. You have to separate yourself from the natural 'Fight or Flight' urges and come back down to earth. The rest of the world is still out there and for the most part, it's calm and happy. I know its hard Jay, but if you don't work that out in your mind, you are in for a life of stress, health issues and sometimes *'mistakes'* that we can't afford in our business. Do you understand what I am saying?"

"Yes sir. Maybe once I understand what precipitated this mess, I will be able to think it through."

It actually took quite a while for Mac to fill Jay in on the whole story. He had gotten every meticulous detail. It was turning daylight before they were done. One thing Jay admired about Mac was that he had a knack for gathering every bit of information available on a matter without making it obvious and without burdening his officers with a lot of info that they didn't need to dwell on and he didn't care to belabor. Once Jay knew that the cause was the Walking Eagle Matter, he felt calm and more than a little bit amused.

On the drive home, Jay thought to himself,

"I guess it couldn't have happened to two more deserving guys."

Then he chuckled.

CHAPTER NINE

All who have died are equal.
(Comanche proverb)

According to Mac, who had gotten the entire story from Butthead and other details from Josie and the officers at the scene, the tale was extraordinary.

It all started early Saturday morning. Butthead had unceremoniously ordered Josey Eagle out of the bed in the bunkhouse and demanded that Josey go fix him breakfast. He gave complete details of exactly what to cook, how to cook it, what condiments must be present, how much of each and how it must all be fresh and hot or he would simply throw it out and Josey would have to start over. Now, this was not the first time that such orders were given to Josey. And normally it would not have caused a problem. But Josey had only been home for a couple of hours because he had stayed out all night at a local dive and came home completely 'Knee-walking' drunk. Every sharp command out of Butthead's mouth was like a dagger driven straight into his brain.

He and Butthead got into a real foul-mouthed argument. One side of the dispute dwelled on headaches, hangovers, tone of voice and a recognition that slavery had been abolished. The other side of the dispute dwelled on the perils of laziness, who was boss, how much money was provided in food, quarters and gasoline, and other not-so-nice things about personal hygiene that cannot be quoted.

Needless to say, breakfast never got cooked and things deteriorated after that. It was a whole day of opposing wills and arguments, intent on belittling the other party with the hope that it would leave scars on the psyche. The final insult was when Josey declared the nickname that he had heard mentioned around town. That A. Butler Hedstrom was appropriately nicknamed "A.Butthead" and everyone in town knew it and they all were laughing at him.

Butthead was so furious that he actually threw a bottle of wine at Josey and didn't miss. Right across the forehead it hit with an accompanying shower of wine and glass, all over Josey. Not to mention the searing pain in an already tortured brain. Josey was so surprised that it took him a minute to realize what had just happened. During which time, Butthead told Josey that he had decided to give him a new Indian name. The name was "Walking Eagle".

"Walking Eagle?" Josey mumbled, still somewhat in shock.

"Yes, don't you know what that means, you pitiful excuse for an Indian lunkhead? It means an Eagle that is so full of crap that he is unable to fly, so he has to walk everywhere. That's you, for sure. Walking Eagle!"

That was the final straw. Josey lost complete control. He roared, turned bright red and struggled to wallow himself up from the overstuffed sofa that was now a mass of broken glass and wine. Butthead realized he had gone too far. He was small, but he was quick and he dashed out the back door of the house and managed to get into his big Cadillac sedan and get the door closed and locked before Josey reached the car.

That didn't stop Josey. He was completely "bonkers." He smashed his giant fist right through the driver side window, pushing a mass of shattered glass and an iron fist right into the side of Butthead's face. Before Josey could get his arm out of the window, Butthead floored it and the Cadillac leaped forward. Josey was dragged along the gravel driveway with glass gouging his arm. Pain, fury, blood and a screaming migraine took control of Josey. He was not a wrangler now, he was a warrior on the warpath. When his arm finally came loose, he ran for his Hummer. He would end this and end Butthead as well, once and for all.

Earlier, Josey had threatened Butthead that if he didn't shut up, he would rip off his head and jam it where the sun doesn't shine. "Now", he felt, was the time to fulfill that promise.

For Butthead, fear and survival were his compelling thoughts. It had begun to turn a little dark and he thought if he could get far enough away, he could call in the cops to protect him from Josey. He dialed the Creek Police since his home was just within their boundaries.

"Police Dept., please state your emergency."

"My name is A. Butler Hedstrom. I think you guys know me. I own the Broken Bar Ranch. I have an emergency.

There is a drunk Indian ranch hand who is threatening my life. I have escaped the ranch in my Black Cadillac Sedan. He is in pursuit in his Black Hummer. I will be taking Route 66 toward Stroud. Please send help. He has promised to kill me. Also, please alert the police in Stroud."

"I know you Mr. Hedstrom and I will alert cars in the area. Just stay calm and let us do our job."

Butthead knew there were cops in Stroud. He smiled and was pleased with himself as he hung up. Then he looked in the rear view mirror and saw the Hummer was behind him, but still some way back. Dusk would soon turn to dark and he hoped his chances for survival would improve. He gave the Cadillac all it had. They were now cruising at over 100 miles per hour.

As the two screamed past the line bordering the Sak & Fox Nation, their positions had not changed much, but you could see another vehicle behind the Hummer with red and blue lights flashing. Butthead knew that one or two cops would not be nearly enough to handle the size and strength of Josey. He would make quick work of one or two cops, guns or not. And Butthead knew that Josey kept a 357 magnum in his glove compartment.

When the call came in to the Creek Police Headquarters, the nearest police cruiser was dispatched to intercept the two cars. Sergeant Johnnie Wolf had barely reached the highway when two vehicles came past him at racetrack speed. He turned on his lights and fell in behind them. They were going so fast that he had no hope of catching up to them, so he called Dispatch for assistance. Soon there were three patrol cars with lights flashing, barreling along at speeds that were not safe for them or for others who may be on the road.

A call went out to the Sac & Fox police in Stroud, advising them of the problem and they immediately set up a road block utilizing three of their force's five cars. Two were regular patrol cars, the third was the unmarked car belonging to the Chief. It was the last car in the line, on the far left side of the pavement. The officers got out and waited. When they heard the roar of the oncoming cars, they knelt down behind their car's hoods with guns drawn. No one was going to get by them. This was a one-of-a-kind event for the Stroud officers and they were going to do their job.

When Butthead saw the cops with guns drawn, he felt that he might get himself shot, since the Stroud guys wouldn't know the whole story. He made an instant decision. He had better take this all the way to Oklahoma City.

As the first of the string of cars came into close proximity, the Stroud cars triggered their lights and sirens to signal the cars to halt. At their speed, it began to look like the two subject vehicles might not be considering stopping. In just a few seconds it was obvious, there was going to be a crash and the guns were not going to help. At the last moment, the Cadillac swerved left, climbed the curb and continued down a sidewalk plowing through garbage cans, mail boxes and benches. The trailing string of cars did the same.

The wide-bodied Hummer did not completely clear the roadway and caught the right rear of the Chief's car. There was a sound almost like an explosion as metal ripped at metal. The Chief's car was spun away about a quarter turn, taking the Chief along with it. Two officers jumped in their cars and joined the parade, while another officer ran to the Chief's aid. He quickly notified the other two officers, who were speeding away, that the Chief was injured. The two were on their radios and were tuned in to the State Emergency Operating Channel which the Creek officers and State were monitoring. The two Stroud officers, with a generous supply of profanity, declared that they were going to catch these two if they had to chase them all the way to Hades and they would make them pay, big time!

The Creek officers chimed in, "Not if we get hold of them first".

Just past Warwick, the whole parade turned onto the I-44 Turnpike. The State Police were already lining up their patrol cars, just northeast of Oklahoma City in a blockade. Some twenty cars or even more, were stationed front to back across a six lane stretch of highway, with coverage from tree line to tree line. There would be no driving around this blockade.

Soon, the parade of vehicles, and flashing police lights were in view. The lead car was swerving as if to find a hole to dash through. There was none. The car began to slow down, but not soon enough. The driver had made a serious misjudgment about braking distance at that speed. At the last second, with all tires sliding, the car spun to the left bringing the entire right side of his car hard up against two of the patrol cars. The front of one and the rear of the next in line. The crash was ear shattering as the lead car came to an instant stop and the two patrol cars were flipped over on their sides.

The Hummer driver was even more inexperienced, or else was determined to crash into the car he was chasing, because he didn't do much braking and did not try to turn. Instead, he rammed straight into the side of the Cadillac, just behind the driver's door. The monster oversized Hummer tires may have been a jazzy modification to the looks of the Hummer, but they only served to help the front end to ride right over the smashed body of the Cadillac and up over the top of the two turned over patrol cars, taking a flight that finally brought him to earth about 30 yards or so, beyond the crash site. It landed on its roof, which immediately sandwiched. Then it spun like a top for several rounds.

Fortunately, two of the patrol cars stopped in time to avoid the wreck. The lead Creek patrol car ploughed into the ruined side of the Cadillac and stopped. The driver, Sgt. Wolf, made a round spider web of cracks in the windshield where his head hit and there were immediate traces of blood.

After that, things kind of went haywire. The Stroud cops, not knowing the condition of their Chief, wanted blood. The Creek cops after doing a quick triage on Sgt. Wolf, wanted blood. The State, who had lost two patrol cars and were in charge of the district where this occurred, wanted blood. And with that raft of emotions running wild, the result was a perfect storm. Tempers flared. Fists flew. The war was on. And a classic story was born that got funnier with each telling.

CHAPTER TEN

**Force, no matter how concealed,
begets resistance.**
(Lakota proverb)

After their discussion, Major McCall had told Jay to go home and take the day off to catch up on some sleep. Jay didn't think he needed to sleep, but the chance to do a little work on the ranch was too attractive to refuse. A day of free time on his mini-ranch was like a vacation to him.

There were weeds to pull in the vegetable garden, some spraying to do on fruit trees and fire ants had decided that everyone was out to lunch, so they attempted a take-over, which he quickly took care of by feeding them some bait that they would soon wish they hadn't touched.

Corn was ready for picking and the hay in the field was ready for baling. His two horses would have all they needed for the winter months, which were normally pretty miserable for humans and non-humans alike. He had a couple of cows that needed shots and some hay bales that were just about ready to be replenished. And there was still a need to check some fences, if time permitted. One day is not enough.

However, it gave Jay time to clear his head and consider the whole Walking Eagle matter. And particularly about A.Butthead. Mac had also shared the entire background story on Butthead. Apparently, he had suffered through some really tough early years, It was truly sad, but not uncommon among the people Jay dealt with on a daily basis. While it in no way excused his actions, it did provide the reasons behind what he had become. The reasons, while unfortunate, cannot overrule the fact that it still involved his own poor choices.

CHAPTER ELEVEN

**So long as mists envelop you, be still
until the sunlight pours through and
dispels the mists. Then act with courage.**
(Chief White Cloud   Ponca)

The Butthead story was, actually, extremely sad. When his father and mother separated, she was only 6 months pregnant with her son. The separation was bitter. His father, who would never be called "Dad" by his only son, was the epitome of the word "Macho". At least in his own mind. Tattoos, beard, gruff voice, foul-mouthed, chain smoker, motorcyclist, addicted to whiskey with a beer chaser, he hated religion, hated politics, hated his marriage and hated the idea of becoming a father.

Out of spite, he began the legal battle over custody by trying to have his wife, who would never be called "Mom" by her only child, committed to an institution as a hopelessly demented waste of space. The fact that it was over their child was of no interest to either one of them. What little money they had was frittered away between the warring attorneys.

He worked for a small motorcycle shop as a mechanic. She was a prison guard at the local State Penitentiary. He told her that if the child was a boy, his name would be "Tiger Menace Hedstrom". He also hated the name "Hedstrom" and planned to change it to "Headstrong". His wife would roar with laughter any time it was mentioned, and the fight would be on.

As you might imagine, A.Butthead's mother was not your typical Southern Belle. She was more like Bonnie Parker with a touch of Belle Starr. She was a foul-mouthed chain smoker, who hated her husband and hated the idea of being a mother. She continually hassled her husband about finding something to charge him with so that she could have the opportunity and pleasure to be his prison guard. They ran out of money before their son was born.

Again, out of spite, she named her son "Alma Butler Hedstrom". The name had consequences. It did several things. All bad. First, it enraged her husband. Second, *she* also hated the name, and finally, it eventually caused the child great difficulty in dealing with the other schoolkids who told him, often, that he had a girl's name. Kids can sometimes be vicious. Alma being the target of harassment and bullying, also caused difficulty for the school teachers. Something had to be done. So, "Alma" became, simply, "A. Butler Hedstrom".

He grew up in a variety of foster homes. Undernourished, undersized and unwanted. He soon discovered that he had a real talent for manipulating people. He was good at it. He worked hard to perfect it. This was his destiny. It was one of the comforts in his young life. He devoted nearly every waking moment to it and was eventually able to get scholarships that got him through college where he majored in Finance. He minored in Manipulation.

Even with scholarships, he had to work his way through college. He had the pleasure of being a dishwasher, assistant janitor, delivery boy and other stellar jobs. He lived off what food he could steal and any borrowed money he could finagle. Money which, of course, he never bothered to repay. He developed not only an immunity to the hatred of others toward him, but actually found some level of enjoyment in it.

Finally, armed with a college degree, he found his real niche in life by serving senior citizens in managing their retirement incomes. It was here that he found that manipulation and ill-gotten money were somehow inexplicably linked. He arranged the purchase of several small parcels of land from his clients, at a price that his elderly friends were convinced was giving them top dollar and that he was doing them a huge favor. These same parcels of land were then offered to his other elderly clients, as a long-term financial advantage. And he assured them that the price they paid was well below market value. He had the forged documents to prove it. The difference was huge. The money just kept rolling in. With some great Investments, which he was able to make by purchasing some insider information, he was fixed for life.

He saw his father only once. It was at his mother's funeral. A.Butthead only went to make sure she was dead. There was certainly no emotional attachment. He was shocked at his father's looks. Fat, sloppy, unkempt, drunk and apparently homeless. His mother would probably have enjoyed seeing her ex like this. His only words for his son were questions.

"What snuffed her?"

"They said she died as a result of dementia."

"Huh. She was born with it. You her son?"

There it was. "Her son", not "My son" or "Our son."

"Yeah" he answered. That was all he could think to say.

His father turned and lumbered out. A. Butler never saw him again.

CHAPTER TWELVE

**If we wonder often,
the gift of knowledge will come.
If we never wonder, knowledge will never find us.**
(Blackfoot proverb)

C hase's phone buzzed.
"Yes." He said quietly. No names. Never on the phone. It was one of the big boss's rules.

"I'm really disappointed in you my friend".

"For what?" The team leader was getting a knot in his stomach.

"Since when did you decide to pick your own targets?"

"I don't understand." Now he was scared.

"I think you do."

Chase was silent.

"We had a clear understanding. You send me requests, I reject or approve. You don't accept any money or make a move until I tell you. Is your memory starting to fail, or do I have a problem here?"

"No. No problem. I just thought ..."

"I don't pay you to think. I pay you to follow orders. You didn't."

"But, I mailed you a note along with the money. I said it was a rush job, the money was good and it looked like a slam dunk."

"Do you know the difference between the word 'reason' and the word 'excuse'?"

"I guess they're the same."

"You guess wrong. An 'excuse' is something you say to justify why you want something 'excused'. Like you want it to be an exception that you think is O.K. The word 'reason' is the circumstance that caused you to have to ask for an exception to start with. Do you get that?"

"I think so."

"That's not good enough. I want you to KNOW so, not just think so."

"I got it, boss. I apologize."

"Apology not accepted. There can be no exceptions. Understand this. You are well paid to do exactly what I say. No more, no less. We will never have this conversation again. Do you understand?"

"Yes I do. And I just want to say …"

(Click)

Chase thought to himself. "O.K., the Washoe hit in Durant was my mistake. It was a good hit. But from now on, only the Boss can make the decisions, no matter what."

CHAPTER THIRTEEN

**We are taught that
God does not care for the petty quarrels of men.**
(Chief Geronimo   Apache)

S everal weeks passed with no major issues. The final closure of the "Walking Eagle Matter" became history. It turned out that the Sac & Fox Chief was bruised and had a few scrapes and a broken arm, but she recovered quickly. She was the Sac & Fox Nation's first female Chief. Mary Grey Eyes.

Sgt. Wolf had to spend a couple of days in the hospital for observation and had a few cuts and bruises. His officers said that his head was the hardest part of his body, so he couldn't be too badly hurt.

There were a few cut lips, black eyes and skinned knuckles among several of the officers on site, but the most surprising thing was that neither Josey nor A. Butthead had a scratch from the wreck, just the damage that they had done earlier to each other. They were shook up, of course, and Butthead had a mysteriously and seriously bruised bottom side. But other than that, they were good to go. Good to go to trial, that is.

Butthead hired a slick, big time lawyer, that cost him premium bucks, but it was well spent since the lawyer argued successfully that he was fleeing for his life and therefore was temporarily insane and had no control over his natural desire to flee for his survival. The court bought it.

Josey unwittingly helped in that defense since he would tell anyone, and did, that he was absolutely going to kill Butthead and that going to jail for a while wasn't going to change that at all. Josey got 5 - 10 years with a list of charges that included everything from speeding, to destroying state and tribal property to attempted murder. With his attitude, parole or time off for good behavior was not in sight.

CHAPTER FOURTEEN

Humankind has not woven the web of life.
We are but one thread within it.
Whatever we do to the web, we do to ourselves.
All things are bound together.
All things connect.
(Chief Seattle   Suquamish)

ay spent another Saturday until real late on farm chores, slept-in and totally missed church on Sunday. But when that happened he would always try to make up for it by reading some in his scriptures that he kept by his bedside. He didn't claim to be a great scripture expert like some he'd met, but he did have faith and since he spent so much time every day with what some would call the dregs of society, he needed that spark of Christianity just to keep his feet planted firmly on the ground. He didn't want to ever lose sight of the fact that most of humanity is pretty darned good. As far as he was concerned, the jury is still out on politicians.

He could have spent several days and still not be caught up. Being a rancher is a lot of work and he loved every minute of it. His home had two large bedrooms, a combination living room/dining room, and a small family room that he used for his office. Only one bathroom, but there was only one of him, so that worked. Closets galore, storage space in a floored attic and all the walls were sheetrock, plain white. A bit of heaven on earth in his way of thinking. Best of all, the big country kitchen was where he spent any time that he wasn't sleeping, puttering around in his office or taking care of the farm.

The kitchen was a single man's dream. Big double sink, a central island where pots and pans and electric gizmos were stored. The only gizmo on the counter was the toaster, since the microwave was built in over the cooktop. The big fridge and bigger freezer was full of farm raised beef, chicken and vegetables. Life was good and he looked forward to retiring some day and just enjoying the quiet life. Quiet was the key word. So, he did what chores he could when time allowed, and then it was back to work.

Mondays at the office were always big work days. There was never a quiet or boring moment around the department. About the time you had a fire put out, another popped up and each one had the potential of growing into a bonfire if it wasn't snuffed out efficiently and effectively.

Fortunately, nothing out of the ordinary happened for several weeks. As it turned out, it was the proverbial "calm before the storm".

CHAPTER FIFTEEN

**We don't inherit the earth from our ancestors,
We borrow it from our children.**
(Native American Saying)

t had been a quiet day. A really lazy day. When Jay received an inquiry
from the Choctaw Police in Durant about an incident at one of the
liquor dives that was near the Choctaw border with Texas. A pickup
truck with Texas plates had pulled up, near closing time, and 5 guys
with hoodies on had run in, beat a guy's head to a bloody pulp and ran
out before anyone knew what was happening. The officer was asking
him if they were aware of anything like that in their Liaison files.

Jay said, "No, we have plenty of people's heads getting used for a
punching bag but not anything like a run-in run-out attack. I'll be glad
to let you know if we stumble across anything."

"Thanks. No big deal, just asking. Thanks anyway." And they
hung up.

Something just didn't smell right about that call. Fights in these
dives happened all the time. Why would they take the time to poll other
agencies to ask about a bar fight. It seemed so odd that he couldn't quite
get his head around it. So, he called one of the good friends that he had
developed on the Choctaw force and asked him if he could share any
info on why the curious interest in this bar fight.

"Look Jay, you didn't hear this from me OK? Our Chief doesn't want to start some kind of panic. You know how the media blows these things up. This has to be between you and me. OK?"

"Sure, no problem. Your request for anonymity is assured. You have my word."

Jay carefully avoided saying that he wouldn't tell anyone, just that he wouldn't indicate it came from his friend, in case he needed to alert Mac to something. He would never break a confidence, no matter what. There is little in life more important than a person's reputation. Uncle Jay had drummed that into him, every chance he got.

His friend spent a few minutes explaining the matter and why it was important that it not leak out to the media.

"Jay, it seems that there is a possibility that a Murder-for-Hire gang is operating out of Texas and there have been a few quiet incidents in Texas that were so remarkably similar, that there is little question now that we have a big problem. Hear me out, Jay. In each case, the persons who were attacked, and I mean, in every case, 'fatally' attacked, were all suspected of various criminal acts that included controlled substance violations, child trafficking, prostitution, pornography and other violent and non-violent crimes. And other than some suspected criminal activities by these victims, there doesn't seem to be any pattern to the killings. It's like crooks are killing crooks. They were so random that some of us are wondering if it might be the act of some do-gooder group that had decided to take the law into their own hands. A group of Vigilantes."

"Friend, I don't see how you are going to keep the lid on this one. Sounds like an FBI deal, to me."

"Probably. And now, there is a new condition. The most recent kill was a Durant gentleman with no criminal background, no ties to any suspected criminal activity and the only thing we could find was that there was a rumor he was cheating on his wife. His name was Walt Washoe. This could have been dismissed as a totally different group, but the M.O. was exactly the same. Five guys run-in, do the deed, run-out and in every case, the murder weapon was a brick. And not just any brick. It was a solid black-painted brick. They say the damage was so bad, the victims were unrecognizable. And they always left the brick in the middle of what once had been a human skull. They say the red blood on the black brick was something you were not likely to forget, once you saw it."

"Look, this is all news to me. We haven't heard a peep. There has to have been a message that someone was trying to send. You think they were either trying to dare the police to catch them, or they were advertising their new occupation?"

"Let's hope it's neither. Call me if you hear anything, Jay."

That last thought was chilling. He had to take the information straight to Major McCall since the last killing was in Oklahoma and was a cross-state-border incident. Mac immediately had him transfer his case load to others. The anger in Mac's voice was obvious. Although on the outside, he was as cool as usual. Mac said that this case was Jay's top priority.

Jay mumbled to himself, "My first action will have to be to hightail it to Durant, locate the dive, gather information and interview a few witnesses. Specially the new widow."

He was torn about whether or not to involve the Choctaw Police. He checked the Choctaw paper and the other papers in the area for any murder reports and luckily, there was one blurb in the county newspaper and it spelled out much of the details, including mention of the truck having Texas tags. That was his passport to investigate. He did decide, however, to make a simple routine call to his friend at Choctaw Police and simply say that since it was a cross-border issue, the Department felt obligated to do their due-diligence and give it a once-over-lightly.

He got no push-back from his friend, though he did tell Jay to make sure to let him know if Jay found anything that they would be interested in and he would pass it on, internally. Jay could tell by his careful choice of words that they wanted to keep it simple and not give away anything that would indicate their intense interest.

"Keep it simple, fine. What is good for the Goose, is good for the Gander", is what his Uncle would say.

CHAPTER SIXTEEN

**I want my people follow after white way.
Some white people do that too.**
(Chief Quanah Parker   Comanche)

A fter the 2 hour drive to Durant, Jay didn't have much trouble locating the dive. And a "dive" it truly was. Low, flat roof, red painted wood plank sides, a gravel parking lot complete with bone-jarring, water-filled pot holes. And a single sign, on a 4 by 8 sheet of plywood saying simply "Beer Shack".

On the side of the building, some equally unskilled and uninspired artist had painted in huge white letters, "BEER SHACK". Definitely a dive.

Inside it was a toss-up about which would make you sick first, the stale beer smell, the occasional whiff of sweat and vomit, or the choking smell of cigarette smoke. It was also dark and hot. And those were the high points. The tables were early attic or late Salvation Army. Nothing matched, nothing was in good condition. You were instantly aware that it would be best not to sit down and not to touch any furniture surfaces.

The bar was pretty standard, except that its condition matched the furniture motif of the seating area. Behind the bar stood a large man, with unkempt hair, and a hairy face. Not talking about a trimmed beard and mustache, saying unshaven for at least the last 90 days. His stained and dirty tee shirt had a big hole in the top, exposing a hairy nipple and a cigarette hung loosely in his cracked lips. His belly hung way over his baggy wrinkled pants. Jay was in jeans and a denim shirt and felt vastly overdressed.

"What'll you have?" He croaked. One eye was shut to avoid the cigarette smoke that was curling up in his face.

"Just some information, actually."

His eyes widened and a slight sneer curled his mouth. He continued wiping the counter with a filthy towel.

"You a cop or just a pretty boy?"

"Well, I have been told that I am not pretty or handsome."

He purposely left out the "Cute" part since he knew that it would be a downhill slide after that and would not end up very pretty.

"But, Yes. I am with the Oklahoma State Police and if you could answer just a couple of questions, I will get out of your hair."

"Listen Dude. If you were in my hair, you would already be laying in one of them mud holes outside. Let's keep it that way".

Jay swallowed hard to keep from saying what he wanted to say. This was obviously going to be a test of his patience. Better that, than the paperwork involved in punching this joker's lights out.

"As you say, sir. I am not looking for trouble. If I was, I would have a group of officers with me and you would be answering my questions down at headquarters. I would prefer to avoid that trouble and I assume you would too."

"What do you want to know? And make it quick. I have a business to run."

Jay wanted to say that with only two customers in the place and one was him, there wasn't a whole lot of business to run, but he discretely refrained. Uncle Jay always told him that "Discretion is the Better Part of Valor."

"You had an incident in here last week where a customer was beaten to death with a brick. Is that true?"

"Yeah, so what?"

"So, would I be correct in saying that such an event is not a regular occurrence here?"

"Yeah, so what?"

"Are you familiar with the victim? Also, how often was he a customer of your establishment?" He was trying to sound very official, like they do on TV. He figured this guy would expect it.

"Yeah, I knew him. His wife too. He came in almost every other night. Never on Saturdays though."

"What was so special about Saturdays?"

He grinned and you could see that what teeth he had left were almost black.

"He had a skirt he liked to visit on Saturdays."

"Who was the lady? Do you know her name?"

"Look, this is a high-class joint. I don't go around blabbing about my customer's personal life."

"Sir, I have to remind you that you can answer my questions here or downtown, but I need the answer, now".

That "downtown" line was right out of the cop shows on TV. Jay figured it would register with this jerk.

"OK." He growled. "Honey Smith, is what she calls herself, but her real name is Myra Quattlebaum." He paused, then, "With a name like that almost anything would be an improvement." Then he laughed out loud.

"May I ask where she lives?"

"Sure, you may ask." He continued wiping.

Now Jay was starting to get aggravated. He grabbed the towel.

"OK DUDE, where does she live?" He said, trying his best not to lose it.

"Two houses down that way." He pointed. "This side of the street."

Jay didn't bother to thank him and left while he could still breathe. If it had been Marijuana smoke he figured he would be *high* by now. Sure enough, two houses down was a really ramshackle house. Worse looking than the Beer Shack. On the mail box in small, felt marker letters was the name "Honey Smith". He parked in the driveway. It was overgrown with tall grass. She apparently had no car.

He got out and walked to the house. It was an unpainted shack, raised on pilings with a small porch and no steps. You had to hike your leg and pull yourself up by the porch support column. "Column" in this case was an unpainted 4 by 4. He knocked and his knock sent the door swinging open.

"Honey?" He called softly. Then louder "HONEY?"

A drunken voice answered. "WHA YA WANT? I'M ASLEEP."

"My name is Jay. I am with the State Police and I want to talk to you."

"HOL' ON. I AIN'T DRESSED."

So, he waited and thought to himself, that this had all the earmarks of being another "classic". While he waited, he sent a text message to the office asking for any records on a "Honey Smith or Myra Quattlebaum". He got a response within a couple of minutes. For Honey Smith, they had a few incidents of Public Intoxication, a couple for Disturbing the Peace and a dropped charge of Simple Assault on a neighbor. Nothing noteworthy.

On Myra, they had a real rap sheet. Starting with Assault with a Deadly Weapon, Drug Possession, one charge of Attempted Murder and an open warrant for Parole Violations. "Now, that one gives me some leverage", he thought. She had been in and out of jail since she was 16 and she was no spring chicken with a reported age of 52. She had done one 5 year prison stretch for the Attempted Murder. This lady was no lady.

Honey/Myra strolled into the room and plopped down on a blanket-covered recliner. She was a mess. She was in her 50's but looked more like 60's. Dirty, partially blond hair with 3 inches of black roots and styled by windstorm. She had the droopy eyelids and big red nose so common to heavy drinkers. Heavy lips with bright red lipstick and extra-long fingernails covered in purple glitter polish. She was wearing fuzzy slippers and a housecoat with a low neckline barely covering her breasts. She was smoking a long brown cigarette. She looked to be about the same size and weight as the bartender at the Beer Shack. His mind leaped immediately from her to the victim. This was Walt's girlfriend? He was totally underwhelmed.

"Get you a beer?" she croaked in a low gravelly voice that had probably seen too many cigarettes over the years.

"No thanks. May I call you Honey or would you prefer Myra?"

He thought he would establish his leverage at the get-go. She didn't blink. She took another long drag off her cigarette while she processed what he just said.

"Honey is what my friends call me. But since you ain't my friend, I don't give a crap what you call me."

"Well, we seem to have that all cleared up", he said. "Good!" He would take it from there.

"Myra", he began, because he certainly didn't want her to think he wanted to be her friend, "I want to make sure that you understand that we can do this right here, or down at Headquarters, I want to give you that choice." This time she blinked.

"Here's fine. How'd ya' find me?"

"I am with the State Police, I know all about you, but I wasn't sure exactly where you lived, so I asked at the Beer Shack."

"So Dutch ratted me out!"

"Not really, we would have found you anyway. He just saved me a little time. So, 'Dutch' is the bartender?"

"Bartender, Owner, Bookkeeper, and overall louse."

"I take it you two don't get along."

"We get along OK. Doesn't mean he ain't a louse."

"I understand that you knew the recently departed Walter Washoe."

"Yeah, I knew Walt. He was an OK guy, if that's what ya' wanna' know."

"Actually I want to know a lot more than that. He was murdered in a very savage and brutal way. I want to know what you know about how it happened and whether or not you were there when it happened. And I want the whole truth. Lying to the police is a felony, as you well know."

"Huh." She took a long draw on her brown cigarette.

"All murders are savage and brutal, didn't anybody ever tell ya'?"

"Were you there when it went down, Myra?"

"Nope, I was just waitin' here for him to stop by."

"That was what day?"

"Friday night, a week ago." She said and took another long drag.

"Friday night, a week ago? But he never showed up?" Jay asked.

She was lying or Dutch was. Walt only came on Saturdays.

"Nope. Never showed up. I heard about it the next mornin'."

"How?"

"How I heard? I guess Dutch told me."

"You guess?"

"OK, Dutch told me."

"When? And don't lie to me. I've already told you we could do this downtown."

"He told me right after he opened up on Saturday mornin'."

"I understand that Walt always came by on Saturdays not Fridays like you just said."

"He changed it. Said it would have to be Friday. He had to meet somebody on Saturday night."

"Meet someone over at the Beer Shack? Who?"

"How am I spose' to know, I ain't his secretary!"

He pictured that in his mind. Myra the secretary. He started to shake his head without thinking.

"What?" She had noticed him shaking.

"Nothing, I was just wondering … if maybe he told his wife who he was meeting."

"He never told her nothin'. They don't communicate."

"How do you know that?"

"Because he told me they had a communication problem. They've had it for years."

"Myra do you know of anyone who had a reason to hurt him, or to kill him?"

"Sure. I know who did it, his lousy wife, Annabelle. That's who."

"How do you know that?"

"Because she tried it before."

"His wife has tried to kill him before?"

"Sure, ask anybody. Ask Dutch."

"I'll do that".

Jay wanted to explore her house a little. Check her bathroom cabinet for drugs.

"Mind if I use your facilities Myra, it was a long drive here."

"Ya' mean the John? Sure, straight down the hall."

56

She no sooner had that out of her mouth than she got a concerned look on her face. He suspected there was something or someone that she didn't want him to see.

Before she could change her mind, he jumped up and headed down the short hallway. The bathroom door was facing him at the end of the hall. He wanted to peek in the open doors down the hall as he went. He glanced in the first doorway and didn't notice anything. As he was about to pass the second doorway he heard a rustle behind him. Before he could turn around something hit him on the head and the world went dark.

CHAPTER SEVENTEEN

Listen to the wind, it talks.
Listen to the silence, it speaks.
Listen to your heart, it knows.
(Native American Saying)

When Jay woke up, he was laying on the floor in the hallway and Myra had a cold rag on his head. He tried to get up, but his head quickly told him that he shouldn't try right now. He had a world-class headache. He felt the back of his head and it was wet. He looked at his fingers and they were bloody. He wondered how long he had been out. Someone had nailed him pretty good. Even as groggy as he was, he had to ask.

"Who hit me, Myra"?

"I think ya' stumbled and fell and hit the back of your head."

"I wasn't walking backwards, Myra. Who hit me from behind?"

"I musta' had a burglar come in while I was asleep. Thank goodness you wuz' here. He mighta' hurt me."

"Myra, I'll ask you one more time. Who hit me?"

"He ran by me and out the door. It had to be a burglar." She stuck to her story.

He managed to struggle to his feet. The room was trying to tilt.

"Turn around Myra! You are under arrest."

Jay pulled her shoulder around and put cuffs on her. He read her the Miranda Rights and marched her out to his car. After she was tucked away, he called the local cops and it only took a few minutes for them to come out and take her off his hands.

They had called the paramedics who insisted that he go to the hospital for an X-ray and stitches. A cop went to the hospital with him and took his statement. They stitched him up and took the X-rays. They said he should, maybe, spend the night for observation in case there was a concussion. He refused and told them he was absolutely fine. He signed a waiver and then left. Every move he made, had the landscape trying to teeter-totter. He had to get back to that house and give it a thorough search.

When he arrived back at Myra's, there was a car in the driveway. He drew his 38 special and quietly stole up to the door. It was open. When he stepped inside, his gun pointed directly at a guy standing by the hallway.

"Whoa!" The guy growled and raised his hands. "What are *you* doin' here?" It was Dutch.

"I might ask you the same question." Jay said as he lowered his gun. But still didn't holster it.

"I was just checkin' on Honey to make sure she was OK"

"Why wouldn't she be OK, Dutch?"

"I knew you were comin' over, and I know she don't like cops. So, I just wanted to check."

"I didn't think you guys liked each other."

"We don't! But she's still my sister."

Well. So Dutch and Myra were brother and sister. That made sense. That's why she looks so much like him. But this also made the case more complex. Jay tried to get more information from Dutch, but he wasn't very talkative. He said he had no idea who had visited her this morning and when Jay asked him about Walt's wife trying to kill him, he claimed he didn't know anything about that. Now, there were two suspects for who could have conked him on the head.

After several more questions, it was apparent that he was not going to get anything else out of Dutch. He decided it was time for some conversation with Major McCall. Jay asked Dutch to leave because this house was now a crime scene.

"What crime" he growled.

"An officer of the law was assaulted here this morning."

"Who?"

"Me."

He left and Jay sat down and called Mac. After bringing him up to date on all that had happened, his first question was about the head injury and how he felt. Just like Mac to do that.

"I'm OK, Mac. I've had stitches before and I think a night's rest and I'll be fine."

"Look, go check-in somewhere and let this go until tomorrow."

"Thanks, but really, I'm fine."

"Jay, when you've rested, it would probably be a good time to use your leverage with Myra. Tell her that in addition to being complicit in an assault on an officer, her Parole Violation Warrant could send her back to prison. She'll break and spill her guts. Then you can go back to Dutch and nail his hide to the wall. The 'games' are over. If they want matching brother and sister cells, we can accommodate them."

For a change, Mac seemed really angry at the situation. That was sort of a surprise. Jay guessed that he was sensitive to his people getting hurt.

"Look, Jay, get the talk with Myra out of the way first, then talk to Walt's widow. We need to get all we can on her previous attempt at killing her husband. She should be our number one person-of-interest."

Since he had not promised Mac that he would go straightaway to a motel, he continued his search. The most important thing right now was to gather information. This took the next two hours. He found a couple of very interesting things that needed checking out. First, He found a diary. Maybe it would not show anything, but it was worth a shot. He also found several bottles of what looked like drugs and a bottle of white powder. No markings or labels on the bottles. More leverage. When Jay thought he had done all he could, he left with the bottles and diary and found a nearby motel. He must have been truly experiencing a slight concussion. Every movement of his head brought on the dizziness. When he got checked in, he took 6 extra strength Tylenols and laid down on the mattress for a second to let the Tylenol take hold, while he flipped through Myra's diary. He woke up at 7 the next morning.

CHAPTER EIGHTEEN

My forefathers were warriors.
From them I took only my birth into this world.
From this tribe I take nothing.
I am the maker of my own destiny.
(Chief Tecumseh   Shawnee)

Jay, normally being an early riser, realized that he had missed both lunch and supper yesterday and was going to have a late breakfast. He was famished. The motel had a little mom and pop diner next door, so after a shower and shave, he walked over and found a nice padded booth. Everything was still trying to tilt. He pigged out. 6 eggs scrambled with cheese and salsa, bacon and sausage and a Blueberry waffle. He was stuffed and his head only hurt when he moved. One more cup of coffee to make sure that every bit of his stomach had something in it, then he paid his bill and was on his way to the station.

Myra was going to be first on his "Gotta Do" list. Right after he checked in with his mom to make sure all was well with her. Checking on his mom was in his blood and they both enjoyed the tradition.

When he got to County lockup, he was ushered right in to an interrogation room where Honey/Myra was brought in after only a few seconds. He was left alone with her, but he knew that there was someone monitoring, somewhere.

So, he needed to be careful what he asked and what he said. "Keep it simple", he repeated to himself.

Myra didn't look quite as sure of herself as she sat down. Her hands were still cuffed.

"Can you at least take these cop bracelets off for a minute?"

"Why should I Myra? The last time I didn't keep my eye on you, I ended up with stitches and a concussion."

"I didn' do it!"

"How do I know that Myra? I was hit from behind. You were the last one I saw that was behind me. I have no one else to blame. You knocked my lights out."

He watched her reaction. You could almost see the wheels turning in her head. Then she took a deep breath and looked in his eyes.

"You don't believe the burglar bit then?"

"Why should I Myra? You were the only person I saw in the house before or after I was hit. What did you use, a baseball bat?"

"I didn't use nothin'. I didn' hit ya'."

"Well, unless you give me reason to go and tag someone else, you are 'It'."

"If I did see somethin' else or know somethin' else, not sayin' I did, but just supposin'. What's in it for me?"

"Well, let me see Myra. You attacked an officer of the State Police. You had drugs in your bathroom cabinet, you have an open warrant for a Parole Violation. I think that may be good for 5 to 10. But you've done that before with no problem, haven't you? Now, what's in it for me Myra?"

"Just thinkin' out loud ya' know. I forgot about the drugs. They belonged to Walt, OK? He shared them with me sometimes."

"I'm running out of time and patience Myra."

"Maybe I know a little somethin' about the Black Brick thing, though. Maybe not… just sayin'."

Now, that made Jay almost forget about his headache.

"Myra, I would still like to know for sure who hit me. So, you tell me what you know and If I think you aren't pulling my leg …AGAIN… then I might put in a word for you at sentencing…just sayin'."

"Let me talk to Dutch."

"Not in this lifetime, sweetie. You are in this one by yourself. No life preservers except what I just offered. And I have to be leaving shortly. This is not an open-ended offer. Tell me now, or I will promise you that the 5 to 10 will probably be closer to the 10 than the 5. I don't like getting my head busted open by anybody."

He couldn't believe it. Myra started to cry. So much for being a hard case. One thing you could say about Myra, she was not stupid. She knew that Jay had her. And she knew that he meant what he said. When she stopped blubbering, she sat up straight and took a deep breath.

"O.K. Mr. State cop. How do I know you will keep me from endin' up just like Walt did? And don't say 'trust me'. I don't. Not you, not any cop. I want some kind of iron clad insurance that if I squeal, I won't end up wearin' a black brick."

"I won't lie to you Myra, all I can do is take your statement and recommend leniency for your help. The Chief and the D.A. are the ones who will decide whether there is cause to help you. Would you be willing to testify in court to what you know, if it comes to that?"

"If it comes to that, yeah. But you can bet the ranch and your boots and your horse, if you got one, that what I do will depend on you protectin' me. There are some bad actors out there and I am scared of 'em"

"Think about it Myra, when word gets out that I have you in custody, and they may *already* know, they may figure that eliminating a problem is better than just guessing what you might say. You might already be in their cross-hairs."

"You gonna' tape this or somethin'?"

"Myra, you can bet your house, and your fuzzy slippers on it. And your poodle if you got one."

For the next hour, Myra spun a tale that in some ways sounded plausible. In some ways not. In her version, Walt was not only supplying her with "recreational drugs", as she called them, but he also was helping her out if she got into a pinch for money. When Jay asked her about their personal relationship, she said simply,

"We were more than just friends, you know. What with that witch of a wife he had, I felt sorry for him. He was lonely, I was lonely, and

I enjoyed his company. He didn't look down his nose at me like the witch did."

"How did she look down on you, did you and she talk?"

"You bet we did. Miss High and Mighty came by and tried to pull her 'better-than-you' crap on me and said she was demandin' that I stop talkin' to Walt, or seein' him. Demandin'! Me! I put that witch right where she belonged. I told her what I thought of her and the way she treated Walt. I went and got a fryin' pan and chased her scrawny rear-end out the door and down the street. She ducked in the Beer Shack and I was right behind her. If it hadn't been for Dutch, that witch would have looked worse than Walt did, after I got through with her. Demandin'! Me! They should have planted one of them black bricks in her witchy face."

"So Dutch was able to calm everything down?"

"Calm down? No way! He said he had never seen me so mad. He had to hold me till she got in her car. I did get a good crack at her car! I may be a woman, but I have an arm like a quarterback and I put my frying pan right in the middle of her back window before she could get very far."

"What happened next?"

She stopped and started to tear up again. "You ain't gonna' believe this, but I actually broke down and cried on my brother's shoulder."

"I saw you cry just a minute ago. I believe you. Stress and anger can do that to a person. It can even bring them to the point that they want to hurt somebody. Bad."

"If you mean you think I could have hurt Walt, you're nuts. He was the only decent man I ever knew. If anybody was mad enough to hurt Walt, it had to be that witch. If I ever get close to her again, I will make her pay. Count on it!"

Jay believed her. She went on to tell him what she had heard about the Black Brick Gang. She said that was what everybody was calling them.

"Rumor has it that if you want somebody hurt. Didn't matter who or where. For the right amount of money, you could have them take care of it. They would go to any state, any building, any home, and beat the target into a bloody pulp. Leavin' the brick in the middle of it is their signature. You better hope they never get a contract on your skinny butt or you can kiss it goodbye. And they'll do it in broad daylight and in front of a crowd. They're completely nuts and good at what they do." Myra said with conviction.

"How do I find them?"

"You don't, they find you."

"What do you mean?"

"Everybody knows. I can't believe you cops don't know."

"Well, I don't. So, tell me."

"You got it fixed to protect me? Listen, they get wind of me helpin' you guys and they will waltz right in here and beat my brains out right in your jail. Right in front of you!"

"How they going to do that Myra? Almost every person in this building carries a gun."

"Rumor has it that they've knocked off Mafia big-shots, Judges, cops, whatever. You can't stop 'em! So, till you got some ironclad plan, I'm done. That's what I want to hear. Tell me the plan and if I like it, I'll talk."

"If I do this, what are you going to give me, Myra?"

"A name and a place for leavin' your request. Then they contact you. After that, it's between you, them and God."

He let Myra go back and enjoy her new surroundings at the department's expense. This was, now, way beyond his pay grade. Major McCall was probably going to have to go to the Feds. He'll hate that.

CHAPTER NINETEEN

Our first teacher is our heart.
(Cheyenne saying)

Jay's next stop was a visit to his least favorite "dive" to re-interview his least favorite bartender, without benefit of some kind of breathing device. Like, maybe a scuba tank. He decided not to eat before he went. Going in that place with a full stomach was to risk losing it. He thought of one of Uncle Jay's favorite comments. "That place could gag a maggot".

Fortunately, the Beer Shack was empty when he got there. Except, for Dutch. He was there wiping the same filthy bar, with the same filthy rag. Jay knew the deep breath he took before he went in was a waste of effort. The place had the same filthy stench.

"Well, if it ain't the pretty boy. Locked up any innocent citizens lately?"

The croaking growl was the same, also. He kept wiping.

"Not yet Dutch, but the day is still young. We need to talk."

"I've done all the talkin' I'm gonna' do!" Still wiping. - Making sure the filth was evenly distributed.

"Dutch, why do I have to keep reminding you that I am here as a courtesy? I would much prefer to do this downtown. You wouldn't mind closing the bar down for a half day or so, would you?"

"You can't do that."

"Try me. It would be my pleasure."

"Ask your questions and then find the door."

"Thank you Dutch, I knew I could count on you to be a helpful citizen."

"Yeah. Count on it."

"First, Dutch, I want to remind you that being untruthful with an officer of the State could subject you to a great deal of unpleasantness. Got it?"

No response, still wiping.

"Dutch, tell me about the little altercation between Myra, excuse me I mean Honey, and Walt's wife Annabelle."

"Which one?"

"OK. Yeah, there was more than one!" Jay said it like he already knew it.

"Didn't Honey tell ya'?" He stopped wiping.

"She told me a little, I just want to hear what you know about the trouble between them." He was fishing.

"You know about the fuss and the fryin' pan deal, right?"

"Yes, but I want to hear your story of what you saw that day and about any other incidents."

"I guess you want to know about all the phone calls too. I didn't hear 'em. I only know what Honey told me."

For the next hour or so, it seemed like forever, Dutch pretty much confirmed what Myra/Honey said about the incident with the frying pan. Then, about the hundred, or so, phone calls from Annabelle, at all times of day and night, threatening, cursing, screaming and so on. Apparently, Annabelle had decided to make life miserable for Honey and get some kind of revenge by doing so.

There were also some rocks thrown through windows, dead cats left on the porch, mailbox stuffed with excrement, and a few other really inventive methods of harassment. Dutch said it had driven Honey to drinking way more than she normally would. He said Annabelle was truly a witch and he felt sorry for all parties involved. He had shaken his head and then started wiping again. Jay decided it was now time to visit the widow, Annabelle Washoe.

CHAPTER TWENTY

**The first peace, which is the most important,
is that which comes within the souls of people.**
(Chief Black Elk   Sioux)

After Jay's questioning, Dutch was really nervous. His nephew, Johnnie Wolf, on the Creek Tribal Police force, had tried to be helpful to Dutch as a family favor. Dutch had explained to him that since Honey was involved with Walt, he wanted to protect her and that he was sure that the culprit who had contracted to have Walt killed, was his wife, Annabelle. She had lots of money and she could probably buy witnesses in her defense. As many as needed. She was the only one who had enough money to pay for the hit. He said Honey had no money, no friends, no witnesses, and that put her in a bad position. She could be charged with Walt's death, with no defense whatsoever.

Dutch was able to convince his nephew of that. So, in order to help Honey, he had his nephew furnish him with any information he could find out, on an on-going basis, on how the investigation was progressing. Also, who all were involved, what this Officer Jay Nation was checking on, when was he in town, when did he leave town, who had he talked to in town and any info on what was going on. This was the inside track he needed to stay informed.

He also had a contact that he used on occasion when he needed some strong-arm methods to collect bar debts or whatever. This shady friend went by the name of "Hoss" and would occasionally stop by the

Beer Shack. Dutch would furnish him free beer and buy marijuana from him. In return, Hoss would furnish him, on occasion, a bag of cocaine at a cheap price since it was for Dutch's sister. Dutch turned a good profit, on the side, selling what she didn't need. For lack of a better description, Hoss was known as a sort of criminal "handy-man".

Through Hoss, he felt he might be able to get the help he needed to help him get Officer Nation out of the investigation. Dutch knew that this cop was a smart cookie and was probably capable of digging up information from anybody about anything. He was afraid that the investigation might expose not only Honey's criminal background, but also what things that he, himself, had been involved in. He had to try to get this pretty boy, Officer Nation, out of the way.

He began to worry about how well he had covered his own tracks. OH, NO! He remembered, he had stupidly given his real name to that Private Investigator that he had hired to get some dirt on Annabelle. He wanted something so that he could use it against her. He had contracted with a Private Investigator at "P.I. Inc.", using his real name, "Topher Eagle". Now there was no question. That Officer Nation had to be totally eliminated.

CHAPTER TWENTY ONE

The life of an Indian is like the wings of the air.
For instance, the coyote is sly, so is the Indian.
The eagle is the same.
(Chief Crazy Horse   Sioux)

The Washoe home was a big change from the last two places Jay had visited. It was a large semi-Victorian with a long curving driveway on what appeared to be considerable acreage. Several large oak trees were spotted here and there and a monstrous Magnolia tree graced the front. No animals or agriculture were evident, although the large barn with some rusting farm equipment out in front, indicated that at some point it had been a working farm. Both the barn and the house needed maintenance. It looked like the owners had fallen on some hard times and just let the place go. The big, wrap-around porch and railings were badly in need of a coat of paint. But otherwise, the house was not all that bad...Yet.

At least this one had no mud holes and it had steps. He could smell the gardenias blooming around the house. Nice.

He knocked on what was still an elegant hardwood door with a huge oval stained glass insert that stretched almost from top to bottom. There was a screen door but it was standing open and had torn screening. The door opened and he was pleasantly surprised. This was, for some reason, not exactly what he expected. Standing there was a very lovely lady, well-dressed in moderate but expensive clothes, some makeup but not gaudy, hair that was very nicely done up and probably prematurely white. She had a pleasant look, slightly smiling, and obvious curiosity in her eyes.

"Mrs. Washoe, I presume."

"Yes, may I help you?" She had a very soft and attractive voice and was apparently well educated. Her manner was gracious, her articulation was precise. He figured that he should try to do the same.

"Mrs. Washoe, I am Officer Nation, with the State Police, and I want to apologize for showing up here with no advance notification. I only arrived in town yesterday and I wanted to come by as quickly as possible to, first, express my regret for your loss and then to let you know that several police departments are working hard trying to find out how this happened and who was responsible. May I come in for a minute?"

"Certainly, officer Nation. May I get you something to drink?" She said as she led him into a parlor.

It looked like it was right out of the early 1900's. He kind of expected that. It seemed to fit her. She waved at a brocade couch with an expensive looking coffee table in front, while she sat in a matching brocade chair beside it.

"Coffee, Tea, water?"

"Thank you mam, but no thanks. I won't be here long and again, I am so sorry for your loss."

"Thank you officer Nation. If you don't mind, I will fix myself a little spot of tea. Midmorning tea is one of my little vices. Please make yourself comfortable. Are you sure you wouldn't want a cup, it is a special blend I get from India, you know."

He felt it would be less than gracious for him to refuse a second time, so he resolved himself to a "Spot of tea". He didn't particularly like tea. He nodded and thanked her. She slipped away and while she was gone he made a quick look around. You can sometimes pick up some useful insight into people's habits and culture by the way they live. He wanted to know more about Walt and their odd relationship. One or the other of them had, at least at some point, been pretty well off. She returned with the tea. He held his breath and took a sip. Sweet, a hint of flowers or something and very hot.

"Delicious, a hint of what, jasmine?" He said, as if he was some kind of connoisseur.

"Close". She smiled, "Actually Pink Lobe Amaranth and a touch of Rose petal."

"Aha."

That was all he could think to say. He assumed Amaranth must be a flower. At least, he hoped that it was. He blew on it slightly, since it was piping hot and sipped again.

"Mrs. Washoe,"

"Please call me Annabelle"

"Thank you, and my name is Jay. Annabelle, I need to ask a few questions.

It will help our investigation and if at any time you feel that you would prefer not to go on, just let me know. OK?"

"I want to help in any way that I can." She said, still smiling.

"First, Annabelle, I have been told that you and your husband may have been experiencing some domestic problems that have possibly been going on for some time now. Is that correct?"

"Well, right to the point! I suppose you have been talking to that dreadful woman Honey Smith!" No smile.

"Yes mam, we have. That's why I wanted to hear your side of the story."

"Of course. I can tell you that woman tried to kill me one day, and if she is capable of that, she is capable of killing Walter! I barely escaped with my life! Had it not been for that low-life brother of hers, she would have! I suppose I owe him for saving my life. Somehow she got her clutches around Walter and he didn't know how to escape her. If anyone is responsible for his murder, she would be my first suspect. She would do it just to spite me!"

"Would you mind telling me your version of how that all came down, and of any other subsequent contact that you may have had with her?"

"Sure, and I suppose you would want to know about contacts with her brother, as well?"

"Yes Annabelle, I would."

Contacts with her brother? This is getting to be like trying to "pick fly specks out of the pepper", as Uncle Jay used to say.

She recounted for him, minute by minute, how the Frying Pan matter had played out and it basically matched the description given by Myra. Then she got into the calls back and forth between her and Dutch. He couldn't tell how much was fact and how much was fiction. His instincts told him to dwell on the overall story and ignore the obvious attempts to implicate Myra and absolve herself.

"I hope you understand that I was the wronged party. I made many useless attempts to get her brother to intercede on my behalf to keep that 'Honey person' away from Walter. It appeared to me that while Dutch didn't seem to have any strong feelings one way or another, he simply preferred to stay out of his sister's private life. The responses I got all seemed to be saying that he didn't want to be involved with any of it.

I couldn't believe it!" She blurted out. "She calls me a witch, while she is a drunk, a dope addict, a home wrecker and a money grubbing ex-con. She only played Walter for a fool and slicked him out of every penny he had."

"Do you mind telling me what your husband's line of work was?"

"He was an entrepreneur."

No elaboration about what he did.

"Entrepreneurs are the movers and shakers of our world, my Uncle used to tell me."

"In Walter's case, he made many unwise investments in schemes that promised big rewards but in the long run nearly drained all the money that I had stashed away for our retirement. You see, my father was a very successful financial consultant and when he passed, since I was an only child, he left me this farm and an embarrassingly large amount of money and stocks. I think that Walter felt like a 'kept man' and always hated the fact that his efforts were mostly failures and he was basically living off my inheritance. I tried for many years to assure him that it was not *my* money, it was *our* money and I did not feel at all bad about how we lived on the inheritance. I don't know if he just never believed me, or that somehow his self-respect was compromised. And I think that woman tried to use it to weasel into our life. Maybe by giving her money and companionship, he felt like he was helping someone else, rather than being the one who needed help."

"Tell me about these phone calls. Did any of them go to Honey or were they all to Dutch?"

"To her? … Once or twice or maybe a few times, I can't remember exactly. I just got so fed up that I called her and probably lost my dignity and let myself down into the gutter where she was. I am not proud of that. However, I desperately loved Walter and I just wanted her out of my life and out of Walter's life. Of course, it didn't do a bit of good. Neither did talking to Walter. So, I began calling Dutch. He never commented very much and when he did, it was always something non-committal and neutral. But at least he listened. It helped to at least have someone to talk to. I called him almost every time that Walter was obviously visiting that woman." Annabelle gave a resigned sigh. "I thought that if I called Dutch enough, he might just be interested in getting me off his back by saying something to his sister. If that ever happened, I am not aware of it."

"When was the last time you talked to Dutch?"

"The evening they killed Walter."

"Can you tell me what was said by both of you?"

"I don't really remember now. It was right after that when I got the call that Walter was dead. I asked the policeman who called me, if Honey did it. He asked a lot of questions about Honey and I told him what she was and how she kept demanding money from my husband. I told him that Walter was flat broke and I had not drawn out any more money for him to give to that ex-con he was seeing.

I assume it made her mad, and if she was drunk, she probably lost her temper and killed him, like she tried to kill me."

"Why would she have killed him if he was a source of income for her? That just doesn't make sense."

"That's easy. She is a crazy, drunk, murderous, ex-con, psycho. She doesn't need any reason!"

"One last question. There have been some incidents of harassment at her property. Was that you?"

"Yes." She held her head up, proudly.

One thing that Jay didn't know, kept coming back to him as he began the drive back to Oklahoma City. How did she know that Honey was an ex-con? Did Dutch let it slip? Did Walt mention it? Could she have, maybe, hired a private investigator to check up on Honey and Walt? Jay needed to find that out. He also needed to check out Myra's claim that Annabelle had once tried to kill Walt.

He used the time, while driving back to Oklahoma City, to call Major McCall and fill him in on all he had learned.

Mac said to see him first thing in the morning and that it was time to set a strategy in place for moving forward. Jay was tired, still not completely recovered from his head trauma, a muddle of info to still be sorted out, yet, really proud that Mac had made it clear that he trusted both him and his judgement. That made it all worthwhile.

CHAPTER TWENTY TWO

The weakness of our enemy makes our strength.
(Cherokee saying)

Business was good and growing. Nearly three years now and the team had had no major hiccups. Chase knew this was not the greatest hideout in the world. Kind of primitive, in a way. However, it served his purpose well enough. It was basically an old barn that the elderly owner had spruced up and converted into a Bed and Breakfast to supplement his Social Security income. Unfortunately, the B&B business had not been good. Other than a few "Freebies", for advertising, there had been no business. None. Zero. It was just too far out of the way. Secluded, almost.

It was on a country road, a few miles west of Antlers Oklahoma, which is on the Indian Nation Turnpike. The owner was really pleased to finally get someone who wanted to pay to stay there and was willing to sign a one-year commitment, with a right to renew. It was at least 100 yards behind the old farmhouse and had a separate, unpaved entrance road. Chase could not have asked for a better spot to set up his headquarters. Such things took on a huge importance when your business is about killing people.

Two of his guys had been with him now for almost 3 years. The newest guy was well over 1 year and the other guy, on his team, who had been the hardest to find and the most critical, had been with them for just over 2 years. And Chase knew from the start that this would be his

"Do-er". His background was perfect. His name was Leonard Justice. He went by "Lonnie". He had been given to Chase by his big boss. So, Chase really didn't have much choice in the matter.

As it turned out, the boss was right, as usual. Always was. Probably why the boss was the boss. Lonnie was the "Do-er". The guy who was designated to "Do" every target. He wasn't armed with a gun on his "Missions". He only carried a brick. Not your ordinary brick. But a brick painted solid black. The others in the team were well armed and were experts with their weapons. Their job was to protect the "Do-er" and see that nothing interfered with him.

It was interesting how Lonnie got on the team. He had been in the Navy. He was a loner. He got into a fight with two seamen aboard ship. Both ended up dead. He was destined for a maximum security Federal Prison but escaped, while in transit. He killed one guard and nearly beat the other one to death. He escaped in the prison transport van which he later abandoned at the Oklahoma border.

Apparently some cop in Oklahoma tracked him down. Chase's big boss arranged for the team to capture him and then offered him a job. Once Lonnie heard the details on how he would handle targeted victims and that they were all scum-bags who deserved whatever they got, he eagerly accepted the job. The fact that he would be paid for doing it was just frosting on the cake.

He created no problems with the other team members. They simply avoided him, which was O.K. with Chase, if that was the way Lonnie wanted it. There was only one small problem on the first few missions. As team leader, Chase, had to make Lonnie understand when to stop pounding. After that, no problems. Chase avoided talking to him as much as possible. However, he knew that the day would come when he would probably have to terminate Lonnie's employment. So, in addition to his sidearm, Chase also had a custom-made 45 caliber derringer tucked away in a hidden ankle holster, with two soft-point dum-dum bullets. These were capable of stopping an enraged elephant. They were about the only thing that could, for sure, do the job on the giant. No one knew about the derringer. Not even the big boss. Loyalty is important, but self-preservation is more important and you never really knew who you could trust in the end.

Chase Stormcloud, on the other hand, was an ex-cop who had served 15 years for 2nd degree murder, extortion and jury tampering. He was Native American, but claimed heritage with no specific tribe. Working for the big boss was special, even though the boss was the one who originally helped put Chase away. Kind of ironic, if you think about it. Chase considered himself a world-class Vigilante.

"Hey Chase, when do we get to meet the 'big boss'?" whined the one they called "Lizard".

"Not gonna' happen, so forget it. The boss has survived this far by keepin' out of the action."

"No problem, just curious."

"Curiosity killed the cat. You would do well to remember that. All you need to know is the mission."

That's what they called the "hits". "Missions". A little military discipline and terminology fit well in Chase's way of thinking.

"Lizard" was the newest member of the team. Almost 6 feet tall and not much over 100 pounds, he was a true scarecrow. He had a whiny voice but could knock the pimiento out of an olive at 15 yards with his Glock 9mm. He was the Annie Oakley of handguns. Early on, Chase had been curious about the nickname, "Lizard". So he asked.

"You know Lizard, I don't think I ever came across that nickname."

Lizard jumped at the chance to go into his spiel.

"Let me tell you, man. When I was young and stupid, I decided to hold up a convenience store. I had it all planned out, or so I thought. I parked my motorcycle at the front door, facing away from the store, and left the engine running. I had removed the license tag to hide my identity. I wore a hoodie and had a borrowed gun. I don't even know if it was loaded, I didn't plan to shoot anybody. But if you hold up a place, you have to show a gun or they don't take you serious. I walked straight up to the register. I showed my gun, and told the guy to give me all his money. I figured that since this was in a high-crime area, the cops would probably take their time responding. What I didn't figure on, was that some owners in a high-crime area, hire off-duty cops to sit in the office and monitor the security cameras.

Before I had time to think, I saw a cop with his gun drawn, coming from the back. I had only one thought. Get to the motorcycle and haul tail. I hadn't moved two steps when he fired. The bullet caught me right in the butt. Took a chunk out, the size of your fist. The prison doctor stuffed it with gauze and let it heal itself. After a few weeks of eating my meals standing up, he closed the opening. He said it looked like the flesh was already rebuilding itself. He said I must be part Lizard. I told him I liked that name and I have been 'Lizard' ever since. My motto in life is 'Use your head, or you might lose your tail'." He roared laughing.

"Lizard, it's a good thing we hired you for your marksmanship and not your brains." Chase said, laughing.

Lizard roared laughing again and they all joined in the laugh. Except Lonnie, of course.

Lonnie had no nickname. Chase was curious about that.

"How come you never took a nickname Lonnie? I think Goliath would be perfect."

"My name's Lonnie". He said quick and firm. And that was the end of that.

As they tended to their equipment, Chase was deep in thought. His other two, Luke and Kaid, were also hired for their marksmanship. They both had gotten a dishonorable discharge from the Army Rangers, for a variety of repeated violations. They weren't as good as Lizard, but they were better than 90% of all other handgun owners. All in all, he was satisfied with his team. He thought to himself, "I guess I'll quit one day, but not now. These guys are gonna' make me rich. They're already making me rich. Each mission is another slug of money that goes into my off-shore account. All told, it amounts to nearly $200,000 now. When it's big enough for me to never have to work another day in my life, then I'll think about quittin'. Till then, Bring It On."

CHAPTER TWENTY THREE

**When you know who you are.
When your mission is clear and
you burn with the inner fire of unbreakable will,
no cold can touch your heart.
No deluge can dampen your purpose.
You know that you are alive.**
(Chief Seattle   Suquamish)

Morning came early on the ranch. It always does. The migraines were almost gone and Jay was pretty well rested. He did something that he didn't think he had ever done before. He actually went to bed with his clothes still on. Now, *that* is tired. A quick shower, then breakfast, and a check on the animals and he was on his way to work. He usually listened to the radio on his way in. He almost lost his concentration on driving when the announcer uttered a "Breaking News" bulletin. He had to pull over. The reporter was explaining about a violent criminal cartel that had apparently committed a number of unusually vicious murders in Texas and Oklahoma and officers were checking records to see if other states were involved. The newscaster said that there was a mounting toll of homicides that bore such a striking resemblance that law enforcement officers nationwide were being alerted. The group was being called the "Black Brick Gang", for reasons not yet released by police officials. He said the FBI had been contacted by the media, but they said they could not comment on an on-going investigation.

Jay floor-boarded it with lights flashing. Someone had leaked. Speculation had begun to run rampant at the major media. They were guessing that since these were cross-border incidents, and if they proved to be linked, this might even rival the infamous "Murder Incorporated" run by Mafia mobster Al Capone, back in the 1920's.

He arrived at HQ and went immediately toward Major McCall's office but was intercepted by Sarah Blackhorse, Mac's secretary, and diverted to the staff conference room. When he got there, a group of people had already been seated and most of them he didn't know.

"Have a seat, Jay." Mac said, "Now that you are here, we can begin by having each of us state our name, rank and affiliation. Sir, perhaps we should start with you." He nodded at the "suit" sitting right beside him.

"My name is Andrew Jernigan, you may call me Andy, and I am attached to the Governor's office in Oklahoma City where I am assigned as liaison Assistant to the Governor on Crime and Indian Affairs. I speak for the Governor on all matters concerning the safety of our Native American citizens. The Governor has asked me to make this "Black Brick" thing my first priority. Eddie?"

"My name is Edward Whitecloud. I am with the Federal Bureau of Investigation in Washington DC where I serve as special assistant to the FBI Director, with a dotted line responsibility to the Secretary of Homeland Security, on all matters concerning Native Americans. You may call me Eddie."

Jay was next in line at the table.

"I'm Indian Nation. That is my real, 'given', name. My friends call me Jay. I am with the Oklahoma State Police and serve as a liaison officer in the relatively new State & Indian Nation Liaison Force, the SINLF. It is headquartered here in this building. I report to Major McCall and Lt. John Two Feathers. John?"

"Lt. John Two Feathers. I work for Major McCall."

The group continued to introduce themselves. He had known Sgt. Wolf representing the Creek Nation for years, and knew as well Chief Mary Grey Eyes from the Sac & Fox Nation. There were also Chiefs from several other Nations including Arapaho, Pawnee, Choctaw, Cherokee, Cheyenne, Comanche, Chickasaw and a few smaller Nations. While there are 37 Nations in Oklahoma, less than half were represented here. That is still, a pretty full room of people. Some were in casual Indian dress. Most were in suits. Since he was the site's Director, Major McCall mentioned that the session was being recorded, and brought the meeting to order and then turned it over to Andy Jernigan, the Governor's Assistant.

"The Governor's Office is already aware of the possible link between our Durant murder and a few others in Texas, Louisiana and Arkansas. We are now looking at cases anywhere in the U.S. Most have the appearance of crooks killing crooks in the old Mafia fashion. Recently, we discovered that there were other murders that did not fit that pattern, but the murder weapon, a brick painted black, as well as the M.O., would indicate that they were perpetrated by the same group. It has begun to look more like 'Murder for Hire'." He then recapped some of the fairly well-confirmed cases. Next he turned his time over to Eddie Whitecloud, FBI, for the most recent update.

Eddie Whitecloud was impressive, both in size and presentation of his information. Proud but gracious. Soft spoken, but with obvious strength of character. Somebody you wouldn't want to mistake for a "push-over". He first detailed the murder of a judge who was a suspected member of the Mafia with ties to the underworld in New Jersey and then the murder of a young woman with no criminal ties that they could discover, but she was recovering from a very contentious relationship involving a serious assault on her "Wife". These all appeared to be unrelated, random acts. Yet, the common denominator, which now seemed to be a link, was the actual or possible breaking of a law.

"To have you understand the seriousness and urgency of this matter, I have to tell you that the ripple effect in Washington has already reached Congress." He said slowly and gravely.

"Wow", Jay thought. "This is HUGE."

Major McCall then called on him to fill everyone in on the investigation of the murder in Durant. You could have heard a pin drop. Jay decided to leave out names and he only gave general information on the parties involved, that he referred to only as, "a bar owner", "a suspected girlfriend" and "the victim's wife". If there was a leak somewhere, He didn't want the media descending on his "persons-of-interest". There followed, several questions and discussions of various aspects of what was known and what was suspected. Then Major McCall dropped a bomb on him.

"A full report is in progress for the FBI and the Governor's office, but for now, I would prefer that Officer Nation be the Task Force point person. He will be working closely with the FBI and State Police, rather than have a raft of individual investigations that could muddy the water and draw unneeded media attention."

His heart was pounding. However, it just made sense to him and apparently to the others, since no one objected. For the present time, it was jointly decided that a general periodic update would be furnished to each Chief and that any murder that had a similar "Modus Operandi" or M.O., needed to be reported immediately to both the FBI and to Mac's office. Normal murder investigative techniques should still be followed, but it would be preferred that no mention be made of the term "Black Brick Gang". Even if it appeared to be such.

The meeting adjourned and a few Chief's stayed behind to question Mac about his new Department and how it all worked.

It was now about 9:00 am and Jay felt as if he had just put in a full day's work. This was big. This was important and he was in charge. So, he had better shake it off and get busy.

"First things first", Uncle Jay always said. And to him, that meant digging into the business about Myra's claim that Annabelle had, at one time, tried to kill Walt and also to find out exactly how she had learned that Honey was an ex-con.

CHAPTER TWENTY FOUR

**What is life? It is the flash of a firefly in the night.
It is the breath of a buffalo in the winter time.
It is the little shadow which runs across the ground
and loses itself in the sunlight.**
(Blackfoot saying)

J ay checked in with his mom. The call nearly scared the living
daylight out of him. She started by saying everything was fine
and gave him the standard invitation for a Sunday feast. Then,
she just casually mentioned a weird phone call that she dismissed as
probably something that was normal in his line of work. This sounded
a little dismissive to Jay, and it also left him feeling more than a little
uneasy. He needed to question her. He needed to know who it was and
exactly what was said.

"Look Mom, it's no big deal, but it might help me in my work
to know anything you can remember. Like, what was said, what the
questions were, just anything you can think of."

She was always happy to oblige him if it was a help to him in his job.

"Well Indy, the call was early in the morning, you see, and the
person failed to leave me their name. But he seemed to be very interested
in your job, what it consisted of, where you were currently located and
whether or not I knew exactly what matter you were working on. I
didn't catch anything particular about the voice. It was just an ordinary
man's voice. And when I asked the man's name, he just hung up. Now,

I don't mean to sound negative, but I am surprised how rude the people you work with can be."

"Mom, I can assure you that this was not a coworker. Just someone I probably owe a phone call to. I think you can forget the whole thing."

After they hung up, he recalled what Myra had told him in the jail in Durant. "You better hope they never get a contract on your skinny butt or you can kiss it goodbye." And now they knew who his mother was. What the...?

He decided not to mention this to Mac. He had enough on his plate. Besides, "forewarned is forearmed". He had heard that somewhere and he hoped it was true.

Jay spent the rest of the morning calling every listed P.I. in the Durant area. There were nearly a hundred. It was when he was about ready to break for a late lunch that he finally struck pay dirt. He had spent hours of droning on with a standard short list of questions. Did they handle infidelity cases? Did they, in the past several months, deal with a client or suspect by the name of Walter or Walt Washoe? Did the names Honey Smith, Myra Quattlebaum, or Annabelle Washoe ring any bells? He had gotten into a routine of running through these quickly and then would scratch that P.I. off his list. He was starting to scratch another one off the list, when the guy got his attention.

"Yeah. I remember a Honey Smith that I put a tail on. I believe the client was not a Smith. I think the last name was 'Eagle', if I remember right. Have to check. If I find it, you want the file?"

Jay gave him the fax number and puzzled over the name "Eagle". He went to lunch. All through lunch he couldn't get it out of his mind. Sure, "Eagle" is not an uncommon last name in Oklahoma. The only one he knew, personally, was in jail for 5 years with a promise to get out and proceed to kill A. Butthead. He knew if that happened, he would have to find and re-arrest Josey Eagle. Even if he felt privately that Josey might have done the world a favor. He decided to wait until the P.I.'s file arrived. Hopefully, it would be there right after lunch. Until then, he needed to find out about the claim by Myra that Annabelle had attempted murder before. He wasn't sure how to start. This time, he needed a little guidance. Back at the office, Mac was out so he cornered

Lt. Two Feathers and told him the dilemma. John was brief, as expected, but helpful.

"Start with Myra" he said.

Jay felt that at this point she was pliable and would feel obligated to help with the details. He knew the only way to do that was to go back to Durant. He left a note with Mac's secretary, Sarah Blackhorse, to let Mac know he was on the way to Durant to re-interview Myra/Honey Smith and why. He asked Sarah to grab the fax from the P.I., when it came in, and re-fax it to the Starlight Motel in Durant. He made a stop by the house, picked up a change of clothes and was on his way.

As he drove toward Durant, he kept going over everything in his head and then remembered that Mac had said he wanted to discuss the path forward. Well, that will have to wait for another day. This was critically important, in his mind. Now that he was the point person on this investigation, he could leave no stone unturned. This had to come first.

It was after he had driven for several miles when it caught his attention that there appeared to be a car following him. He pulled into a truck stop and went inside to a window where he could observe his car, without being seen from outside. The car that he was suspicious of, a dilapidated dark colored Toyota, pulled up to the pump and a hooded guy got out and started pumping some gas, positioning himself where he could observe both the front door and Jay's car.

Jay hurried back to his car and quickly cranked and left while the guy was still fumbling, trying to hang up the hose. After a half mile, the Toyota was still not in sight when Jay spotted a small group of trees in the median between the north and southbound lanes. He quickly left the road and parked out-of-sight behind the trees and surrounding scrub. In less than a minute, the Toyota came roaring by. The car was an eyesore, but the engine was obviously upgraded for power.

He slipped out of the scrub when the Toyota was almost out of sight and tailed him all the way into Durant, drawing closer as traffic thickened.

The car pulled off at a convenience store and the man, in a hoodie, went inside. Jay parked just down the street. When the guy came out,

Jay continued tailing him. The Toyota drove slowly past the Beer Shack and then headed in the direction of the Washoe farm. Jay didn't figure the car would stop. It didn't. The car continued back into downtown and parked again at the convenience store. Jay quickly took a picture of the car tag and sped off to the police station. When he arrived and checked in with the officer on duty, he stopped by a clerk's desk.

"Hi. Back again. Could you do me a big favor? First, would you check out the tag number on this picture that I took? And I would like to have Honey Smith brought up to an interrogation room. I have a few questions I need to discuss with her."

"Sure thing." She said, smiling.

When Myra arrived, the only change he noticed was that her manner of dress had improved greatly. The orange jail coverall, with the bold black letters "CPD", was clean and sort of matched her hair. She appeared surprised to see him.

"You again? You got the plan for me to look at?"

"Not yet Myra. My boss wants just a little more information in order to make his decision."

"Listen bub. You got all I know except for a name and place, and you ain't gettin' that till I see a plan for my protection. You're wastin' my time." She started to get up.

"Myra, you probably are going to need our protection, whether you tell me or not. But if you want to take your chances with the Black Brick Gang, that's up to you."

"Never trust a cop. I shoulda' known. Whaddya' want?"

"You told me, last time we talked, that Annabelle had tried to kill Walt once before. I want the details. And no exaggerations or guesses. I want just the facts. And I am going to check those out, so tell it to me straight."

She sat back down and her manner changed from surly to resignation.

"OK. You want to tape this?"

"You bet." And he did.

"Walt showed up one Saturday night with a cut on his head and he was bleedin', real bad. I did what I could, but the bleedin' wouldn't stop and it looked like it went all the way to the bone. I called Dutch and he came right over. He said Walt needed stiches and he needed them right away.

He said Walt could bleed to death if we didn't. He called the EMT. When the ambulance got there, one of the medics put pressure on it with a gauze pad and towel. They started a drip in his arm and took him to the emergency room in Durant. I stayed home and waited. Dutch went back to the Beer Shack. I didn't find out until the next day what happened at the hospital.

I asked Walt about it later, about what kinda' story he gave the hospital. He said he told 'em that a heavy piece of farm equipment he was workin' on came loose and crowned him. He told 'em he couldn't see it but he could feel blood runnin', so he called friends who tried to help and they called the EMT's. Musta' sounded reasonable to the hospital. So he escaped havin' to get the police involved. Then he told me what had really happened."

She stopped for a drink of water, then continued.

"Seems he and the witch had a big fight. She was hittin' him with her fists, but he didn't fight back. He couldn't hit a woman. She was cursin' him, callin' him names and callin' me names. Walt finally sat down in a kitchen chair and was sittin' there when she hit him, from behind, on the head with somethin'. He woke up on the floor. She was gone. He knew he was bleedin' like a stuck pig. He made it to his car and headed for my house. Walt told me if he had stayed home and hadn't woke up when he did, that he prob'ly woulda' bled to death. He said me and Dutch saved his life, as far as he was concerned. An' the witch got away with it. Scott Free! Dutch had to pay the hospital bill. I couldn't and Annabelle wouldn't. That's all I know."

They took her back to her cell. He wasn't sure how much of this was true, but the hospital and EMT records should tell him what he needed to know. If it all pans out, he would need to confront Annabelle again. And this time he might have to take the gloves off.

He picked up the License plate info from the clerk and had her run a Criminal Records check. The man's name was Alessandro Fernandez. He went by the nickname "Hoss". He lived in Texas, but his rap sheet showed a whole list of crimes and convictions in Texas, Oklahoma and Louisiana. They included Auto Theft, Bad Checks, Assault with a Deadly Weapon, Robbery and a laundry list of minor offenses. Some included drugs. He was suspected of being a "go-to" guy if you wanted some dirty work or a "Hit" done and didn't want to have your name involved. He was widely considered a criminal Handy-Man.

Time to visit Annabelle and get this over with. "Hoss" would have to wait. Who hired him? Was it one of Jay's persons-of-interest, or could it be the Black Brick Gang themselves? Didn't seem like their style. This is probably a lone bad actor.

CHAPTER TWENTY FIVE

A brave man dies once, a coward many times.
(Native American saying)

Jay began working through the next items on his mental list. First thing was to drop by the Hospital. At the hospital, he wasn't able to get much. The Admin office said they could only say that they had treated a patient on that night by the name of Walter Washoe. They couldn't divulge anything more, without a warrant. He could do that later, if needed.

The next stop was the Ambulance service, where he thought he might have better luck talking to one of the EMT's, directly, to avoid all of the warrant issues. He waited until the guys left on foot for lunch and followed them to the local City Café. There were four of them and they chose to sit at the counter, rather than at a table. That made things easier.

He sat down on the end stool beside them and ordered a hamburger. They were going over some of their recent calls. Jay commented that he was a State cop and some of the stories he could tell, people would not believe. Some he could hardly believe himself.

He told them about the burglar who had worked so hard he needed to rest and fell asleep on the victim's bed, where the cops found him snoring away, after the victims had discovered him and quietly called 911. They all laughed.

He told them that it was really tragic what had happened to such a great guy, recently. Walter Washoe.

"You knew Walt?"

"Yes. Well, I knew his wife, actually. But not all that well. I had heard though, that he was a nice guy."

"You couldn't find one better!"

"Were you guys involved in finding him?"

"No, he was too far gone for us to do anything. We didn't even get a call."

"He probably was just getting over that nasty cut on his head." Jay was fishing.

"That should have been healed long before now! But it was a bad one." One of them said.

"Lucky he got to the Beer Shack before he passed out!" Jay said.

"We didn't get him from the Beer Shack, we got him from his girlfriend's house nearby. Honey, that's his girlfriend, said it was his wife that crowned him. Whatever she used, she really gave him a smack. Surprised it didn't kill him."

"How long ago was that? I somehow thought it was recent."

"Nope, probably a year or so ago. Time flies."

He finished his hamburger while they were still laughing about the sleepy burglar. He was ready to confront Annabelle. It was looking to him like either one of them, Honey or Annabelle, had opportunity and motive. Even though Anabelle was more and more becoming his chief suspect.

As he drove out to the Washoe farm, he kept a watch in his rear view mirror. It looked like he had lost the tail for now. To make sure, when he got to the Washoe farm, he pulled all the way around behind the house to park. No use bringing any more trouble to Annabelle. She was in enough trouble, already. By the time he had walked around front, she had already opened the door and was waiting.

"You parked all the way around back, Jay."

"Yes Annabelle. I didn't think you would want neighbors driving by to see a cop car in your driveway."

91

"Well, thank you. That was very thoughtful. Would you like some tea?"

"No thanks. Matter fact, I just finished lunch. I'm good for now."

They sat down in their same positions as the last time.

"What can I help you with, Jay?"

"Annabelle, I am a little confused. I hope you can help me understand something. I heard a complaint while I was interviewing Honey Smith."

"That pitiful excuse for a woman. If she has any complaints, she probably deserved them."

"Well this is a little more serious, Annabelle. She claimed that about a year or so ago, you had attempted to kill your husband. Took a baseball bat or something to his head while his back was turned."

"That is scurrilous, baseless and another example of her obvious hatred of my marriage to Walter."

"Actually, I checked it out. The Durant hospital has a record of it, as did the EMT squad."

She was speechless and began fiddling with her handkerchief. She avoided his eyes.

"Annabelle, I want the truth. This will come out eventually, whether you want it to or not."

She held her handkerchief to her eyes and you could see her body jerk in silent sobs. He gave her a minute, then,

"Annabelle?"

She took her handkerchief away, took a deep breath and looked him in the eyes. Her eyes were red from crying.

"Isn't it enough that I have lost the love of my life, without dredging up some mistake from the past that doesn't help anything and certainly won't help find his killers?"

"I am just trying to get all the facts, Annabelle. Help me understand what happened."

"OK. I have to be honest and admit that sometimes I have spells of a violent temper. Especially when I think that I have been purposely wronged. I admit that, openly and without shame. It is what it is. But, when I say violent temper, I am not saying I would kill someone. I might yell or curse or throw things. I might even slap or ball up my fist and hit someone. But I always regret it and apologize after. And yes, sometimes I directed it at poor Walter. But I would never have tried to kill him. I might have tried to kill that witch. But no, never Walter. He was a poor misguided and used-pawn in her game of chess. I hope you can get enough evidence to put her away for the rest of her life. She has condemned me for the rest of mine." She began to cry again.

"Maybe I'm gullible", he thought, "but I can't really decide which one of them killed Walter, or rather ordered his execution. Knowing now what I know about the Black Brick Gang, the killers were obviously them. The problem, now, was who ordered it and paid for it. Honey was broke, but she could have borrowed money from Dutch, maybe. Annabelle could, certainly, have found the money to pay for it. But both of them also had reasons to not do it. Of course, both had opportunity. Both had a mean streak that was sometimes uncontrollable."

He was certain that Annabelle conked Walt a year ago with something, but she will never admit it. Surely, Annabelle and Myra couldn't have conspired to have it done. What would that accomplish? No, either one could feasibly be clients of The Black Brick Gang, but neither one seemed to be a 100% slam-dunk. Jay tried to comfort Annabelle, as much as he could, then made his apologies and left.

He went to the Starlight Motel where He had stayed before. The fax from his office was waiting for him. He settled in to read the P.I. file. He gave his mom a call so she wouldn't worry and to let her know he was now in Durant and would spend the night at the Starlight and would probably be back in town tomorrow.

He ate later at the diner next door and just rested in the booth for a while and ran over everything that had happened today. He tried making a lot of notes on ideas and suspicions. It was getting late and he still had to finish the P.I. file. As he was leaving the diner, just by chance, he noticed a ragtag Toyota parked on the shoulder across the street. There was no doubt. It was "Hoss" Fernandez's car. He had been "found".

Jay thought about walking across the street and confronting Hoss. But then, that was dumb. Hoss could plug him and be gone before the echo stopped. He decided to go back to his room and set a trap. If this guy was serious about doing him in, he wanted to be ready.

CHAPTER TWENTY SIX

A danger foreseen is half-avoided.
(Cheyenne saying)

He had his service revolver and in the trunk he grabbed a bag containing his 12 gauge shotgun and as luck would have it, he still had his automatic pistol that he used around the farm. Armed with a shock bomb and a couple of tear gas canisters, he felt ready for The Black Brick Gang and certainly ready for "Hoss".

He didn't change for bed. Instead, he took the extra blanket from the Motel closet, a bunch of towels and his spare clothes and placed them under the sheets to look like a body was in the bed. He turned out the lights and positioned myself just inside the partition to the hanging clothes area. He crouched in a sitting position with all of his armament around him. If "Hoss" was a spotter, and the Gang broke in, he felt he could take them all out with only a reasonable risk. If "Hoss" came in alone, Jay would take his legs out from under him and hold him for the cops and EMT.

He didn't have to wait long. With a crash, his door was smashed open and a single hooded figure rushed in, firing at the form on the bed. Jay picked up his shotgun and before Hoss was through emptying his gun into the dummy, the shotgun tore into his legs. Hoss let out a blood curdling scream. Jay quickly relieved him of his gun. His pant legs were in tatters and blood was literally pouring out of him. Jay put a tourniquet around each leg, then cuffed him and called Durant police.

They were there in less than 5 minutes. Pretty good for a small town police force, after normal working hours.

Jay didn't bother to question Hoss. That would come later. He was relieved that it wasn't the Gang. Maybe he was just feeling a little paranoid. Time would tell.

The next morning, before he visited with Hoss, he called Mac and filled him in.

"O.K." Mac said. "Enough is enough. I am sending John Two Feathers down and two of our spare officers, as well as the Fed, Eddie Whitecloud. I apologize for burdening you with the Fed. But Eddie seems like a competent guy and maybe his experience and his contacts would come in handy."

Jay could tell that Mac was really agitated. "No problem, Mac. Right now, Hoss is the only good lead we have, unless I pick up something in the P.I. report. I haven't finished reading it yet."

"Jay, I want you to set up a report schedule to call me mid-day every day and a call before you retire for the night every night. Watch your back and think of it as a huge bullseye until this thing is put to bed."

He appreciated Mac's concern, even though it did seem a little overkill.

Hoss was still in the hospital. He almost didn't make it. It is amazing what a load of Double Ought buckshot can do to human flesh. He had lost part of one foot and most of the muscle from the other leg. The nurse asked if he had maybe stepped on a land mine. He was awake and cogent, although pretty well doped up for pain and awaiting surgery. Jay wasn't waiting for John, Eddie and the other two.

"Hoss?"

He opened his eyes. A questioning stare.

"Who are you?"

"I am the guy you thought you were killing last night. Looks like I almost returned the favor."

"You ruined me dude. What am I supposed to do now? I can't even make a living."

"If you are looking for pity or an apology, you'd best ask someone other than the guy you tried to kill, dude."

This was the best and only suspect and his hide was now Jay's.

"Who hired you?" Jay said.

"You know where you can stick your questions." He closed his eyes. Jay sat down on the edge of his bed.

"Listen Hoss. I don't know what they told you when they hired you, but I am a State Police Officer and you are an attempted murderer."

"Whoop tee doo. Am I supposed to be impressed? Leave me alone. If I need you I'll call 911."

Jay "accidentally" bumped his leg. Hoss yelled, jerked and almost rolled out of bed.

"Sorry, Hoss. But you might as well get used to pain. In prison, you won't be able to run from anybody who wants to hurt you. You are a lifer's dream come true. A slave you don't have to worry about turning on you. But you may not even make it to prison. You may not make it out of this hospital."

"What are you talking about?" He looked like he was hyperventilating.

"Ever heard of the Black Brick Gang?"

"Yeah, so what?" He had a pained expression.

"I am the Chief Investigator for the State Police and I am working directly with the FBI on the Gang. Once they know I have you in custody and the media says you know all about the Gang and are ready to cut a deal, your life will not be worth a plugged nickel. I bet your employer failed to cover that with you. To him, you are expendable. Peripheral Damage. Tough luck. There is a possibility that we can help each other. Doesn't matter to me. We have other leads. To me, also, you are expendable. And by the way, we are posting no guards at your door. If you can't help us, the Gang can have you. When they show up, just try calling 911."

"Look, I don't know anything about the Gang. I've heard of 'em and that's all. I ain't cuttin' no deals either." The distress on his face didn't match his words.

"OK Hoss. You can try to tell that to them when they show up. I'll read in the papers whether or not you were successful. Eat hearty today Hoss. It may be your last meal. I have a press conference with the local media. You are about to be on the front page." As Jay rose to leave, Hoss hollered.

"Hold on a minute. You can't do that. I have rights. You'd be killing me."

"Hoss, you need to tell that to somebody that cares. I don't. By the way, I'm sure you know how they do it. They smash your face in with a Black Brick. You don't die quickly. It takes a while for the brain to stop working. You will probably be screaming, but without a working mouth or jaws, you won't actually be making any noise. Heck of a way to die, Hoss. Sorry, I have to run, got a news conference".

He grabbed Jay's sleeve, his eyes were brimming and red. It didn't take long to get his statement.

He would never know that the News Conference was just a little white fib. It had served its purpose. Hoss said an Indian Dude, by the name of Eagle, had contacted him and promised him $5,000 to do the hit. Jay was disappointed. He thought he was worth a lot more than that.

The money was to be dropped off for Hoss in an envelope at a local Beer Joint after the job was done. He got few instructions. Just a name, where the target probably would be staying, and where he probably would be visiting and when the job would have to be done, due to Jay's travel schedule.

Somehow, this Eagle person knew a lot about that schedule and his habits. That is insider info. Jay didn't just smell a leak, he knew it.

After a stop at the Durant Police Station to fill out some paperwork for them, he decided he needed to go back to his room and finish that P.I. Report, just to make sure he wasn't leaving some stones unturned. There were now three issues for him to consider.

First, who ordered the killing of Walt Washoe? Second, who is telling people who didn't like to see Jay laying on this side of the turf, what his schedule is. And third, how do you find and stop the Black Brick Gang.

CHAPTER TWENTY SEVEN

**If a man is as wise as a serpent,
he can afford to be as harmless as a dove.**
(Cheyenne saying)

B ack in his room and before he could get more than a few pages scanned of the P.I. report, Eddie, John and two officers showed up. After introductions and a phone conversation about the case with the local Chief, Eddie, John and the two officers wanted to go see the Motel crime scene and then see the three points of interest, the Beer Shack, Honey's house and the Washoe farm. That took the rest of the day. They had a chance to chat briefly with Dutch and Annabelle. Then they all retired to a private meeting room at the local Holiday Inn, where supper was ordered in. The FBI picked up the tab. Steak with all the trimmings.

Jay smiled, "I love this job." He announced.

The two spare officers were both females. Both Choctaws. One was Ona Little Bird, the other was Naya Little Bird. They were cousins. Both had excelled at the Police Academy and were currently unassigned, so they got assigned to this case. Eddie and Jay got into a deep discussion about motives and what motivates a murder-for-hire criminal. Eddie had studied both the Mafia and the high-profile serial killers that made the news, like the Boston Strangler, Ted Bundy, Jack the Ripper and others.

His view of the Black Brick Gang was that money was not their first concern. He felt that they were a group of Sociopaths, who had somehow found each other. Possibly, in prison or in the military. And they had a feeling of low self-esteem, from some kind of abuse in their younger lives. High on their list was a need to feel important, powerful, in control of others and a need to draw public attention to their worth. Even if that worth was negative or fear-producing. Therefore, their method of painful, shocking murder and their advertising of what they did and who did it. Eddie was a treasure trove of info.

A lot of that was a little beyond Jay's pay grade, but he couldn't disagree. To him, they were just nuts and it was his job to put a stop to their agenda. He told Eddie that he knew that most nut cases, like this gang, don't get any better. They just get worse and worse, until they start making mistakes. That was when they tripped themselves up. That is how you catch them. Eddie didn't disagree.

That night, instead of a Motel, they all stayed at the Holiday Inn. Again, on the Feds nickel. The night was uneventful. In the morning, it was decided that after breakfast everyone would read the P.I. report and then split up the investigation.

One critical item was to try to pick up some trace of a criminal named Eagle. Another, was to find out where the money had come from to pay Hoss. Eddie was going to push for a plan for Honey to enter the witness protection program for a while, at least until they could put together a "Sting" and the Gang was gathered up and put away.

There was a leaker to contend with, who probably had some connection to all of this. A leaker could not only screw up an investigation, but it could be a problem that could not just "hinder" them, but could get someone hurt or worse. They were convinced that although they knew that Walt was killed by the Gang, the most critical thing was to find out who ordered it. And after all of the efforts so far, with two prime suspects, they were no closer today than on day one.

Jay had a head start on the others, since he had already waded through several pages of the Private Investigator's times and dates, where he was and what he saw or didn't see. Mostly boring. Jay didn't know why anyone would want to be a P.I. The team made notes of anything that caught their interest, but very little seemed to jump off the page at them. The one thing that did catch everyone's attention was the client that the P.I. was working for. They had a name, but no address or phone number. His name was Topher Eagle. A common last name, but an uncommon first name. The Little Bird cousins said that they would run that one to ground. And they retired to their room to work.

Eddie went to the Hotel's Business Center, found a corner work table, got into his satellite hot spot and started his work. John and Jay got on the horn with Mac and began strategizing a path forward. Mac said the media was going nuts and were accusing every terrorist organization in the world, the Russians and possibly even some alien beings from outer space who were angry over our capture of their astronauts that we were holding in Area 51. It was a circus.

Jay hoped that Eddie's work on getting Myra/Honey into the Witness Protection Program, would be approved. Her info could help resolve their other concerns. The Black Brick Gang had to be identified, and brought to justice.

He gave his mom a call to let her know that he would be out of town for several days. She said OK. Then the call got serious.

"Oh yes, I met that nice friend of yours the other evening."

"Who?"

"I can't recall his name. It was kind of a late visit, but I know how your job sometimes requires late hours. He said he worked with you. So I guessed that he was a cop too. He said he had some very urgent information for you, but he couldn't remember where you told him you'd be staying. I told him it was something like Sunlight or Skylight or something like that. I offered to call you and get the right name but he said he knew the place and had stayed there himself. He was very nice. I told him I would let you know he had stopped by. He said please don't, it would just worry you, unnecessarily. Oh goodness, I guess I forgot about that part. Oh well, now you know anyway. So, no harm done."

"No harm done Mom." So that was how Hoss knew he was at the Starlight Motel.

"Did you see what kind of car he was in?"

"Funny thing, he didn't park out front. He parked down in front of the Lewis's house. Seemed odd. But I did see him drive away. It was not a cop car."

CHAPTER TWENTY EIGHT

**I have learned that the point of life's walk
Is not where or how far I move my feet,
but how I am moved in my heart.**
(Anasazi Foundation)

Now, with Hoss being shot, Dutch was worried. The State cop was going to end up putting Honey in jail. She was trouble, but she was family. About the only close family he had ever had. Obviously, this was one tough cop. Not easily scared off and apparently well able to take care of himself. Without Hoss, Dutch had no access to the gang. Dutch's first idea was to find out exactly which hospital room Hoss was in. He could tell Dutch how to get hold of the gang.

Dutch's nephew told him that Hoss was still in the Hospital and in what room. Great having a nephew on the Creek police force. Armed with that info, he decided to swing by the hospital and question Hoss.

When he got to the hospital and approached the room, he saw an officer sitting just outside the door. He recognized the officer and knew that he would be recognized since they had been involved in a couple of incidents at the Beer Shack and the two of them had no use for each other. In fact, that cop would welcome the chance to tell others that there was something going on between Hoss and Dutch.

He kept walking right by the door, making no eye contact and when he reached the end of the hall, he took the stairwell and left the hospital. Now he didn't know exactly what he was going to do. Perhaps he should just wait until Hoss got out of the hospital and then try to get word to him that he needed the contact info for the Gang. But that would take too long. Probably by that time, Officer Nation would have put two and two together and dug up things that were best left buried.

With the help of his nephew, he was able to get into the Choctaw County lockup for a visit with his sister. They termed it, "Compassionate Exemption." After all, she was his only beloved sibling. Dutch had never developed the skill of communicating graciously. When she was escorted in, he grunted and slipped a small liquor flask from his pocket and gave it to Myra.

"I'll put it on your tab."

"What's goin' on, Dutch?"

"Whaddya' mean?"

"With your friends from the State Cops."

"They ain't my friends, they may be yours." He said.

"They ain't mine either."

"Maybe somebody should get in touch with that Black Brick Gang and put a brick through that cop's face. But, I guess that's not somethin' you look up in the Yella' Pages." Dutch was fishing.

"They're easy enough to get hold of." She said.

"Yeah?"

"Yeah. I've got a name and a contact point. I could go get 'em myself if I ever had a need to. But I guess I'll never need to. I wouldn't even do that to the witch, although she deserves it. I'll leave that up to the next person she makes mad."

"I've always wondered how they got hold of that bunch. What did you say that guy's name was?"

"I didn't say. And you probably don't want to know."

"Well, there's no such thing as too much information. Who knows? I may be able to sell that information to somebody, some day. If I do, I'll split it with you."

"Yeah, I won't hold my breath till that happens."

"No, no kiddin, what's the guy's name?"

"Dutch, come on."

They chatted about her situation for a while, then he kept insisting in a casual way until she finally gave him the name and the contact point.

"OK, thanks. So what do I do? What's the procedure?" Said Dutch.

"You write down what you want done and who you want it done to."

"Then what?"

"Then you just put it in an envelope and put this contact's name on it and leave it with the bartender. He will see that it gets to the right people. Exactly seven days later you pick that same envelope back up. It will have the price of their services written on the inside flap. You put the money in the envelope, same name, same bartender, all the same info. He may be a part of the Gang, I don't know. Then you go home and forget about it. They don't miss. I am told, that for the next few days, you should stay far away from the target and always have an alibi for where you were at all times."

"Oh well, you never know. I may be able to sell the info someday to somebody and if I do, I know you don't believe this, but if I do, I will split it with you. Scouts honor."

"You were never a scout."

CHAPTER TWENTY NINE

You must speak straight so that your words may go as sunlight to our hearts.
(Cochise   Apache   Chief)

It took a lot longer than Jay anticipated. After weeks of digging, the cousins, Ona and Naya Little Bird, created a compilation of all the information that they, John, Eddie and Jay had dug up. It was a wealth of data, requiring days of phone calling, travel, and many face-to-face interviews. It explained a lot. Everybody settled in to hear their report before it was sent out to the other Task Force members.

"First, we really appreciate all the time you guys threw in to the research. If you hadn't pitched in on the phone calling and face-to-face interviews, we probably would not have gotten as far along as we did. Can't thank you enough." Said Naya.

"OK, here is what we have so far." Said Ona.

"Just to be precise, as far as I am concerned, it is 100% accurate. However, most of it is hearsay and would not stand up in court. At least it gives us some background and direction. This came from many sources. We got just about every branch of Homeland Security involved in one way or another. Eddie was our champion, there," said Naya.

The two filled in around each other as they unfolded the story.

"Myra Quattlebaum was her married name. Her maiden name was Eagle, same as Dutch. A fairly common name where they came from. Myra hated Dutch and probably for good cause. Her first marriage was to a wife beater. 'Abusive' would be an understatement. Her husband was a drunk and beat Myra almost nightly. When he would hurt Myra, Dutch would hurt him. But he couldn't stop. He just kept on beating on her and then getting beaten by Dutch.

Finally, he couldn't take Dutch's beatings anymore, as they got progressively worse. He packed up and left. Myra blamed Dutch for her husband running off. She stopped having anything to do with her brother, even though he was doing it for her own good. She had come to accept the beatings because as an abused wife, she thought that it was probably her fault. Myra took to the bottle. Bad friends, bad choices.

She spent 5 years in prison for Attempted Murder. When she got out, she had no job, no place to live and nowhere to go. So, she swallowed her pride and went to see Dutch. He found her a place to stay. He, apparently, had always had trouble expressing his feelings. He was a rough, tough guy by anybody's standards. He knew he was. He also knew that Myra hated him and would never appreciate any help from him after she got herself squared away.

But she was his sister. He had to try to do *something*. He figured Walter Washoe might be the perfect go-between. Walt had an unhappy marriage, no money of his own, and was a caring, giving sort of guy. He knew this because Walt was a regular at the Beer Shack and he liked to talk.

Dutch explained the problem to Walt and swore him to secrecy. Walt had agreed to do whatever was needed. Dutch mentioned to Myra that Walt was a great guy and might be willing to help her some. Dutch would then feed Walter money, from time to time, when Myra was in any kind of financial bind.

For a while, Walter even secretly shared some of his own money. But, that soon stopped, because Walter had no money of his own. Whatever he got, was from his wife's trust fund. She made sure that he never had any money. She apparently wanted to keep him broke and dependent. Myra and Walt developed emotionally supportive relationship.

Walter became the 'good guy' by helping Myra, because she never knew the money was from Dutch. She thought that Walter cared about her. They needed each other for their own reasons. When she was sometimes really down, depressed, or wanted to just give up, Walter would let Dutch know and Dutch would slip him some marijuana and an occasional snort of cocaine to try to help her get through it. Myra had Dutch absolutely wrapped around her not-so-little finger, she just didn't know it. Both Hoss and Annabelle had contributed details on this.

The name 'Dutch' came to him in an odd way. His mother was full-blooded Creek. Their dad was full-blooded German. Myra and Dutch were German/Creek Americans. Early in life, his name proved a problem for Dutch. His father had named him Kristophe. The German name for Christopher. His dad pronounced it 'Chris-Toph-Uh'. Dutch hated the German pronunciation. Kids in school had trouble with it too, so they just called him Christopher. He did not like the name Christopher. And he especially hated the nickname Chris. His dad had a habit of calling him that only when drunk or when he wanted to take his anger out on his son. Finally, Dutch decided that he had to change his name. And since he didn't like Chris or Kris, he took the last part of what the kids called him and began calling himself 'Topher'. He grew up as Topher Eagle.

Myra didn't like that name. She said it sounded too much like Gopher. So, Myra began calling him Dutch, because of his German background. It stuck, and soon, it was the only name people knew him by. He adopted the name and insisted, sometimes violently, that this was his only name.

According to Hoss, somewhere along the line, Dutch made the decision that either Walt or Annabelle needed to 'Go away'. The whole situation was making life hard on him, on Walter, on Annabelle and ultimately on Myra. Myra was becoming more and more unhappy and depressed.

Dutch had earlier hired a private detective to get information on Annabelle and make sure that there was nothing that could link 'Honey Smith' to 'Myra Quattlebaum' that might make her more of a suspect. The whole Annabelle thing was driving Myra to hide behind drugs and alcohol. She felt like she was causing trouble for the one man in her life that cared about her, Walt Washoe.

Several people, including Hoss, said that Dutch loved Myra as a sister, even though he couldn't bring himself to show it. Apparently he hated that he had set the deal up with Walt and now it was falling apart because of Annabelle.

Walt became depressed, because of the trouble his wife was causing him and Myra. He told Dutch he was going to confess to his wife about the whole deal. Dutch had never been aware that Walt was also giving Myra money that he had hidden or stolen from Annabelle until she told him on one of her harassment calls.

For sure, Myra held a grudge against Dutch for her marriage breakup. If she found out that he had set up Walt as a go-between to funnel her money, it would be the last straw. She would either do something horrible to herself or just pack up and leave and he would have no way to watch over her. He couldn't let any of it get out. Plus, he was now getting constant harassing calls from Annabelle.

Dutch felt it was his responsibility to fix it, since he had set Walt up. So, in his way of thinking, the only way he could fix it all, was to contact the Black Brick Gang. He didn't know how, but he knew he could work through Hoss Fernandez to get something done. He offered Hoss $1,000 to contact the gang and get their price so that he could pay to have Walt taken care of. Basically Myra was Dutch's only close family. Although, he had a nephew who worked with the Muscogee Creek Reservation Police. Dutch decided to pay the gang to clean up his mess. That's all we have, up to this point." The cousins both said.

After copies of the report were distributed to their little group, the cousins strongly reemphasized, that the investigation was nearly all hearsay. All of the connection between Dutch and the Gang was undocumented. Even though it seemed to be known by some informants and it had taken a lot of interviews and arm-twisting to dig it all out. Having the info and being able to prove it in court were two separate things.

At least they now had the name of who had probably ordered the hit on Walt. Whoever ordered the hit on Jay at the motel was still somewhat up in the air. Even though Hoss had dropped the last name of "Eagle", there was still no hard evidence that it was Topher Eagle. Hoss had done it, for sure, but the proof that Dutch paid for it was, simply, not there. And if Dutch was squarely in the middle of all this, how much could his nephew, Johnnie Wolf, be involved. Was he the "Leaker"? They still had no idea who the gang members were, or where they were located. They needed to lay their hands on a Gang member. And most likely, when they tried to get one, they would have to get them all.

Jay decided to start with the potential leaker. Sgt. Johnnie Wolf. They sent the entire report and Jay's suspicion about the leaker, to Mac and the other top level persons on the task force. With that done, for now, everybody could return to their own areas and start running down leads on the Gang.

CHAPTER THIRTY

**As long as the sun shines and the waters flow,
this land will be here to give life to men and animals.**
(Chief Crowfoot   Siksika)

Jay was happy to be getting back to the farm. He had some friends watching over things, but this had been dragging on too long. Another, needed, day off. A famer or a rancher has a busy life. And when you are both, there is simply never enough time. The good thing was that it kept him healthy and his muscles hard and he needed that.

His house was his my most prized possession. Surrounded by grass with a clump of pecan trees out front that kind of isolated it from the road, it was obviously designed by someone who, like Jay, enjoyed the simple comforts of life. Lots of trees here and there that made a comforting white noise when the wind blew.

His home was kind of unique for the area. A solid log house with shuttered windows and wood floors of some kind of hardwood that had a nice grain and soft brown color. The light colored shingles on the roof helped to deflect some of the summer sun. His 100 acres was almost too big. However, the price was right and Uncle Jay endorsed it as being "just right" for him. And in his mind, it was beautiful. It had some low, rolling hills, some fertile fields and a clear, spring-fed stream near the back of the property. The barn was fairly large for a small farm. Red sides, a dirt floor with a hay loft and a shiny tin roof that never leaked.

It was only about 50 yards behind the house, so it was convenient, yet distant enough.

He was working in the hay loft, when He got a call from Mac.

"I hate to interrupt you on your day off, but I guess in our line of work it happens."

"What's up?"

"We have some surprise visitors. I need you to see how fast you can get here. I can't go into detail right now. I will fill you in when you get here."

A quick change and he was on his way. He decided not to use the sirens and just drive as quickly as safety would allow. Mac sounded upset. That was not like him. The visitors must be an unwelcome event. He knew Mac didn't like surprises. This had to be something pretty important to upset him like this, not to mention disturbing Jay's day off. When he arrived, he was again intercepted by Mac's secretary, Sarah.

"Hurry to the conference room, they're waiting on you."

"Fine. Seems like this is getting to be a habit." Jay said with a smile.

She did not return the smile.

He expected to see a similar group of Chiefs from the various nations and maybe a few feds and of course, John. Nope. There were only 4 including Mac. There was a lady and 2 guys who looked like Feds. No wonder the surprise didn't sit well with Mac. Jay would have been pissed. In fact, he was pissed. Mac, on the other hand, looked calm and focused on the outside. Jay had been with him long enough to see that something had gotten to him and that sent up warning flags. The obligatory introductions proceeded and when they got to the girl, Jay offered her his hand for a handshake, as he had done for the others. She ignored it.

"Well, this is certainly going to be interesting." He thought.

It was. He was told that she would be working with him as co-director of the operation and that Jay would still report to Mac and she would report directly to the Feds. They wanted an update through yesterday. After Jay had updated them on where they stood in the investigation, they all took a short break. He cornered Mac and asked him what was going on.

"Look, Jay. This came direct from the top. It is a complete surprise to me." He wore a frown. He was upset.

"O.K., so how does this affect me and the investigation?"

"Just find a way to work with her. Share everything, as you do with me. And let me know if she doesn't reciprocate."

Jay couldn't just let this drop. He called an acquaintance of his in the Washington FBI office, who he had met a couple of years back when he attended a seminar on interrogation methods, put on by Homeland Security in Virginia. They had hit it off and ended up spending time discussing the seminar. He was about Jay's age, a great guy, friendly, professional and a really good cop, for a Fed. He took Jay's call right away. After some small talk, he asked how the Gang investigation was coming along. Jay was surprised that he knew about it. Jay brought him up to date with what he could share. After a few questions and answers, it was time to get down to business.

"Jay, I know you didn't just call to say 'Howdy'. How can I help you?"

"Well, I have a new addition to our team. An Agent Thorpe, from somewhere in your building."

"Who?" he said and there was a short pause.

"Agent Brittini Thorpe." Silence. "You still there?"

"Yeah. Sorry. Just trying to let that soak in for a minute."

"Is there something I should know?" He felt his anxiety rising.

"No, not really … She is a good investigator, probably one of the best. Maybe THE best in the FBI. Someone really wants this to get settled."

"What are you not telling me, guy?"

"O.K. You didn't hear this from me, alright? That has to be the way it is."

"Seems to be a lot of that in this investigation", Jay thought to himself.

"No problem. This conversation never happened … now, what?'

"Like I said, she is absolutely the best thing that could happen to a sticky investigation. But … ", he hesitated again. "She has a bit of a 'rep'. You will probably find that out pretty quick."

"I think I already have. She has a thing about shaking hands. Go on."

"That's pretty typical. Don't expect her to be friendly, cut you any slack, or accept anything you say at face value.

And especially don't get on her bad side. She is a hell-cat. No, 'vicious' would be a better description. She normally works alone. No one else has been able to stand to be partners with her for more than a week before they ask to be reassigned."

"I see. A glory-hog."

"No, glory is not an issue for her. First of all she knows she is good. However, and take this seriously, if she thinks that you are interfering with her work she will wring you out and dump you. Not for glory. Just for getting the job done. And she doesn't go by 'Brittini', by the way. She expects, no..., she *demands* that you call her 'Britt'. Around here we call her 'Brat'. But not to her face, of course. Several good agents have had their records smudged by trying to put her in her place. Don't try it. Help her. Share everything with her, and I mean *everything*. Ask her for whatever you need, but be careful. It doesn't take much to get yourself tagged as a bother to her investigation."

"But, we are Co-Directors", Jay hastened to add.

"That's O.K. Just know this. She plays strictly by the rules. She will not try to get in your way. Don't get in hers. If there is a fork in the road, it would be my suggestion to let her decide which fork to take. You can ask her 'why', that's just good police work and she won't object. Make it sound like information gathering and not like you are challenging her decision. I know, that as cops, we are historically hard-headed, hard-charging and hard to argue with. Don't be that way with her. Also, don't let anything slip by you. Work at least as hard and as long as she does. If you can do all of that, you might be O.K. The operative word is 'might'."

"Wow. Is there anything else that might set her off?"

"Yes. Treat her like a cop, not like a female. I don't know why, but that's an issue with her."

"Any special reason that you know of?"

"Just rumors. She was married once, is what I heard. That may have something to do with it. No kids, just marriage and a divorce. But don't dare try to discuss anything personal with her. And remember, this conversation never happened."

"What conversation?" Jay said with a smirk, "Sorry bud, I must have reached a wrong number."

"Yeah, you did. Good luck."

CHAPTER THIRTY ONE

**Beware of the man who does not talk,
and the dog that does not bark.**
(Cheyenne proverb)

Mac was giving her a tour of the facility and a look at the evidence that they had, so far. She was back in a few minutes. She was all business.

"We need to talk." She said.

"Want to go for a cup of coffee? There is a Deli right across the street." He tested.

"I don't want coffee, I want to talk. To you." No smile. Just a raised eyebrow as she waited for an answer.

"The conference room is empty right now."

"Is it bugged?"

"Only when we want it to be. I'll show you where the switch is."

Once they were in the conference room, he noticed that she had no pad or pen.

"Can I get you a pad and pen?"

"My memory is perfect." She said. Not as if she was bragging. It was just a solid fact.

"O.K., good. Let's talk."

"What do you know about me?"

"I just met you."

"If you are a good cop, you will probably want to check me out with someone. But I will save you some time. Here is what I expect. We are Co-Directors. That's fine with me. I will count on your local knowledge and the background you've developed so far on this case. We will solve it. I emphasize 'WE'. I will fully cooperate with you and expect no less than the same from you. This is not a game to me. We have to be professional and we have to be better than good. You will get that from me. If I can't get the same from you, then I will tell you … once. After that if you don't agree or respond, I will come down on you like a ton of bricks and you will spend the rest of your career writing parking tickets. That is not a threat. That is a promise. Do we understand each other?"

"Well, I understand you, but what do you understand about me?"

"I have checked you out. I know more about you than your boss or co-workers do. I think you are a good cop. That's all I need to know. Personalities are for TV shows.

This is real life. Work with me and we will make it happen. Interfere with me and you will regret it."

"Brittini …"

"My name is Britt. Remember it." She barked.

Britt, I accept what you said as a statement of fact, rather than a threat. So I have no problem with it. Threats are for TV shows."

A hint of a smile played at her lips, but didn't quite make it.

"Good. Let's get to work." She said.

For the next several hours Britt went over every Document, report, or piece of evidence, in detail. She asked what seemed like a zillion questions. At one point Jay began to get drowsy and his chin touched his chest.

"Look Jay, if this is boring you, go home." She barked.

"No, I'm fine."

"Then show at least a modicum of interest." She barked again.

"Modicum" He thought, "sounds like a disease. If I have to communicate with her, I guess I'll need a dictionary."

Late that evening, as he was leaving, he found a dictionary in the small library in their lunchroom. After he got home and the farm chores and animals were taken care of, he fixed himself a big breakfast-supper.

He had somehow skipped both lunch and supper. And then he got into bed with the book.

"Here it is", He said out loud to the dictionary, yawning. It had only taken him a few seconds to find it.

"Why didn't she just say a *modest amount of interest*?" He grumbled, out loud.

He began thinking of all the ways he could use that word. Finally, he put the book down and thought to himself, "what I need right now, is a 'modicum' of sleep." He was smiling as he drifted off. The next morning, the alarm went off at 6:00 am. He dressed quickly, grabbed a cup of coffee and got to the office just before 7:00 am. She was already there.

"Sorry", he said, "I slept-in this morning. Must have been something I ate."

Again, the hint of a smile. "No problem, just don't make a habit of it".

He couldn't quite figure if she was serious or kidding. "No matter", he thought. "I will be here at 6:00 tomorrow, Miss Agent. Two can play this game."

The day turned out to be much like the previous one. Except, he actually found her questions helpful. The direction her questions would go, was helping him to start putting some of the pieces together. Her questions suggested possibilities that he had simply not considered.

"Maybe she is as good as advertised", he thought.

"Britt, I was just thinking. I had an idea about how we might find them. This may not be worth even considering, but these guys don't seem to be local, so if they are hiding out somewhere, it's possible that the local location is only temporary. Unless, they are constantly on the move. The confidence level, or arrogance they have shown would seem to me to suggest that they have taken up a main location, possibly in Oklahoma or north Texas. If that's the case, then they probably secured it from someone who could offer them privacy, seclusion and space for at least 5 persons. Do you think checking rental offerings over the past year could be a good use of time?"

"Hmm. Possibly. It would mean going over a huge amount of data.

But who knows, it might pay off." She said with a look of concentration as she played it over in her mind.

"Does the FBI data base have the capability of handling that kind of search or are we on our own?"

"It's not a matter of capability, it's more a matter of getting them to commit. The analysts usually have a heavy research load and sometimes results can take almost too long to be of any value on something as hot as this. I'll call Eddie Whitecloud, it would probably have to come from him." She picked up her phone and began to punch in a number.

Jay went for coffee to avoid even the possibility that she might object to him listening in on her private conversation. Getting hammered was not his favorite way of starting off the day. Especially from her. He didn't get her a cup. She would probably pour it in his lap. Accidently, of course. He had actually made a couple of accidental spills like that, in his lap, in the past. It was not a pretty picture. He didn't want to do an Indian war dance in front of her.

By the time he got back, she was done.

"Was he in?" Jay asked, avoiding asking her what he said.

"Yes. He thought that it was a good idea, but he said that even with him pushing it, it was still going to take a lot of time. He agreed that it should include the top half of Texas, just to be sure to make the effort thorough enough."

"Any estimate on time?" He dared to ask.

"No. Nothing definite, but he said maybe a few weeks."

He tried not to look disappointed, although he was. "Perhaps in the meantime, I could call the area Sheriffs and pick their brains. I think they would appreciate our asking for their help on this."

"O.K." She said, "That fits the category of 'leaving no stone unturned.'"

"I appreciate your approval", he said.

"Don't let it go to your head." She said as she went back to reviewing files.

He thought to himself, "Not to worry, Miss Agent, I'm just thankful for your overwhelming show of appreciation."

She looked up. "There are a lot of holes. We need to plug them up.

We need to go back to Durant. But first, tell me something. Since the media has this in their sights now, how do we know we won't get some 'crazy' involved who decides to use a black brick to do-in his wife or boss or someone who he thinks offended him?"

"Oh. I thought it was in the reports or I would have mentioned it. Perhaps it's somewhere you haven't gotten to yet. What we have not released to the press, is that on the bottom of each brick, in small white letters, we found the victim's name. There would not be any doubt, going forward, even if a 'copycat' killer emerges. If that clue is ever mentioned among ourselves, which is discouraged, we simply say 'The Logo'."

"Hmm. How perspicacious. Well, that's something, anyway."

"What?" He thought to himself. "What does she mean 'that's something anyway'? And what the heck does '*perspicacious*' mean? Back to the dictionary, I guess. This lady is not just tough, she is an 'enigma'. Look that up in your Funk & Wagnall, Miss Britt."

They began gathering their things for the 2 ½ hour drive to Durant. He knew she probably wouldn't think about lunch, so he grabbed a few candy bars from the vending machine in the lunchroom. And on impulse, the dictionary.

No change of clothes, so he assumed they were not going to stay overnight. If he had assumed incorrectly, he soon would learn another lesson.

The drive was quiet. The one question he did ask, went unanswered, which gave him an idea of the intensity of her thought process. For the record, they did skip lunch.

"First, let's stop at the station and let them know that we are in town. What was the Assistant Chief's name again?" She asked.

"So much for the perfect memory", he thought.

"His name is Ben Pushmataha. I understand he has been on the force for over 30 years."

"Does the last name mean anything?"

"No, I don't think so. It's just a 'Chatah' name. The word 'Chatah' is the actual Indian version of the word Choctaw. It means 'proud'."

"I know what Chatah means. I *am* Native American".

"I didn't know." He said meekly. "I guess the name "Thorpe' threw me."

"Ever hear of the name 'Jim Thorpe'? She asked.

"A little"

"Voted the greatest athlete of the first half of the 20th century. Two Olympic Gold Medals, First President of the NFL."

"Any relation?" He asked without thinking.

"He was Sac & Fox. He was my great grandfather." End of conversation.

CHAPTER THIRTY TWO

**When you rise in the morning, give thanks for the light,
For your life, for your strength. If you see no reason to
give thanks, the fault lies in yourself.**
(Chief Tecumseh   Shawnee)

Assistant Chief Ben Pushmataha destroyed what was left of Jay's day.

"I'm sure you've heard by now. It's making the rounds." Said Ben.

"Heard what?" Jay asked.

"About your friend. He announced today that he is running for Mayor"

"Who?"

"Mr. A. Butler Hedstrom."

"What?" Jay roared. "No way. He's not qualified to be a dog catcher."

"Unfortunately, a lot of them haven't been, but if you have the money ..."

"Who is A. Butler Hedstrom?" Britt asked.

"I'll fill you in tonight. Right now my mind is Jello." He said.

"Well, get it in gear. We have work to do." She said. "Sir, I think Jay sent you a message about looking into any rental property that might have served as a Headquarters for the Gang. Any thoughts?"

"No", he said. "Nothing comes to mind, but I'll keep digging. I would be flabbergasted if it turned out that they were in my area. Basically, all we have are hotels and motels. None are secluded. We also have a lot of trailers and rental houses. Only a few which could be considered secluded and we know most all of those folks. The few we don't, we are checking out. I don't think we're gonna' find them close around here, so I am widening the search area."

"O.K. Can we see Myra /Honey for a few minutes?" She asked.

"Sure, interview room number 2. I'll have her brought out. You know the way, Officer Nation."

Jay led the way. It only took a few seconds for Myra to be brought out. She was handcuffed. What happened then was his second shock of the day.

"Hi, Myra" Britt said with a big smile, the first he had ever seen. "How they treating you?"

"O.K. I guess. The food's good. Can you take these cop bracelets off? They hurt." Myra said

"Sure Myra, Sorry. Rules. You know how cops like rules." Britt said. And with that she unlocked the handcuffs.

"Thanks. You seem nicer than your friend there." She looked daggers at him.

"Yeah, he's a State cop, I'm FBI. Makes a difference. But I'm working on him." Britt said and looked at him with a smile, but she had fire in her eyes.

"You got a plan? He don't." Myra said, again looking daggers at him.

"As a matter of fact, we do." Said Britt. "Just came through this morning."

"Whatcha got? And it better be good." Myra said

"With the help of my folks in Washington, we have you set up under the Witness Protection Program. In case you aren't familiar with it, you will be given a new home, a new name, a job and protected lodging until the Gang and their associates can be brought to trial. In the meantime, until we can work out some details and hear your story, the safest place for you is right here. And no more handcuffs." She concluded with a smile.

"O.K. As soon as I see that in writing with a signature on it, I will tell the lady everything I know." She said, as she looked at Jay with sheer contempt. And then was taken back to her cell.

"What about her caving my head in?" He asked rather bluntly.

Her smile was gone, the real Britt was back in town. "Maybe next time, you won't turn your back on a potentially violent suspect."

"I did not get any heads-up from anybody on the Witness Protection Program for her." He said with a little edge in his voice.

"Not confirmed yet, but Eddie said he had a promise that it would be approved today or tomorrow. He'll call us when it is. Don't get your britches in an uproar. Let's go see Annabelle and Dutch." She said.

His britches *were* in an uproar. He still felt a little slighted. He couldn't stop himself. "By the way, who was that nice lady I was with in the interview room?"

No response. He didn't expect one. 'Perspicacious' he repeated to himself. Good thing he thought to bring his dictionary along. It might be even something he would like. You never know with her.

They stopped first at The Beer Shack. He couldn't wait to see how she would react to the hospitality and surroundings. He smiled to himself. Dutch was there. Wiping with the same filthy rag. He must only own one. Same stink, same décor, different shirt that was also ragged and dirty. Cigarette hanging from his lips. One eye closed. Deja-Vu.

"Whatta ya have." He croaked.

"Your best champagne, for the lady, Courvoissier Cognac for me. It was Napoleon's favorite, you know." Jay was yanking Dutch's chain, hard.

"You're no Napoleon." He fired back.

"I see you gentlemen know each other. Good. My name is Agent Britt Thorpe. I'm with the FBI. We need to ask you a few questions." No smile, no handshake.

"Bein' FBI, I suppose you ain't into drinkin' on the job." Growled Dutch.

"My drinking habits are not your concern. However, your drinking habits and your drug dealing are my concern." Britt had his attention. He stopped wiping.

"Thorpe. I know some Thorpe's up around Stroud. You kin?"

"Not your concern." Britt said firmly, still not showing any emotion.

"I already answered a hunnert' or two questions to your partner there. What now, you wanna know what my grandma died from?" Dutch was in rare form. But so was Britt.

"It could come to that." Said Britt, "And maybe a lot more."

"Rats." Dutch said with a crooked grin on his face.

"What about rats?" Jay said, he thought he had missed something.

"What she died of. Rats chewed on her. Got infected. Died of pneumonia." Anything else?" He started wiping again.

This time Jay grabbed the rag and threw it over his shoulder. "I've told you before dude, the Interrogation room down at the station is cooler and smells better. You want to lock up and go with us or cut the smart mouth?"

Again, Britt had the hint of a smile. "O.K. whacha wanna know." Dutch said and he was now looking directly at Jay and if looks could kill, he would be a dead man.

"You can start", Britt said calmly, "By telling us about the drugs we found in Myra's bathroom cabinet."

"They were Walt's". He growled.

"We have information that you were the one who supplied them to Walt." She said, again, calmly.

"You can't prove that. Unless you ask Walt." He grinned.

"As a matter of fact, we can prove it." She said now more sternly. "We found several sets of fingerprints. One set was yours. One was Walt's. One was Myra's. She had cocaine in her blood test."

"You here to arrest me?" He muttered, the arrogance gone.

"We might." Jay said. "Depends on how cooperative you are. Dealing drugs could get you some heavy duty jail time."

"A guy drops by now and then. I swap him some beer for a little coke for my sister. He knows she has an emotional problem. But that ain't dealin', no money changes hands." He said.

"You apparently didn't read the law on that," Britt said, "You exchanged it for something of value. You paid for it in beer. You're still guilty. The fact that you gave it away to someone else doesn't change your culpability."

"Who was it that you got it from? We want a name." Jay said.

"His name is "Hoss". That's all I know him as. He ain't a regular. Just drops in now and then."

"Describe him", Jay said.

"We don't normally get stats on our customers." He said.

"Do the best you can." Said Britt.

"Hispanic, dark complexion, beard, always wears a hoodie, even in hot weather. I guess he don't like to be noticed. About 5 foot 9 or so. Maybe 160 pounds. Hard to tell with the hoodie. That's about all I can tell you."

"How does he get here?" Jay asked.

"Whaddya mean?"

"What kind of car?"

"I don't know. I'm in here. I got a glimpse once, through the door. Dark color. Old. A real jalopy. Burns a cloud of smoke."

"We'll be back." Britt said and they returned to their cruiser.

"Well Jay, that confirms some of what the cousins dug up and what Hoss told you. I think Dutch wants you dead. And you would be, if Hoss hadn't screwed up."

"What did he screw up? He did what he was told to do, except he killed some blankets instead of me."

"O.K., I'll give you that one. Good job, getting ahead of him."

"I appreciate the compliment."

"Don't let it go to your head. What if you hadn't noticed the car across the street from the diner?"

Jay guessed that was another point for her. Not that he was keeping score.

As they pulled into Annabelle's driveway. Britt said, "Nice house. Must have cost a pretty penny when it was new."

"The inside is nice, if you like the early 1900's look. You might like her tea. It has a touch of Pink Lobe Amaranth and rose petals. From India you know." Out of the corner of his eye, he caught Britt jerking here head in his direction. He pretended he hadn't seen her stare.

Annabelle answered the door. Gracious and well-groomed as usual, she greeted them with a genuine smile. She could have made a killing selling cars. They were escorted into the parlor.

"What a lovely place." Said Britt. And it sounded like she meant it.

"Thank you. I love it." Said Annabelle.

"My name is Agent Britt Thorpe. I am with the FBI. And of course you already know Jay. We have a few more questions if you don't mind."

"You must have some tea. It has Amaranth and a touch of rose petal."

"From India?" asked Britt.

"As a matter of fact, yes." Annabelle smiled as she glided away.

Jay looked at Britt and smiled.

"What?" She said.

"Great memory."

Annabelle returned with the tea. No lemon or cream, just a little sugar.

Tea was not Jay's deal, but it wasn't all that bad when you got used to it.

"Have you gotten enough yet to put that horrible woman into prison?"

"Not yet, Annabelle, but we're working on it." He said.

"Well, with the FBI involved, it shouldn't take long."

"No mam, we hope not." Said Britt. "Tell me, Mrs. Washoe, …"

"Please, call me Annabelle. And if you don't mind, can I call you Britt?"

You could sense the conflict as Britt hesitated. She was struggling with the whole 'personal' thing.

"I guess that would be O.K." she said hesitantly and looked at Jay.

He tried not to smile by taking a long sip of tea. He hoped he wouldn't choke. Britt would probably hope that he did. His cell phone began to buzz. He noticed that the call was from Chief Bill Yellow Feather from Durant. He excused himself and stepped out.

"Yes sir. Jay here."

"Meet me in Atoka as soon as possible. There's been an incident."

"In Atoka?"

"Yes. The Sheriff there called me first because he was aware of that hit we had on Walt Washoe. Appears to be exactly the same. I advised them to call no one else until we get there. I asked them to take the victim's wife into protective custody to avoid a media circus. She said that she saw the Gang and their car."

The Chief filled Jay in on the details he had so far. He had gotten quite bit from the judge's wife. Including the fact that one of the Gang was shot.

"Black Brick Gang." Said Jay

"Yes, looks like it. Let me finish giving you what I know so far."

Afterward, Jay returned to the parlor. "That was an emergency call. I apologize Annabelle, but we will have to reschedule this for now. I will call you."

Britt had a questioning look on her face.

"I'll fill you in." He said. They left, quickly.

"What is it?"

"That was Chief Yellow Feather from Durant. There's been another hit. In Atoka. He is on his way and asked us to meet him there."

"Black Brick Gang? Verified?"

"He said it looks like it. I don't know that he is aware of 'The Logo'."

"The victim?"

"County Judge Freeman Hunter. This could be the break that we've been looking for".

"Why is that?" Britt asked.

"Louise, the judge's wife, heard a strange noise outside. She and the Judge were both NRA members and proficient with weapons. They had guns in the house. She grabbed a hunting rifle and stepped out the door. Her husband's car was still in the driveway. He should already have been gone to work. Then she saw movement on the other side of his car. A group of black clad men ran out and headed for the street where a car was waiting. They had guns. She fired and hit one guy in the back. He was the last one getting into the car as it began to pull off. He fell. The car slowed for a second but she began putting shots into the car and it squealed away. She ran around the Judge's car and almost passed out.

It was her husband, but his head was a mass of blood. Her first impulse was to bend over and try to help him, but she knew it was useless. Her next impulse was to go to the downed killer and finish unloading her rifle into his face. But when she saw that he was probably fatally injured, she called 911."

In a few minutes they were just coming into Atoka and Britt was in contact with the Chief who said he would watch for them as they came through town and would lead them to the site. When the Chief and Jay's cruiser got there the Local Chief had the area cordoned off as neighbors were beginning to gather.

"You guys have a tent?" Jay asked the Sheriff.

"No, but I'm sure the funeral parlor has some."

"Get one of your guys to run and pick one up. One with weather side curtains. We don't want to advertise the full extent of the damage to the Judge's head."

"I understand. We thought of that and we draped a blanket over him for now. I'll go send one of my guys for a tent." He started to walk away. Something clicked in Jay's mind …

"Hold up a second … "

"We have to talk to his wife. She will need to verify to the media that he was fatally attack, but if asked about the manner of death, she needs to say she doesn't know, and that they should ask the police. Also, it is important for her to get the word out that she shot the killer in the back with a .30-06 hunting rifle and that she is sure he is dead. We need to try to avoid setting up either her or the injured guy as potential targets for the Gang."

"I'll take care of that." Said the Chief. "I'll take her in my car to a safe house in Durant. They won't be looking for her there. Once the media realizes that no one is home, they will move to the county jail here. I will fill the Sheriff in on telling the media that there is 'No Comment' on an on-going investigation."

"Great." Said Jay. "How about the injured guy, is he dead or dying?"

"According to what I've found out, he is in critical condition. His backbone is blown to pieces, some of the bone fragments penetrated organs. It doesn't look good. If he does survive, he will be a vegetable from the waist down."

"Where is he now?" Britt asked. "We have to talk to him as soon as possible."

"The local hospital is working on him. If they can stabilize him, they will helicopter him to Oklahoma City where they have the doctors and equipment to handle this kind of injury. But first they have to stop all the bleeding. That hollow point slug tore him to pieces." Said the Chief. "Gotta go. Got to get Mrs. Hunter out of here." And he hurried away.

Britt spoke calmly, "The Gang knows he's down. We need to report that he was pronounced dead at the scene. The media needs to think it was a grudge shooting. We can't state that, but we can hint at the possibility. No other details. We can say for now that '*she*' is too traumatized by her husband's death for interviews and the police can't comment on an on-going investigation. They'll scream and threaten, but we need to control this."

"What about reporting it to the rest of the team? We know we have a leaker." Said Jay.

"We need to figure that out. I'll call Eddie Whitecloud. We are on real sticky ground here. If we get jumped on, he can cover our backs. If he says 'No', we'll just have to take our chances." Britt said.

"How can he say no?"

"Politics."

Forensics was setting up under the tent. Jay needed a chance to examine the brick for "The Logo" without making it too obvious. After they verified that there were no fingerprints, they cleaned the brick and handed it to Jay. Britt placed herself between them and the brick. Jay checked the bottom corners. You could barely make it out. But there was no question. In hardly readable tiny white letters it said "J.Hunter".

Britt called Eddie. They now had a confirmed Black Brick Gang killing. When she was done, she was not smiling.

"He said this was too hot for him to make the decision. He is going to have to go up the ladder." Disappointment was on her otherwise poker face.

"Meanwhile, we stay the course as planned." Jay said.

"I agree"

"For me, that means not telling Mac. I don't like that."

"It is what it is." She said, heading for the car.

CHAPTER THIRTY THREE

**Old age is not as honorable as death,
but most people prefer it.**
(Crow saying)

Chase's phone buzzed.

"Yes."

"You know, of course, that this is a disaster." The big boss said.

"Yes," Chase gulped.

"You also know that our deal was that you would be paid a bonus for every 'clean' mission. Do you think this could, by any stretch of the imagination, be called a 'clean' mission?"

"No."

"Do you even realize how it may be impossible to replace L … I mean your guy?"

"Yes, I do."

"I want you to personally verify that he is actually dead and that this is not some federal trick to try to get something out of him."

"Yes. We can do that."

"Apparently you misunderstood. There was no 'We' mentioned. I said, 'I want YOU PERSONALLY to do it.' I think that plainly suggests a one-man operation, does it not?"

"Yes. I am just trying to understand how I can start asking a lot of questions without creating suspicion."

"Good. So, then, don't start asking a lot of questions. If I might suggest something, there are people who have to know the logistics of moving his body either to a funeral home or a hospital. You might want to check out employees of the local hospital and mortuary by either befriending them, or getting them drunk, or just beating the crap out of them. Torture is not out of the question. I want you to see the body, personally, or send me his head. How you do it is up to you. I want better results than this last debacle. Are we clear?"

"Yes. I am on it."

"Keep me informed, daily"

"No problem."

"Oh and one more thing. This is twice you have disappointed me. Don't make any more blunders. Three strikes and you're out."

(Click)

Chase was angry. "OK Boss", he thought, "Next time I will take out family, neighbors and any observers. You want fireworks, I'll give you fireworks".

Buffalo Skull

Ghost Dance Drum

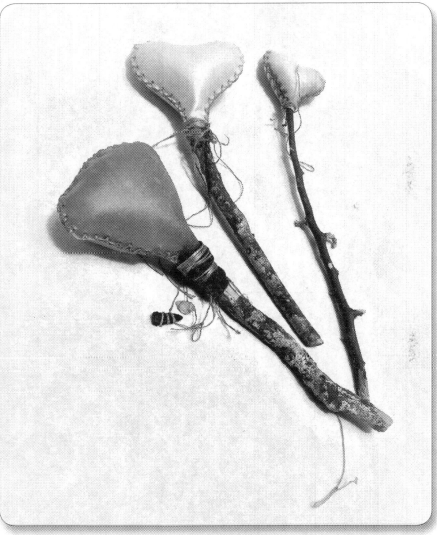

Dance Rattles

Spider woman

Stone Carving

Dance Cuffs

Storage Bowl

CHAPTER THIRTY FOUR

**I salute the light within your eyes where
the whole Universe dwells.
For when you are at that center within you
and I am at that place within me,
we shall be one.**
(Chief Crazy Horse   Lakota Sioux)

Jay couldn't believe that he was sitting in a very nice restaurant in Durant, with a very attractive enigma sitting across from him. He thought for sure they would either skip supper, or grab a to-go Taco somewhere. Not tonight. It was plush Italian.

"Is this a split-the-check outing, or are the Feds picking up the check?"

"If you don't order any $100 wine, I think the Feds can afford it."

"Great, just don't make a habit of it." He said, checking her memory.

"Touché'. I have to give you credit, Jay. Most people can't stand my attitude. I run them off in a week." She said, not smiling, just peering over her water glass.

"Who said that I *can* stand your attitude? You're a cop." He waited.

She was quiet. Deep in thought. Then she looked up and he awaited either a smart response, or a tongue lashing. He got neither.

"Let's order." She said.

They had a wonderful meal. Chicken Cacciatore for her, Lasagna for him. Tiramisu for desert and an after dinner cup of Cappuccino.

He filled her in on his knowledge of Butthead and the little demolition derby that he and Josie had on a bunch of cars. She even smiled a little. After they were done, no small cheap motel was in store. They found two rooms available at the Durant Casino's hotel. They agreed to meet for breakfast in the Casino's restaurant. He settled-in for his nightly perusal of the dictionary. He was beginning to enjoy finding new words. 'Perspicacious' meant a keen mental perception. It was a compliment after all. Now, for a modicum of sleep.

They didn't talk much at breakfast, and he certainly didn't want to think of what he saw in Atoka. Not over breakfast. Britt picked up the tab for rooms and breakfast. Jay still thought, "I love this job".

They drove to the Durant station and met with Chief Yellow Feather and his Assistant, Lt. Pushmataha. They had a discussion about the case. Britt and Jay wanted to know all they could about Judge Hunter and his activities. Mrs. Hunter was in a safe house with a plain-clothes deputy on duty there. She was distraught, as could be expected, but she understood the program and what they were trying to do. The injured gang member was in a drug induced coma to help his chances of recovery. He was critical and doctors would make no estimate of his chances. All they said was, "he should be dead'."

As to Judge Hunter, The Chief said there probably was a laundry list of folks who would cheer at his funeral. But, the only ones who stood out were a few connected with issues at the Casino. There had been some problems concerning unreported muggings and out-and-out robberies of patrons. There had been hints of prostitution and card sharks, but so far, none had turned out to be legitimate claims. According to the Atoka Sheriff, the feeling was that when a guy gets drunk and either blows all his money or gets taken in by a prostitute, that the first thing they want to do when they sober up, is blame the Casino.

The big problem was not so much about proof, as it was about some of the supervisors sometimes failing to report problems to local authorities, so that they could be investigated. Judge Hunter was on their case, big time. However, in many instances, the complaint of the victim was just not actionable. "He said, she said". So the judge was not popular with Casino employees or with victims. He just wanted things reported that needed to be reported.

Could this be a lead? Who knows? The only way to know, for sure, would be to have a shot at the injured gang member. *If* he survives. And *if* he is willing to talk. As they headed toward Annabelle's place, Jay was feeling glum. He was quiet and there was a frown on his normally pleasant face.

"Jay, is there a problem I should know about?"

"No, why do you ask?"

"Because you look like someone just killed your pet."

"I don't have a pet."

"You don't have horses on your ranch?"

"Yes, but they are not pets. They're friends."

She had to think on that for a minute.

"O.K. then, what's up?"

"I don't feel good about keeping this from Mac."

"I think it's necessary for control."

"Mac has been my mentor. He is the most decent man I know, other than my Uncle. He has always shared information with me and I have always done the same with him. I kind of feel like I am betraying his confidence in me. I'm a believer in loyalty. He has always been loyal to me and I would not want him to ever think that I would not be loyal to him. I realize it is a personal hang up of mine, but it is just me. That's who I am. Or thought I was."

The rest of the ride, nothing was said. Jay figured that he had just crossed the line with this lady. Or cop or whatever she is. But, so be it. If she wants him booted out, so be it.

CHAPTER THIRTY FIVE

**I am tired of talk that leads to nothing.
Good words do not last long, until they
amount to something**
(Chief Joseph   Nez Perce)

Annabelle was home. She ushered them right in. When they were settled in the parlor, the obligatory cup of tea was prepared. He couldn't say that he had learned to love tea, but it's O.K. If he kept coming back, he'd probably learn to love it out of self-defense.

"I hope your emergency went well." Annabelle said, politely.

"Oh. Yes. Thank you. Sorry we had to leave so rudely, but unfortunately it's part of the job." He said.

"I totally understand." She replied.

Britt got right to the point. "Annabelle, were you aware that Walt was providing Honey Smith with drugs?"

Annabelle appeared stunned. "That's not possible. Walter had nothing to do with drugs. Ever." Her eyes were wide and her mouth was open. "No, you are wrong. Money maybe, but that's all."

"Unfortunately, we have evidence. Cocaine containers with Walter's fingerprints." Britt said.

Annabelle lowered her head and began to cry. Jay's heart went out to her. She really didn't know. This was not the Walt that she thought she knew.

"I want that woman to pay. She is responsible for Walter's death, one way or another. She is a piece of trash that needs to be locked away forever." She started sobbing again.

Jay couldn't help himself. He went over and put his arm around her.

"Annabelle, I promise you, when we are done, Honey will get what she deserves."

He looked at Britt. She had no expression on her face. They left after a few more words with Annabelle. As they were leaving, they got a call from Atoka. Jay put it on speaker phone. It was the doctor.

"He was able to tell us that his name was 'Lizard'. That was all we could get out of him and we dared not push him. He is still critical. If nothing goes wrong and he continues to stabilize, we should be able to fly him to Oklahoma City tomorrow." The Doctor said.

"O.K., He will need a police escort. I will cover that with the Sheriff. And there must be no leaks. He is still listed as deceased, until we can get more information on what is going on."

"No problem, he is not in our system. Not even as a John Doe."

"Thanks Doc." Britt said and they hung up.

"You gonna' pass that on?"

"Yes." Britt said. "To Eddie and to Chief Yellow Feather. No one else."

"You know how I feel about that."

"I know, Jay. I can't help that. But you will have to trust me on this one. We know there is a leak somewhere. We can't risk it until we have a chance to squeeze something out of this guy 'Lizard'."

"I just want you to know that this is a little out of character for me. It's the 'Loyalty' thing. I will work it out in my own head. I just will feel better when we can be open and honest with Mac. I owe him so much."

"I agree that Mac is a decent guy. There is nothing wrong with loyalty as long as it isn't 'obsequious'."

"Crap". He thought. "Back to the dictionary."

"What next?" Jay asked. This was the proverbial "fork in the road".

"Let's go confront Hoss. Then we need to head out for Oklahoma City."

"Great. I am on the second day with these clothes. I guess you feel the same."

"Here's a little tip. I always keep a change of clothes in my little computer roll-around. Obviously you were not a Boy Scout."

"I wasn't. What's that got to do with it?"

"Boy Scout Motto. 'Be Prepared'."

Lesson learned. One more point for her.

Hoss was not glad to see them. He was still guarded and was handcuffed to the bed. He looked like hell.

"What do you want?" He growled. I spilled my gut to ya'. Ain't that enough?"

"There is never enough when it comes to the truth, Hoss."

"Who's the lady?"

Jay started to say she's no lady, she's a cop, but thought better of it.

"Hoss, this is Agent Thorpe from the FBI. She is heading up the Federal interest in the Black Brick Gang."

"Mucho Gusto" said Hoss.

"El gusto es mio" Brit said. Then she fired off.

"How much were you offered to get the Black Brick Gang to kill Walt."

"A lot. And, as I told your officer there, I was offered $5,000 to do Walt myself."

"Is that your regular price for murder?"

"I don't know what you mean."

"Isn't that what you were offered to Kill Officer Nation?"

He looked at Jay and then looked down. "Yes."

"How much for the Gang hit?"

"$10,000."

"So you took the $10,000 and gave it to the Gang."

"No. I never took money to hit Walt. The guy musta' made his own contact."

"How much did he give you to tell him who to contact, and where?"

"I didn't, I tol' ya'. He musta' took care of it on his own."

"Your 'guy' is Dutch, correct."

A pause, then, "Yeah."

"And you know nothing about how the Walt hit was set up?"

"Nope. Plus, I liked Walt. He was a straight shooter. Took good care of Honey when nobody else would."

"You don't consider Officer Nation a straight shooter?" She asked.

"He's a cop."

"Yeah. So am I, Hoss. Two more questions. Have you had any contact with Annabelle Washoe? And second, was it you in Honey's house when Officer Nation was attacked?"

"No and No." Hoss said.

As we exited, Jay stopped at the Nurse's station and asked about Hoss's prognosis on being able to leave the hospital for his trial.

"Not for a few more weeks", she said.

That worried him. Especially since he knew they had a leak.

CHAPTER THIRTY SIX

**The tragedy of life is not death,
but what we let die in us while we live.**
(Chief Tecumseh   Shawnee)

On the ride back to Oklahoma City, Jay needed to talk about the next steps.

"I want to see what I can find out about Sgt. Johnnie Wolf's involvement in the leaks. At this point, he probably doesn't even know that he is suspected."

"Good idea." She said. "Why don't you take the lead on questioning, since you have a greater background and relationship with Sgt. Wolf?"

"This is going to be a little hard for me, since Johnnie has always been someone I trusted and respected. He was on the original group that set up the task force. He was party to all the information we had as it was being developed. He lost his wife to cancer and has a very sick daughter named Blossom… Leukemia."

To himself, he thought, "Maybe I'm too soft-hearted for this job, I need to think about that."

He broke the silence. "We are gonna' be late getting in. I am already getting sleepy."

"Jay. You are definitely a Diurnal person." She said and laid her head back and closed her eyes. 'Power Nap'." She announced.

He thought to himself, "'Diurnal'. Definitely not a compliment. Back to the dictionary."

It was well after midnight when they got back to the station and he dropped Britt off at her car. He found out one thing, she doesn't snore.

After checking on the animals, he took a quick shower, ate and settled in bed with his dictionary.

"What were the words?" He thought. "Oh yeah. Diurnal and Obsequious."

Diurnal meant active during daylight. The opposite is Nocturnal, active after dark, he already knew that one. Bats are nocturnal.

"I'm no bat or vampire, so I guess it was a compliment." Next, Obsequious.

She had said, "as long as you're not obsequious." According to the dictionary, *Obsequious* means "Servile or Fawning."

"Wait a minute", "Loyalty doesn't make you someone's servant. And I don't fawn, bow, or prostrate myself at Mac's feet. This woman is going to drive me to drink."

With that, he conked out. After only a few hours of sleep, the alarm went off at 5:00 am. Jay didn't jump right out of bed like he usually did. He groaned and rolled onto the edge and just sat for a minute or two. He shaved off two days of beard and skipped breakfast. One cup of coffee to go. He got in at about 6:05am. She was already there.

"Spent the night here, huh." He said.

"Nope. Just wanted to clear up a few things before you got in. I assume you got enough rest officer Nation?"

"Power Nap." He said, as he headed for the coffee machine.

He didn't look at her, but he could feel her grinning.

"I called Atoka, she said. They will be transporting Lizard today. ETA about noon. That gives us a little less than 6 hours to knock out the interview with Sgt. Wolf and get back. Is that enough time?"

"Plenty". I'm ready to roll when you are."

"Need for me to drive?" She asked.

"No, I'm good."

As they got into the cruiser, he said what he felt he had to say.

"By the way, I did want to clear up one or two things. Loyalty does not necessarily mean obsequious. At least not in my case. And I am a diurnal person, for sure. I admit that, and as Annabelle would say, 'Openly and without shame'."

Jay smiled. And was rewarded with a quick return grin.

"Well", he thought, "and as Britt would say, 'That's at least something'."

Sgt. Wolf was on patrol. They asked if he could join them and the Lt. on duty said he would call him in. He got there in about 5 minutes. They needed to watch their time. He joined them in one of the Interrogation rooms.

"Hi guys. Kind of a surprise visit." He looked at Britt. "I don't think we've met. Sgt. Johnnie Wolf, My pleasure."

"Agent Britt Thorpe. FBI." His body seemed to stiffen.

"This about the Gang investigation?" He looked concerned.

"Yes it is Johnnie." Jay answered and was looking straight into his eyes.

"How can I help?" He shifted uneasily in his seat.

If you were a profiler, you would have to say that he was acting guilty.

"How's the daughter?"

"About the same. The Chemo seems to be helping. Can't tell for sure, just going by what the doctors say. She isn't in any pain, but she is thin, pale and has lost some of her beautiful hair." Johnnie put his hand to his eyes which had begun to tear up.

"Must be expensive as well as heart-breaking, Johnnie." Jay said with some compassion.

"Very. Both."

"Johnnie, I won't beat around the bush. I think you know why we're here. And I want to tell you, up front, that my friendship with you and my understanding about your daughter's condition, make this hard for me. But I'm a cop. And I have to do my job. I hope you understand that."

He looked up. His eyes were red and wet. "Jay, you don't have kids, so you can't even imagine what it's like to watch your child withering away. You can't just stand by and not try to fix things in any way that you can."

"You're right Johnnie. I can't even imagine. I want you to tell me about it. How it started and who was involved. You owe me that. And I will listen without blame. I owe *you* that."

"It all started a year or so ago. I was already hurting financially. Insurance had run out. I was in debt up to my ears, trying to take care of the doctor bills and medicine. I was at my rope's end. Then I got a call. I was offered more money than I could have imagined. I could finally set my finances straight and get my precious daughter taken care of. I had no other options, so I agreed. I would be like a personnel placement person. I would find the kind of people they were looking for and send them their rap sheets. I made it clear up front that it was all I was willing to do. What they did with the info was up to them and I wanted no part in what they were gonna do with it. Do you understand? It wasn't until they started killing people that I began to suspicion that this was about the Black Brick Gang."

There was a stunned silence. He was openly crying now. Jay's mind was racing. They came here to confront him about possibly leaking info to Dutch, since Johnnie was Dutch's nephew. This was completely unexpected. He was deeply involved in the organization of the Gang. Jay had to stop and think.

"Johnnie, I want to give you a minute to compose yourself. I know this is hard for you. I get that. Perhaps we can handle this without it jeopardizing the welfare of your daughter. Sit here for a minute or two. Britt and I will get some coffee and I will bring you one."

CHAPTER THIRTY SEVEN

Is it wrong for me to love my own?
Is it wicked for me because my skin
is red? Because I am Sioux?
Because I was born where my father lived?
Because I would die for my people and my country?
God made me an Indian.
(Chief Sitting Bull   Lakota Sioux)

They stepped out. Jay got a cup of coffee and took it in to Johnnie and told him they would be right back. Britt and Jay went outside.

"Britt, I would appreciate your guidance on this. It can be our best possible lead to get to the Gang. If we arrest him, the person in charge of the gang will know and that means Johnnie's life will be in jeopardy. We now have four people we have to protect from harm. Hoss, Mrs. Hunter, Lizard and now Johnnie. Not to mention the both of us."

"We can start with his written statement." Britt was staring off into space and thinking. "We won't cuff him, but we need to tell the Lieutenant on duty that we want to 'borrow' him for a while. That his help is critical in our investigation. We need to take him to our office, put a locator bracelet on his ankle and pretend to all concerned that he is helping us."

"Now we *have* to tell Mac."

"Jay. I haven't been completely open with you. For a while we considered everyone in the office as a 'leaker' suspect. Even you. The first thing we did was start gathering who called who, what cell phone transmissions originated at the homes or offices of each person in your office. I can tell you now, that you are cleared, so is John Two Feathers. He apparently rarely calls anybody. But we know that several cell calls hit the cell tower originating at your offices and contacting a throw-away cell phone in Durant. I couldn't tell you before because you were a suspect. That's why I have been playing this so close and not involving anyone else at your offices."

"Listen, it can't be Mac. You know, yourself, that he is professional, caring and a career officer working toward retirement. I would give my life for him."

"I understand that Jay. And I tend to agree. But until he is cleared, as you and John Two Feathers are, he can't be told any of this. I am truly sorry."

"We have to tell John Two Feathers at least."

"Let's tell him together. I feel I should be the one to do it."

"O.K. I'm good with that. Let's get back inside and get his statement."

The statement took a while. Britt asked him to include anything he might have fed to Dutch, also. Then they asked him to go home, pack some clothes and meet them at the office in Oklahoma City. They still had time to make it back before Lizard arrived. They had no time to stop by the office and just visit.

Mac was out, thankfully. Jay didn't look forward to talking to him right now. Britt asked John Two Feathers to come with them. She told him that they had something to discuss with him. They arrived at the hospital just as the helicopter bearing Lizard was being unloaded into the emergency entrance. Two Durant plain clothes officers were overseeing the transfer. Jay checked with them and thanked them for their help and reminded them that this whole transfer was confidential. It didn't happen. At least until the Gang was caught or eliminated. They agreed and left. Jay and the others accompanied the stretcher into the ICU.

John had not said anything up to now, He finally asked. "What's going on?"

Britt took over. "What I am about to tell you is confidential and would carry severe Federal penalties if you fail to keep it that way. I think I know your history well enough, John, to know I don't need to say that, but it is my job to do so. And it is also my job to ask if you understand."

"Yup". Said John with a furrowed brow.

Britt proceeded to tell him the whole story about Lizard's capture and injury. Also about Sgt. Johnnie Wolf's confession. He said nothing. When Britt explained about the cell phone tracing and the mysterious calls, his first response was the same as Jay's had been.

"You can't think its Mac?"

"I don't currently think so, but until we know more, as Director, excuse me, *Co-Director* of this Investigation, I can't rule anyone out. Even the janitor."

"O.K." He said.

"It may be a couple of days before we can safely question Lizard. Until then, I am going to ask Chief Yellow Feather to detail two plain clothes detectives to schedule 24/7 protection of him. As far as all of us are concerned, this all never happened," Britt emphasized. "John, Sgt. Wolf should be getting here any minute. We need to see if there is some way to pursue this and still keep it quiet. He is willing to help in any way he can."

"Does he know who it is?" John asked.

"He said yes, but he can't prove it and wants to keep it to himself for now, to protect his daughter. I can understand that. We need to set up a trap with Sgt. Wolf. Wasn't my idea. It was his." She said.

Jay's cell phone buzzed. It was Chief Yellow Feather. "Hi, Chief."

Before Jay could say any more, the Chief blurted out, "We have a new problem. Actually two problems."

"What's up?"

CHAPTER THIRTY EIGHT

A very great vision is needed and the man who has it must follow it as the eagle seeks the deepest blue of the sky.
(Chief Crazy Horse   Lakota Sioux)

"Two guys stormed the hospital. Shot one of my guards, outside Hoss's room. There was another guard just coming out of the bathroom who got off a spray of shots and the two guys bolted. Security cameras caught the guys jumping in a dark sedan and roaring away. There were two other guys in the car. Has to be the gang."

"How's your guy?"

"Luckiest guy in the world. The bullet should have gone right through his heart. Instead, he was planning to take his wife's cell phone in for service. His phone and hers were in his shirt pocket. Bullet went through both and lodged in his ribs. He is in surgery right now. He'll hurt for a while, but he'll make it. We have a good description. I'll shoot you the information.

Second problem, we have a 'missing person' report. Normally not a big deal. Except this one is on the staff at the Atoka County Coroner's office. I smell a big problem."

"Thanks Chief and sorry about your guy. We need to move Hoss, as soon as possible, to a more secure federal hospital. We'll have Eddie Whitecloud get in touch with you. As far as the other, we have to assume, for now, that we have been compromised. These guys are getting desperate. Is there any way you could spare two plain clothes guys to protect the one we've got, 'Lizard'?"

"My guys are hyped. No problem, if you need more than two, let me know. I'll have them there in a couple of hours or so."

"Thanks Chief."

Sgt. Wolf had arrived. Jay shared the information that he got from the Chief with everyone there.

"I am so sorry. I feel like this is all my fault." Said Sgt. Wolf. "I should have reported this as soon as I had suspicions. These injuries and deaths are my fault."

"We don't have time to talk about who's at fault. We have some desperate lunatics on our hands and none of us are safe. Let's talk about setting a trap. Sgt Wolf, we need to talk about what you have in mind." Said Britt.

A nurse approached them. "Are you the guys here about Mr. Lizard?"

"Yes mam." Jay said.

"They said you wanted to be notified if there was any change in his condition. Well, there has been."

"Oh No. Is he O.K.?"

"Yes, in fact he is surprisingly much improved. He asked for water."

"He's talking?' asked Britt.

"Talking? We can't get him to stop. The guy must be like a cat with 9 lives."

"Actually, more like a lizard." Jay said.

CHAPTER THIRTY NINE

Listen or your tongue will make you deaf.
(Cherokee proverb)

Jay and Britt hurried to Lizard's room. You could hear him talking as they came in the door. He was on his favorite subject. Himself. His voice sounded a little weak, but he was explaining to the doctor and two nurses, how he got the nickname "Lizard".

"So that's how I got it. I lose something, I just grow it back. Somebody blew my backbone away, I'll just have to grow another one."

"Doctor", Britt said, "I am Agent Britt Thorpe, FBI. Is he well enough that we can have a few minutes alone with him?"

"Maybe 10 minutes. No more, but call me if he seems to be fading. His condition is still considered critical."

The room cleared except for the officers. He was not handcuffed to the bed. He didn't need to be. He wasn't going anywhere.

"Lizard, I'm Agent Thorpe, we need to ask you some questions. You have the right to have an attorney present if you'd like."

"Nope, I'm good. Say, are you curious how I got my name?"

"I think I already know, but I'd be glad to hear you tell it after we get some questions out of the way."

"Good. It's a real grabber."

"I'll bet it is." She gave him a big toothy smile.

Jay couldn't help telling himself. "Apparently the Britt I know has left the building."

Britt continued, smiling. "To begin with, where have you been staying?"

"I think they call it Durant."

"Do you have an address?"

"Don't know if they have one. Never heard it said."

"Surely you must have seen some road signs or something."

"Nope. You see, I have to sit in the back. Only the giant and the boss sit in the front."

"What's it like? Is it a house or a trailer or what?"

"Ain't a house or trailer, it's a barn."

"Do you know what general direction it is from town?"

"Nope. Say, could I have some water?"

"We'll ask the Doc for you. How many guys are in your Gang?"

"Ain't a Gang. It's a Mission Team."

"A Mission Team? You do Missions?"

"Yep, very military. You see, the world is full of bad guys. Cops just can't seem to get them taken care of. Slick lawyers and such let them get away with anything. We are Vigilantes. You know what Vigilantes do, right?"

"I think so. You tell me."

"We get done what the cops can't. You got a bad guy that ain't doin' the right thing and is doin' bad things and hurtin' people and makin' the world a worse place to live in, Vigilantes are the ones who fix it. Make it right. We're soldiers. We're on the front lines. We're kinda' like heroes in a way."

"Who is your boss?"

"Chase. Don't know his last name. But he's not the big boss."

"Who is the big boss?

"Don't know. Never seen the big boss. Chase says by stayin' out of the action, that's what keeps the boss safe."

"How long have you been a Vigilante"?"

"Several months. I was the last one to join the team. I'm a better shot than any of them. Includin' Chase."

"How many of these bad people have you shot since you've been on the team?"

"Never had to shoot anybody. Not yet."

"Who does all the killing then?"

"Just the giant, he's the official 'Do-er'."

"What's his name?"

"Don't remember. I've never talked to him."

"Never talked to him?"

"Nope."

"Why Is that?"

"He tried to kill me on our first Mission."

"How did that happen?"

"Simple. They didn't tell me that he had claim on the passenger seat. I hollered 'shotgun' and got in the front.

He lifted me out with one hand, by the throat and if it hadn't been for Chase, I would have been choked to death on the spot."

"Strong guy huh?"

"Strongest I ever seen."

"How about the other two?"

"Great guys. Good soldiers. Between me and them, the giant ain't got nothing to worry about. Doesn't even have to carry a gun. Just the brick."

"How do you get your targets, I mean your 'Missions'?"

"Chase gets a buzz on his cell phone. He steps outside. Comes back in and he gives us our mission."

"How do you get paid?"

"We get it right after we complete a 'clean' job."

"How do you mean 'clean'?"

"We get in, do the job, get out and go home. Clean."

"Looks like today was not a 'clean' job."

"No, we got in, did the job, but didn't get away clean. Probably won't get paid. None of us."

"Probably right. 'You', for sure."

As they left the room, Jay told Britt that he wished they had taped all of that. She pulled a small recorder from her shirt pocket.

"We did."

"You must have been a Girl Scout."

"How'd you guess?"

They got permission to use one of the hospital's conference rooms and gathered around a table to put a plan together.

CHAPTER FORTY

**Have I done everything I could
to earn my grandchild's fondness?**
(Chief Dan George   Salish)

"Sgt. Wolf, What kind of a trap did you have in mind?" Britt asked.

"They probably already know that Lizard survived. We need to get the word out that Chief Yellow Feather orchestrated a move, without our knowledge, to this hospital because they were better able to treat the injury. The right doctors and the right equipment. I can call that in to the Gang's boss. It's possible that only the few of us know about all this. Not yet, anyway. Then, we have the hospital put a "John Doe" into the system, dated late last night, showing the room number. We put our people on duty as doctors and nurses. The hospital should have plenty of uniforms we can use.

We put a mannequin, with pajamas and a wig, in the bed. No guard outside the room. We then put a uniformed officer out in the hall, with Kevlar protection on under his uniform and SWAT body armor on the outside. He is at the nurse's station talking to a nurse. 'Our' nurse. Some spotters in the lobby and some others on the security cameras looking for 2 or 3 guys. We now have a pretty good description thanks to Mrs. Hunter. Probably only 2 guys since the giant would attract attention. The leader will be driving the getaway car. When we spot them, we will watch the cameras and when they hit the floor and get off we will have the guard announce loudly that he has to make a quick pit stop, but if the nurse will watch the door, he'll be right back. Make sure the room is far enough from the nurse's station and the elevator, so that they wouldn't need to shoot the guard. All the fake doctors and nurses will either have a gun on them or easily reachable."

"What about the regular doctors and nurses?" Jay asked.

'When we spot the guys, we'll put them into an empty room." Said Britt.

"What if they take the stairs up?"

"They won't." Johnnie said. "The stairs are monitored on the security cameras. Let's get the hospital informed now, get their suggestion on a room and then check it out.

We need to get some officers over here pretty quick. They can't come from here. The quickest would probably be some of my guys from Okmulgee. The guys only need to know that this is a special assignment."

"How do we get the word out that will spark immediate action?" Britt asked.

Jay said, "Good question, Britt. It's time for Johnnie to call his contact. And time for us to report to our own units that we have caught a gang member and he is alive. That he has been in a medically induced coma and that Chief Yellow Feather didn't alert us until just now. He had his hands full with a dead judge, the recent victim of the gang. We'll report that the doctors are saying that the prognosis is good. And they are bringing the killer out of the coma, as we speak. We'll say that we should be able to question him this evening. Probably close to midnight."

Jay made the call to Mac, got a recording. Good. He left a message with all details. Johnnie made his call to his contact.

CHAPTER FORTY ONE

**Those that lie down with dogs,
Get up with fleas.**
(Blackfoot saying)

C hase's cell phone buzzed.

"Yes."

"I've been waiting for your call. The hit on Hoss didn't pan out, but I hope you had better luck with the girl from the coroner's office."

"Not 30 seconds ago, she broke. Lonnie made her suffer. She is a mess right now. Bleeding everywhere. I am going to have to put her out of her misery. I have an old abandoned well not far out the back. I'll have him put her in there."

"Good, what did she tell you?"

"Lizard was hurt bad. They took him to the hospital in Atoka, then transported him to Oklahoma City."

"As soon as we get rid of her body, we are takin' off for the hospital in Oklahoma City. I was going to confirm that when I reported in."

"I can't put it more strongly than this. Lizard has to die. Whatever you have to do to accomplish that, do it. That is your mission. Use your best option. I am not going to rule out explosives. Do I make myself clear?"

"Absolutely."

"Keep me posted." (Click)

The boss's throw-away cell phone buzzes.

"Yes?"

"Only got a minute", Johnnie whispered. "They got one of your guys. He's at the hospital in Oklahoma City. He is unconscious right now, but they expect him to be awake by late tonight. That's all I know right now. Thought you would want to know."

"Thanks, friend. I already knew. However, thanks anyway."

(Click)

CHAPTER FORTY TWO

**He who would do great things
should not attempt them alone.**
(Blackfoot saying)

Britt hung up from her update to Eddie Whitecloud. She had a peculiar look on her face and her brow was wrinkled.

"What's up?" Jay asked.

"As I was finishing up my update to Eddie, he asked me to hold a minute. When he came back he said his guy in Phone Tracing Group told him that a call just went out from your office area to that same throwaway cell phone. I am hoping it was the action we wanted. It's about 2 ½ hours from Durant to here. We have at least that much time to get ready. Possibly a little more. But we should be prepared."

Jay's Cell phone buzzed. "Britt, Its Mac."

"Answer it."

"Hey boss. I was just fixing to call you. Did you get my message?"

"No. I'm sorry Jay, I've been home most of the day. I wasn't feeling very good today so I knocked off about noon and came home. The little wife insisted. I told my secretary to let you know, as soon as you checked in. Sometimes when I am home, I put the darn phone down and forget where I left it. Guess I'm getting old and forgetful. I see you left me a message. You want to wait a second while I check it, or do you want to just let me know what it says."

"No, let me just read it to you." And he did.

160

"Sounds like a real mess. If you need for me to come in, I will."

"No, right now we have everything under control. Just waiting for this Lizard guy to wake up. I'll keep you posted after we have a chance to question him. Shouldn't be but a few hours. Britt and I will probably grab a bite somewhere and come back before midnight."

"O.K. Did you let anybody else know what has happened?"

"Not yet boss. Unless Eddie Whitecloud passed it on. Britt got a call from him about the same time we found out Lizard was here and alive. He must have heard through the guys in Atoka. I just hope it doesn't get leaked."

"Let's hope."

"I apologize for not contacting you earlier, but things just have been crazy today. I'll cover it all with you when I see you."

"Jay, you don't owe me any apology. I expect you to be good. I don't expect you to be the apotheosis of law enforcement. I have told you that many times."

"I know boss. And I appreciate it. I'll keep in touch."

Jay didn't have to look up *apotheosis*. The best of the best. He looked it up a long, long time ago. Mac loves that word.

"So, what did he say? I heard your side of it." Said Britt.

"He left work at around noon. Didn't keep his cell phone with him for a while at home. I'm relieved. That call had to have come from someone other than him. I'm thinking now it has to be his secretary, Sarah. He tells her everything. He almost has to. She is his right hand. Sometimes both of his hands. She caught the Fax from the PI. She always knows where I am staying. At this point, we just don't know for certain. Can't worry about it now. Let's get ready. I think it is coming down tonight."

Everything just fell into place. The mannequin was in place. The fake doctors and nurses were in a couple of rooms waiting for the swap. Extra spotters were in the parking lot and extra eyes were deployed in the security room, one person on each monitor. Everyone had their radios on and blue tooth earplugs monitoring a special channel they had set up for tonight. Everyone was trying to act cool, but you could sense the tension.

"Unit 1, side parking lot. Two 'possibles' just exiting a black sedan."

"Unit 2, I got 'em. Headed my way. Wearing long black coats. Not cold enough for coats. I am laying my head back on the seat like I'm asleep. Should be to the front door in about 2."

"Unit 4, in the Lobby. I see them approaching the door. They are looking all around. I am reading a newspaper and have a pot of flowers between my feet. They are checking me out."

"Unit 13 here, this is Jay. Get those doctors and nurses into their rooms. Fake Docs and nurses to your places. Uniform, you in place?

"Unit 10, Uniform. Yes sir, they are moving. Holler when the elevator doors start to open."

"Unit 13 here. O.K., Uniform, you are the most vulnerable. Take no chances. Start walking away and talking loud as soon as the doors open."

"Unit 10, Uniform. 10-4"

"Unit 3, lobby. I'm near the elevator. They have stopped. Looking around. Walked over to the stairwell. Discussed something. Looking around. Now, headed back toward the elevator. Punched the button. Getting in. Door closed. Headed your way. We will stay here in case they change their mind."

"Unit 7, Security room. We have been following them. Have them on elevator camera. It's them for sure.

Something under their coats. Can't tell what. ETA 20 seconds or so."

"Unit 13, Jay. Fake doctors and nurses get set."

"Unit 7 security room. Doors should open in 5, 4, 3, 2, 1, Opening."

Loud voice. "Hah, Hah, Hah. That's a real laugh. Look, will you watch that door for me for a minute, I have to make a pit stop or I'm gonna wet my pants."

"Unit 8 Security room. Uniform walking away as he talks. Suspects standing in front of the elevator door.

Whispering to each other. Uniform going into bathroom at far end of hall."

It was at that instant that all hell broke loose. The two suspects each pulled a huge weapon from under their coats. Two rocket propelled grenades, "RPG's" launched. One went right through the door of the room that was supposed to hold their witness. The other went into the wall adjoining the nurse's station. There were two huge ear-shattering explosions in the small enclosed area. Jay and Britt felt the tremor from where they stood two floors below.

"What the …", Jay exclaimed.

"Jay, you stay here to protect our witness in case this is a diversion. I'm going up." Said Britt. And she left the room on the run.

The smoke was so thick you couldn't see anything. Debris was everywhere. Suddenly the sprinklers came on. Slowly the smoke was dissipating. There were groans coming from the nurse's station. The room where the grenade went in, was on fire. The room on the other side of the nurse's station was on fire. The doors were laying out in the hall. Britt checked the hall for the suspects. They were gone. She opened the doors where the real doctors and nurses were waiting and told them their help was needed at the Nurse's station. 5 officers were down, two had bloody faces. Two were unconscious. One was holding his ears and looking stunned. The nurses and doctors began triage.

"This is Jay, what's happening."

"This is Unit 7 Security room. Two suspects took the elevator down. Got to their car and took off."

"Anybody in pursuit?"

"This is Unit 1. I am in pursuit, Unit 2 is right behind me. I see two other cars with lights flashing, somewhere behind us.

"That's us, Units 3 and 4. We have radioed ahead to all cars in the area.

When we know which way they are headed, we will try to arrange a road block. They are not going to get away."

"Jay again. Try to take them alive if you can do so without risking your life. Remember, these guys are psychopaths and think they are vigilante heroes."

"Unit 10, can you send a couple of your monitor officers up to guard Lizard."

"This is Unit 10. They are on their way."

"Unit 1 here. We just got broadsided by a guy running a red light.

Lost Unit 2 also, he was right behind me. I am pretty bunged up. Don't know about 2. I can't get my door open to go check. Oh crap, my car is on fire."

"Unit 3 stop and assist Units 1 and 2. Unit 4, try to catch up to the suspects."

"This is Unit 4. There's a problem. The road is blocked by the accident.

I'm trying to take the sidewalk to get around them. I don't see their taillights any more. We may have lost them."

"This can't be happening", Jay thought. He found Britt. She was with the injured officers.

"Did you hear?" He asked.

"Yeah, two more officers hurt and the suspects may have gotten away. I just talked to Eddie Whitecloud. He is on his way down. This is not a good career move for either one of us. We need to find that barn before they decide to move. We are running out of time."

Jay called Chief Yellow Feather in Durant and gave him the bad news.

"Chief, time is of the essence now. Before these guys decide to tuck tail and run, we need to find that barn."

"You know Jay. I've been thinking about that. And just this afternoon, a thought came to me. You can't carry out military precision missions when you are walking around in cow poop. I figured they may have converted a barn or rented one that was already converted.

I knew at once where they might be. So, I called a guy I know, over toward Antlers, who tried for a while to make some extra money with a bed and breakfast. I called him to see if he had ever made it work. Had to leave a message. He just returned my call and said 'In fact I did. Got some fellas gave me a year lease on my B&B.' I told him I was glad for him. And wished him well. I don't know why I didn't think of it earlier.

His B&B is a converted barn, between Antlers and Durant, A little south of Stroud."

CHAPTER FORTY THREE

**Man's law changes with his understanding of man.
Only the laws of the spirit remain always the same.**
(Crow saying)

Early the next day, the Chief had gathered a group of officers in the Durant Police station Conference Room. There were some extra officers from surrounding cities who wanted to help. There was standing room only. The Chief took to the Podium. Britt and Jay were standing right behind him. They had been up all night.

"O.K. here is what we've got. The Black Brick Gang appears to be hiding out in the barn that used to be the old Bed and Breakfast. I think most of you guys know the one. We are passing around a flyer with the location marked on it in case you don't. There should be 4 guys in there. They are armed and extremely dangerous. They are serial killers and they are well-trained. Mostly ex-military. With the added guys from the surrounding area, we have about 50 officers plus the two reps from the State and Federal task force. There will be two helicopters overhead, once we engage. There are police cruisers scattered around the nearby roads. If the guys try to run, we should be able to spot them. I will turn this over now to Jay with the State and Agent Thorpe with the FBI."

Jay stepped up. "I'll speak first. These are not your normal run-of-the-mill lunatics. They are well-trained, well-armed, efficient and ruthless. Treat them as such and we can make this a successful operation. Agent Thorpe?"

"We have eyes on us from here to FBI Headquarters in Washington, D.C. and maybe beyond. What we do today will probably make the training manuals for State and Federal Training Academies. More importantly, we need to get these guys off the street. Your actions today will probably make history. I remember a very smart person saying, 'Do it, Do it right and Do it right now'. So, Let's Do it."

"We'll meet out front. You all have been fully armed and equipped". Said the Chief.

As he was heading out front, he asked his desk sergeant if she had been able to reach Ben, his 2nd in command.

"Not yet Chief, but I will keep trying and have him meet you at the barn." She said.

The group moved out. There were over 30 cars. It looked like some kind of a military parade. Except it was made up of several different Police departments.

After the previous night's disaster, Jay felt that this was probably their last chance to redeem the failures they've had up to now. He kept remembering what Britt had said. "Definitely not a good career move." She was right, as usual.

The Durant Chief's assistant. Lt. Ben Pushmataha, was in the area when the call came through to approach the target barn with caution. He immediately hit his lights and went barreling toward the spot. He was very familiar with the old man who owned the place and hoped that nothing had happened to him. He barely slowed down to turn into the barn road. The owner was a relative of a relative of his. He had loved the old man like a brother. When he reached the barn clearing, he slid to a stop with the car turned sideways to the road. He was as close to the barn as he dared to get. He got out of his cruiser and with bullhorn in hand, called out to the occupants.

"This is the Choctaw police. Come out with your hands up. I promise that no harm will come to you, if you surrender peacefully."

Not a sound from the barn. He wondered if the Chief had acted on bad information. He saw no vehicles, unless they were parked behind the barn.

"Listen, I have over 50 men on their way here. If you don't surrender yourself to me, right now, I can't guarantee your safety once the whole force arrives. I have never shot a man in my career and I don't want to start today. Please come on out with your hands in the air. I will not shoot you. Look", he said as he stepped out from behind the car with his hands and gun in the air. He slowly holstered his weapon and then kept both hands in the air. "Look now, I have holstered my gun. I will not harm you. But when the others who are on their way get here, they might. I won't. Let me take you into protective custody. I will put you in my cruiser and get you to the station. You have my word. Please hurry, I can hear their sirens. They will be here any minute."

He took two steps forward. A shot rang out, just as the other cruisers began arriving in the clearing. Lt. Pushmahata dropped to the ground. A small hole in his forehead began to trickle blood. The cruisers formed a semi-circle in the front of the clearing. Chief Yellow feather ordered his men to encircle the house and lay down to make a smaller target. He then ran to the downed officer, grabbed his legs and dragged him behind his cruiser. Britt and Jay joined the Chief, behind Ben's cruiser. Britt checked Ben for signs of life. She looked at Jay and then the Chief and shook her head. He was gone. The Chief took the bullhorn.

"This is Chief Yellow Feather of the Choctaw Nation. Come out with your hands up. I will count to ten and then we will turn that barn into a pile of splinters. We have more than enough fire power to do so."

After 10 seconds, no response.

"O.K. men. Blow the place apart." The Chief said over the bullhorn.

The sound was deafening. You would think there was a war going on. Holes began appearing in the barn boards.

Windows shattered. Still, the firing continued. Then he ordered a cease fire.

"If there is anyone still alive in there, come out with your hands in the air." He said over the bullhorn.

After 10 seconds, no response.

Over the bullhorn again. "Fire at will."

Again the firing began. This time they kept it up until it looked like the barn might actually cave in. The big guns had come out. Big game rifles and 357 magnums. Barn boards were shattering. You could begin to actually see inside the barn in several places.

"Hold up." It sounded like someone was screaming from inside the barn.

"Hold up, we're comin' out."

"Cease fire", hollered the Chief. Most of the firing stopped, but not all.

"Cease fire", the chief said again, this time over the bullhorn. "They're comin' out." Now it worked. All firing stopped.

The barn doors swung open with a creak. The officers gathered at the front with guns pointed at the doors. Two men limped out. One holding the other up. Both men had blood on their shirt fronts.

"On your face with your arms over your head", the Chief was saying. But it was almost too late, they had already started to slump toward the ground. They crumpled into a heap.

"O.K. everybody in the barn. Find the other two." The Chief ordered. "And somebody call an E.M.T."

They began to check the two injured men. They were in pretty bad shape. Officers handcuffed and ankle shackled them anyway. It only took 4 or 5 minutes to clear the barn. There was no one else inside.

"Where are the other two?" Britt asked the two Gang members.

"Don't know. They were near the back door, last we saw." One gasped.

"Chief, I think they slipped out the back while we were focusing on the guys coming out the front." Britt said.

"O.K. listen up you guys." The Chief said. "Half of you go with Agent Thorpe, half with Jay. Comb the woods behind the barn. If they are injured, they may not have gotten far."

The two groups, with Britt and Jay in the lead, started to jog toward the woods.

Britt held up her hand and spoke.

"O.K. guys. Most of you know how to track and trail deer. Humans are no different. Look for tracks, broken branches or blood trails. Jog, don't walk. Stay in a sweep line. Don't lose sight of the guys next to you. Don't fall behind the line. Don't charge ahead of the line. Stay 8 or 10 feet apart. Maintain the line. We don't want to lose anybody to 'friendly fire'. If you see something holler, loud. Let's go."

When they got into the woods, the real search began. Within 100 yards or so, they came to a stream. There were no signs that the guys had crossed. But those two were trained on stealth. So, the group crossed the creek and continued on. Jay had a thought. He hollered out to everybody.

"I am going upstream. To make sure they didn't take to the creek to throw us off."

After a couple of hundred yards, he saw a slight spill of dirt, on the other side, from the bank above. Could be them, could be an animal. Only one way to know. He had to check it out. He had been well trained on the reservation, as a young kid, in the ways of Indian hunters. He knew how to track game quickly and quietly. After about 20 minutes He was about to give up when he thought he heard a rustling of bushes up ahead. He became even more stealthy. He spotted a dark shadow and saw the branches moving. He wasn't taking any chances. He crouched and with a two handed grip, fired 4 shots into the bushes he saw moving. He heard a grunt and a thump.

"I got him." He thought. His shots had hit home.

He still crept forward slowly, with his gun pointed. Then Jay spotted him and lowered his gun. His bullets had hit home alright. Laying ahead, on the trail, was an 8 point Buck deer. It was making small coughing sounds and its ribs were heaving. Blood was trickling from its nose and mouth. A "lung" shot. He couldn't stand the sight of the deer suffering like that. He put one more mercy shot through its head. Then he charged ahead for another half hour or so. No sign of anything. He returned to the deer.

He always kept his sheath knife as sharp as a razor. He gutted the poor animal, leaving inside only the liver which appeared to be healthy. He cut its rear legs and removed the musk glands to keep from tainting the meat. Then he began dragging it by its antlers, back toward the barn. That took a while. Twilight had just begun to set in by the time he got back. He was exhausted. He drug it to the cruisers and then laid back on the ground and tried to catch his breath. Britt walked up, shook her head and walked away.

The Chief looked down at him and shook his head.

"What". Jay said

"You were hunting gang members, remember? Not deer." The Chief said with a straight face. "Looks like you were the only one to capture anything."

Jay related the whole story to him.

"What you gonna' do with it?" the Chief said.

"Nothing." Jay said. "Let your guys take it to a deer processor and then distribute it to the needy. No sense in wasting it."

The Chief helped his guys load the carcass across the hood of a cruiser and it departed for Durant.

"Three down, two to go" Said the Chief. "I gotta' get back to the station and start on the paperwork. I need to check on the two we got. I hope they make it. You are aware, the Chief said gravely, that this is going to get you some big time ribbing for a long time?"

"Yeah. I probably deserve it."

They found rooms at the Holiday Inn Express. He finally got a good night's sleep and didn't even have to read the dictionary. He met Britt in the restaurant at 6:00 am. He was getting used to it. She looked angry.

"What's up, Britt? You look a little angry." He asked.

"Why shouldn't I be?"

A rhetorical question, or does she expect an answer? He tried the latter.

"O.K. Let's see. First, we caught a killer, then we caught 3 members of 'Murder Incorporated of Oklahoma', then we destroyed their hideout. That may not be 'the apotheosis of police work, but it is pretty darned good."

"They didn't give Elliott Ness a hero badge for catching a bunch of Mafia Gang members. He didn't get a hero badge until he put Al Capone away."

"I guess I don't understand." Jay said quietly.

"I'm FBI. Technically, I am the highest ranking officer on this investigation. You are State, you are second highest. An officer has died. We were part of it. This will go on both of our records, we did nothing wrong, but it happened on our watch."

"So, what do we do?"

"Our jobs. Only better."

"You know, I'm sorry. I guess I wasn't thinking. You are totally correct. I see your point. It's like wrestling. No trophies or accolades for doing well. The trophies go to the winners. This was not the win we were trying for."

She didn't respond.

He added, "Let's tackle the two we got yesterday, if they are well enough to talk. Or, even if they aren't well enough to talk."

They ate in silence. He could see that Britt was upset.

Jay spoke quietly. "I don't know why I didn't notice that the officers who were at the back corner of the barn, watching the back door, came running around the front to help with the gang coming out. I saw them, but I really didn't 'See' them. We knew these guys better than the Chief. I knew what they were capable of. That will never happen again. That, I *do not* promise to *you*. That, I promise to *myself*."

Britt said nothing.

CHAPTER FORTY FOUR

**Poverty is a noose that strangles humility
and breeds disrespect for God and man.**
(Sioux saying)

They drove straight to the Hospital. The Chief was already there. He looked strained.

"Morning Chief" Jay said. "How are the prisoners?"

"Recovering. I had the unpleasant duty this morning of visiting with Ben's wife and family members. Some of them wanted to mount a hanging party. Can't say as I blame them."

"Are the prisoners well enough to talk?"

"If they are breathing, they are well enough to talk as far as I am concerned."

"Let's do it." Britt said, still angry and frowning.

They checked at the Nurse's station and were told that both guys had serious, but not life-threatening wounds.

"You can ask whatever you want and spend whatever time it takes." She said.

The nurse almost seemed like she would prefer that they be questioned right into their graves. The staff all knew Ben and his family.

Their room was a high security room. There was a small entrance foyer where a guard was posted and then it opened into a fairly regular hospital room with two beds. The differences that struck you right off, were the heavily barred windows, the heavy steel framed bed and the ample tie-points for chains. It reminded Jay of a medieval torture chamber. And he was tempted to use it as one. There was no door on the bathroom, no adjustable shower head and no chairs. It was not visitor friendly.

The prisoners appeared to be in their 30's, no facial hair and medium build. Black straight hair and dark complexion. Definitely Native American. The Chief had gotten information from their fingerprint check. The Federal Data base said they were ex-Army Rangers and it had a pretty good bit of information on them. The Chief was awaiting their complete military files from the Rangers.

"I am Officer Jay Nation with the State Crime Task Force."

"I know who you are." One of them said.

"Good, I am here to ask you a few questions. You have the right to have an attorney present, if you prefer. We will be tape recording this session."

He then read them their Miranda Rights.

"And I am Agent Thorpe with the FBI's Crime Task Force."

The two guys looked at each other and then the older one spoke. "I am Kaid Nashoba. This is my brother Luke." We don't need no lawyers. You have us dead to rights. Ask your questions."

Jay took first crack. "First of all, I understand you are brothers, ex-Army Rangers, and you are of the Chickasaw Nation. You were born in Tishomingo, Oklahoma. Your last names, Nashoba, means 'Wolf'. So, do I have all that right, so far?"

"That's right", said Luke.

"You were dishonorably discharged, correct?" Britt asked.

"Yeah, it was sort of like what you guys call a 'plea bargain'." Said Kaid.

"How so?" Asked Britt.

"It's a long story." Said Kaid.

"We're in no hurry, and you guys aren't going anywhere, so let's have it." Jay said.

"We were good soldiers. The problems were caused by them camel jockeys." Said Luke.

"You mean the Muslims." Said Britt.

"O.K. We weren't angels, O.K.? We did some stuff. Everybody was doin' stuff."

"We just did what we needed to do." Said Kaid.

"Like what?" Jay asked.

"Like, we had a lot of supplies, O.K.? Like food and stuff. Medicine, clothes, like that. Those folks had nothin'. So we helped 'em out. We sold 'em stuff that they needed." Said Kaid.

"We weren't the only ones doin' it." Objected Luke.

"We got caught a few times, but they needed *us* more than they needed the supplies." Said Kaid.

"So, what got you discharged?" Asked Britt.

"We both had girlfriends. They caused us to get discharged." Said Luke.

"How could they get you discharged?" Jay asked.

"The unit Doc made everybody get tests. Word had it that the camel … Muslims had hired girls to give venereal diseases to the troops. We tested 'positive'." Said Kaid.

"We weren't even sick." Complained Luke. "At least, not right then."

"So, we met 'em after dark and we killed 'em." Kaid said simply.

"They were enemy combatants, plain and simple. Trying to kill our Rangers, no different than if they had guns. No tellin' how many lives we saved." Said Luke.

"But the jackasses in HQ didn't see it that way." Said Kaid.

"You ever heard of 'Due-Process'?" Asked Britt.

"'In war, you ain't got time for Due-Process. We did what was right." Said Kaid.

"How did they catch you?" Jay was genuinely curious.

"The brass knew we had girlfriends and knew who they were. So did the townspeople, who got up in arms when the girls turned up dead and they complained to our Major. He didn't have a witness or enough evidence to charge us with murder, which it *wasn't* in my book, but to satisfy the townspeople he asked them for proof that we had sold them some supplies. They had plenty of proof. We were court martialed to save face. We was railroaded." Said Kaid.

"When you're dishonorably discharged, you can't get no decent job.

But we knew we had done right, and when we had a way to right other wrongs, we jumped at the chance to join the Gang. Plus, the money was good, it was a military-like operation and until now, we never had to fire our guns." Added Luke.

"What can you tell us about the Gang?" Asked Britt.

"Nothin'." They both said at the same time.

"Look, we might be able to make things easier for you if you cooperate." Jay said.

"Hah! Help us? You gotta be kiddin'. We're both looking at a death sentence. How you expect to help that?" Said Luke.

"I don't know, Maybe the D.A. would consider a life sentence for your cooperation. I can ask."

"Don't bother." Said Luke. "We already got a life sentence."

"What do you mean?" Asked Britt.

"You never asked us what we tested positive for. With appeals, we will die before they get a chance to fry us." Said Kaid.

"What do you have", Jay asked.

"AIDS." They both said at the same time.

"One last thing, which one of you shot the officer?" asked Britt.

"We both shot at him." Said Luke.

"I'm a better shot than you are little brother. It was probably me." Said Kaid.

"No way. I was aiming right at the spot where the slug hit. Had to be me."

"Definitely Sociopaths", Jay thought to himself. Interview over, he and Britt left the brothers still arguing over who did it.

"Maybe, a hanging party is not that bad of an idea." Jay said out loud. But mostly to himself. "By the way, Britt, since we have no way to get anything more out of these two screwballs, we should be able to report this to everybody on the team, without jeopardizing our investigation, right?"

"Sounds good to me. Go for it." Said Britt. Still obviously rankled.

"Gotta get her out of this funk." He thought.

"When is Eddie coming in?" He asked.

"Not till tomorrow morning."

"Would you mind if we run by my ranch for just a minute, before we hit the office? I have kind of been neglecting it recently. I need to take a quick look at the animals and the garden. Then we can buzz off."

"No problem." She sank back into her funk.

CHAPTER FORTY FIVE

**We are Indians and we have no banks,
but when we have plenty of money or blankets,
we give them away to other chiefs and people,
and by and by they return them with interest
and our hearts feel good.
Our way of giving is our bank.**
(Chief Maquinna   Nootka)

The ride back to Oklahoma City was quiet. Jay's ranch was just about halfway between Stroud and the office. Not too far from Shawnee, so it wasn't much out of the way. Britt had called in a report to Eddie's secretary and asked if she would get it out to all of the Task Force members. Until Eddie arrived, they were at loose ends.

Jay's thoughts drifted back to Johnnie Wolf. That matter was still unresolved. Right now, He was working with Lt. John Two Feathers. Doing outside calls and providing liaison between our office and the officers injured in the "Hospital Debacle". That was the tag name that stuck. It was insulting, but accurate. It was a "debacle", all right. No other word for it. No one anticipated Rocket Propelled Grenades or "RPG's" as they're called. Not even the Feds. That was only supposed to happen in the Middle East. FBI Forensics was still working on finding where they were made and how they might have gotten into the hands of the Gang.

They checked in with Johnnie, at the office, the news from the hospital was mostly good. The patrolmen who were Units 1 and 2 were fine, just shaken up. The cruisers on the other hand were a total loss. All five of the downed officers at the hospital had ruptured ear drums. The two worst injured were the two guys with the blood all over their faces. It was from the glass partitions at the nurse's station. They would have small pock mark scars for the rest of their life. But at least they didn't have any eye damage. The two that were unconscious, were victims of the pressure of the blast, giving them both concussions. Which they will shake, after a few days of headaches. No one died. So, all in all, it was going to turn out not nearly as bad as it initially looked. The one who had no cuts and remained conscious but couldn't hear, will probably have to have some inner ear surgery on one of his ears and may have to wear hearing aids for the rest of his days. Again, No deaths. Yet. Except, of course Lt. Ben Pushmataha and the Judge. That was sickening. Jay and Britt were going to have that on their minds for a long, long time. They rolled into his driveway and he took his time approaching the house.

Britt sat up. "How much property." She asked.

"About 100 acres, give or take a few. Goes back to the tops of those hills you see in the distance."

"This is huge." She said, obviously impressed.

"Almost too big for me, but it is actually pretty small as ranches go."

"I see a horse standing at the corner of your fence."

"Oh, that's just my buddy. I have two horses. One male, one female. That one at the fence is spoiled rotten. I am expected to produce at least one apple a day, or I am in trouble. The beggar."

"What are their names?"

"I don't see the male right now, that ones the female."

"I love the color, white and brown with a little black."

"She's a paint. The stallion is named 'Hank'. I'm surprised he's not here begging for apples too."

"What's her name?"

"I named her 'Butch'."

"Why Butch, for a girl?"

"Even as a little pony she would take no crap from Hank. He respects her bites as well as her kicks."

"Good for her."

She was actually smiling. Not the phony one, for show, when she is interviewing suspects. But a real, genuine smile. Now, ain't that something?

Jay pulled around back where she could see the barn. She was mesmerized.

"I would think that being Sac & Fox, farms and ranches and such would be kind of 'old hat' for you."

"I was raised in town." She said. "In an apartment. I never even saw a real live horse till I was 10 years old. Can I peek inside?"

"Sure thing. Follow me."

He fixed them both a quick cup of coffee in the kitchen and they sat on the porch. Hank finally showed up.

"I better go get a couple of apples or I am gonna' be in deep trouble."

"You grow them yourself?"

"Yep. Apples, peaches, pecans, walnuts. Like I tell folks, it is a farm *and* a ranch. And that keeps me hopping."

"What else do you grow?"

"Just about everything. Berries, vegetables, chickens, cows. I don't have to go shopping for much."

"Obviously you can't possibly consume all of that. Do you peddle groceries on the side, too? A gentleman produce farmer?"

"Well, I don't eat all that much. I share some with my mom and Uncle Jay. I freeze a lot of it. The weather can get nasty in the winter and a lot of folks just barely scrape by, even when the weather's good. I share a lot with folks who need it. I am not gonna let any of my neighbors starve, or anybody else if I can help it. I can't cure the ills of the world, but I do what I can."

"You are an interesting person, Officer Nation. Our file says your given name is 'Indian'. I would assume that there must be a story there somewhere."

"There certainly is. And maybe before you head back to the marble halls, we may find the time for me to elaborate. But for now, let me show you the rest of the house, real quick, and then we have to head toward the office."

"How about the horse apples?"

"Oh yeah. House first, so that I can grab some apples, then we will feed them as we leave. Sound good?"

"Sounds great. Let me feed them"

A quick tour of the house and then they fed the horses. Jay told her to feed Butch first or she would give Hank a lickin' he wouldn't forget. This time she actually laughed. First time he ever heard her laugh. Maybe the last. For some strange reason, the sound of it made him feel sad.

CHAPTER FORTY SIX

**Show respect to all people,
but grovel to none.**
(Chief Tecumseh   Shawnee)

Back at the office, Jay had a chance to sit down with Mac for a few minutes. He was his usual, gentle self. Jay filled him in on how much Britt had taught him and how much he had taught himself, in the last few weeks. The good things, as well as the not-so-good things. Some things he held back. Not because he didn't trust Mac, he did. But because he didn't want to talk about the things that he had been hiding from him. Maybe someday he would "Fess-Up" as the saying goes, but for now, he thought he'd just leave it be.

When Eddie arrived, Jay was up to his eyeballs with checking out some things for Johnnie Wolf and checking in on Myra and Annabelle. Myra was getting fairly obnoxious about getting back to her house. When he had a minute, he had a quick chat with Britt and Eddie. They decided to head out for a session with Myra tomorrow. Jay filled Mac in on the plan.

"Well Jay, they travel in luxury from what I hear." He said, "Nice hotels, nice restaurants. The whole nine yards."

"Yeah, but we are back to separate checks now. So if they go for luxury suites, which Eddie probably will want to do, then I am going back to the Starlight. And breakfast tacos, lunch hotdogs and pre-made salads from the grocery store."

"I understand the Salvation Army serves a mean vegetable soup." Mac said, "And don't forget the 99 cent menu at Mac Donald's." Mac laughed a hearty laugh.

Little did he know, that Jay had already explored those "99 cent epicurean delights." Sure enough, Mac was right again. When they arrived in Durant, Eddie checked in at the Casino Hotel. Britt also checked in. Jay respectfully declined to join them.

"My travel budget is about exhausted for the month and to turn in a receipt from a Casino is not a good career move, right now." He explained. "I will be staying at the Starlight Motel. My usual stomping grounds. Besides, I have some history there."

He had no sooner checked in, than he got a text from Britt saying that he did not need to come back and pick them up. Eddie had decided to rent a car to make logistics easier. He could just meet them at the station. This time, he had thought to bring several changes of clothes and assorted travel necessities. Also, experience had taught him to fully arm his trunk with weapons.

They all, somehow, managed to get to the station at exactly the same time. They met in the parking lot and went inside. There was still a somber mood in the office. No one was smiling very much. There was a black wreath hanging on a door down the hall. Jay assumed that it was Ben's office door. On the Desk Sergeant's desk was a wicker basket, full of condolence cards. He realized that any display of joviality, right now, would be inappropriate. They were still in mourning, and may continue to be for quite a while. There was a little sign, informing everyone that they could contribute to the fund for the construction of a memorial and bust, for Lt. Ben Pushmataha. There was a glass container, already brimming with various denominations of bills. Jay added a $20, as did Eddie and Britt. The Desk Sergeant noticed and mouthed a silent "Thank you". It was the least they could do to honor his, over 30 years of service. Jay could probably do more and he would.

"We would like to check in with the Chief if he isn't busy", Jay said.

"He is out right now. Over at the Pushmataha's house. Chief and his wife."

"No problem, we are actually here to have a conversation with Myra Quattlebaum." Britt said.

"Oh, you mean Honey. O.K., I'll have someone bring her up. Conference room 2. You know where it is, Jay."

He led them to Conference room 2.

"Bugged?" Britt asked.

"Probably." He said.

Myra was led in, handcuffed, which Britt quickly removed.

"Thanks." Honey said to Britt. "I hope you guys have somethin' in writin' for me. If not, you've wasted your time and money."

"As matter of fact, we do, Honey." Said Eddie. "You may be interested to know that we have almost waited too long."

Myra looked stunned. "Whaddya mean?" She sputtered.

"You probably haven't heard. Three Members of the gang are in custody. Their headquarters is demolished and we are pursuing the last two." Eddie said.

Myra thought for a minute. "You mean the last 3."

That statement hung in the air for a few seconds. Eddie looked at Jay and then at Britt. The obvious question was, how did she know that there was a third person, the big boss of the Gang?

Eddie went with it. "Yeah, three. Not to mention the bartender who collects the 'Mission Requests' at some location which you are about to provide us with. That actually makes the count 4. We will want to know all that you know about all 4, if we make this deal come to pass."

"I can help you a lot with 1. Maybe a little on another one. Can't tell you anythin' on the other 2. Can't tell you about somebody I don't know or don't know about." She said.

"2 will be fine, said Eddie. We aren't going to ask you about the Gang members that carry out the operations. It makes sense that you wouldn't know much about them. That's O.K. But we want your info on the other 2 and some account of how you came to know about them." Eddie made his requirement clear.

"Let me see them papers." Myra said.

Britt removed the documents from her Computer case.

"Here you are, Myra. Let me know if you have any questions."

183

"I ain't stupid you know. My language ain't all proper-like, but I'll know if you're tryin' somethin'." She spit out.

"Trust us Myra, we want this thing to be over as much as you do." Jay said.

"You know where you can stick your 'trust'. I already tol' ya' I don't trust any cop. Especially not you. Maybe the lady, a little. Seems like she keeps her promises, so far." Myra had begun to read the documents.

She looked up. "I don't see nothin' in here about you accusin' me of swattin' you in the head. That has to be part of this."

"Jay looked at Eddie." He had not seen the document up until now.

"It's in there, Myra." Said Eddie. "Read the part about relieving you of any responsibility for acts or statements made or committed during the investigation." Eddie pointed to it on the page.

"Oh yeah. O.K., I guess that about covers it. Let's get started. You gonna tape it again?"

"Yes mam." Said Eddie.

"Whatcha' gonna' do with all these tapes? Hot shot there gonna write a book or something?" She looked at Jay and grinned.

"Could be Myra. If I do, I'll cut you in on the profits." He said.

"Right. I won't hold my breath." She said

Britt had begun taping. A hint of a smile was on her lips. Again, it didn't quite make it. She was enjoying this.

As the story began to unfold. A lot of things made sense. A lot of it was anecdotal stuff that they already knew about. She knew that Dutch had a serious business relationship with Hoss. Dutch had gotten into drug distribution almost by accident. Hoss was his source. Hoss was very involved with things like prostitution, drug distribution and money laundering, over at the Casino. His clients would sometimes need drugs that Hoss had, but couldn't find time to deliver, so as a favor to a friend, and supplier, Dutch began letting addicts and dealers pick up packages at the Beer Shack and leave the money with Dutch for Hoss to pick up later.

After that went on for a while, Hoss talked him into buying a small supply to keep on hand and mark it up a little for his own profit. It was easy, good pay, low risk. These were Hoss's clients and if there was ever a problem, Hoss took care of it personally with the client.

"How big was the business?" Eddie asked.

"I can't tell you the exact numbers", she said, "but it was in the thousands and it was steady money."

"The police didn't try to crack down on the Casino?" Eddie asked.

"According to Dutch, there was enough money at stake that the cops turned their backs, like cops will do. Anyway, Dutch used Hoss for collections and vengeance, when he thought it was required. The Casino didn't fear the cops.

They had a highly placed insider who managed to use enough influence to keep the Casino in the clear. If Dutch is correct, and he got this from Hoss, the insider was rakin' in hundreds of thousands on the deal. Course, both of them skunks are known to exaggerate."

"Interesting Myra, and we will look into it, but that's not what we are really here for. You need to tell us all you know about the two who you mentioned.

The request taker and the big boss."

"I'll write the name of the bartender and his bar on a piece of paper. I ain't goin' on tape on this. The insider will find out and know who told it."

Britt handed her a blank sheet of paper and a pen. "Write" she said.

Myra wrote the name of the bar and bartender and handed it back. Eddie slipped it into his shirt pocket and looked into Myra's eyes.

"That's close to half of what you promised, Myra. I want to know how you found out about this bartender and then the name of the insider and how you came to know that."

"I checked out the Black Brick guys to get a price for Dutch. He wanted to compare the price I got, with the price he was getting' from Hoss. He liked Hoss and used him, but he never trusted him. Hoss would stop by sometimes at my place. I got him so out-of-it, one night, on coke and grass, that he spilled the bar and bartender to me.

Dutch had several guys that he wanted to know the cost, on what it would take to whack 'em. One was a judge who was makin' it hard on the Casino folks. The Casino wanted to know. Dutch got 1,000 bucks for each price he got from the bartender. The final contract was somethin' that Dutch didn't get involved in, as far as I know. If Hoss tried to take out pretty boy here, you can bet it was Dutch who first put him up to it. I don't think Dutch had anything to do with Walt's death. I don't think he wanted Hoss to really kill anybody, either. That may have been Hoss's idea. Hoss didn't trust nobody.

As far as the insider, I don't have a name, but I know that whoever it was, they were at the top of the heap. Maybe even THE top, in Officer Nation's group. I found that out from Dutch, who found it out from Hoss, who found it out from the bartender who dealt directly with the Gang. I don't know why they would lie. It's no skin off their backs.

That's all I know. Swear to God. Can I have the paper now?"

Eddie handed her a copy, "I've signed it, you can sign it or not, it's just your copy. Here is the original that I have already signed. You can sign on the 'x'."

"So when can I leave?" She said as she signed.

"Right now, if you don't mind having a big target on your back. It will take a couple of days to set up the 'safe house'. It may not be in Durant. *Probably* not. But when it is all set, we will come get you and get you settled in."

"Make it fast. This place is driving me nuts."

As they left, they made their apologies to the Desk Sergeant about missing the Chief and asked her to thank him again, for his help in breaking up the Gang.

In the parking lot, they decided to meet at the Casino's Inn and discuss the path forward. Jay was understandably disturbed over the thought that Myra had not cleared Mac. She didn't hurt him, but she certainly didn't help him either. He still thought the culprit might be Mac's secretary, and he kept thinking whether or not Johnnie Wolf should be back on the list of suspects. All they had was his version of things. Eddie was able to get a small meeting room at the Casino. It felt peculiar to be there, considering it being the hot-bed of crime in the area.

"Have you considered that all of these rooms may be bugged?" Jay said.

"Didn't think about that." Said Eddie.

"Me either." Said Britt.

"Maybe we should move this to my Motel. I can pretty well tell you that it won't be bugged. They don't have a conference room, but we can meet in my room." He said.

"Let's do it." Said Eddie.

Eddie drove to a steak house he knew about and they had a very nice, early supper. Eddie insisted on picking up the check. Jay offered to pay his part, but Eddie said absolutely not. Jay thought, "I still love this job".

It was semi-dark and raining as twilight began to fade. They gathered in Jay's room. They went over Myra's tape and he felt more and more like it was Mac's secretary, Sarah, who they needed to investigate. This went on for a couple of hours. It was getting late. There was a crack of thunder. The lights went out.

"Well, I guess the meeting's over." Said Eddie with a smile.

"O.K. said Britt. So, I think we all agree that our next interview should be with the bartender?" Britt asked.

"Let's meet here at 7:00 am tomorrow morning. That will give me time to check my emails and texts." Said Eddie. "I am bushed. Airplanes do that to me."

He pulled a disposable rain coat with hoodie from his Computer bag.

Something about Feds, they love these roll-around computer bags. You never know what they will pull out of it next.

"Reminds me of Mary Poppins' carpet bag", Jay thought.

"Eddie, if you don't mind, I have a few more things to discuss with Jay." Britt said. "Jay could I get you to give me a ride to the Casino when we are done?"

"Sure thing, Britt. Eddie, thanks for your help today, that interview went extremely well." Jay said.

"Good teamwork, for sure." Eddie said.

He pulled on his raincoat hoodie and made his way out of the dark room and out the door.

Within 5 seconds, a spray of bullets shattered the picture window and started shattering things in the room.

"Down." Britt shouted.

They both hit the floor. The shots subsided. Jay crawled to the door, lifted his arm to the knob and opened the door slowly. Anticipating another round of bullets at any second.

"Jay. You O.K.?" Britt said quietly.

"Yeah. You?"

"Yeah."

"I'm going out." He said, "Cover me."

Jay heard her coming up behind him. It took another flash of lightning to see what had happened. Eddie Whitecloud was laying on the walk just beyond his door.

"Britt. They got Eddie. Call 911."

He crawled over to Eddie and called his name. He was unresponsive. Jay felt his jugular vein. He couldn't feel a pulse. Could just be weak. He noticed a bloody rain puddle under Eddie's head. He stayed on the pavement by his side, gun drawn until the ambulance arrived. Behind it were a string of police cruisers. He holstered his gun and he and Britt began answering questions. There wasn't much to say. It was dark. It was raining. Eddie stepped out. Somebody gunned him down. They never saw a shooter, a car, or anything. With the rain and lightning, they didn't even hear a car drive away. If it was a car. It had to be this guy Chase.

"Why would they try to shoot Eddie?" Britt said. They couldn't know he was here unless they followed us from the restaurant."

"They didn't follow us. After the Hoss deal I always check behind me. It's a habit. They weren't after Eddie. In the dark, with a hoodie, they thought it was me."

The Chief arrived and after they filled him in, He said.

"That's it. I've had enough. I am going with you tomorrow to visit the bartender. We will get what info we need or I will turn him over to the Pushmataha family warriors. They would skin him alive, square inch, by square inch. We are bringing this to a head, now." The Chief stormed off.

"I think he means it." Jay said.

"I am afraid so." Britt said.

"Let's report this to the Task Force." He said. 'We may be about to force someone's hand."

Eddie was pronounced Dead-On-Arrival. This had all the earmarks of an Al Capone hit. They had killed a very high-ranking Fed. Jay called Mac.

"Do you need me to come down?" He asked.

"No sir, we have a line on who the middle man is, between the Gang and their customers. We are interviewing him tomorrow."

"O.K. Jay, Keep me posted." He said and hung up.

"How does this Chase know about you and where you are staying?" said Britt.

"I don't know. Remember what the brothers said? 'We know who you are'. I've been wondering about that ever since they said it."

"You are the target." Britt said almost to herself.

"Yeah. Appears so. Must mean we are getting close to the big boss."

"We are going to get even closer tomorrow. We need to go in armed and with backup."

"I agree. You are right-on. As you always are. Not a compliment, just a fact."

Britt answered with no emotion showing on her face. "I have my moments. Look Jay, your room is a wreck. Eddie's room is already paid for. You might as well stay there tonight. Breakfast at 6:00 am. I'll go now and take the rental car to the Casino. See you in the morning. Watch your back." She left.

He quickly gathered up his stuff and stopped by the Motel office. The owner was there. Jay told him he was checking out. He was too embarrassed to ask for a refund.

As he turned in his key, the owner said almost apologetically.

"Officer Nation, I have no quarrel with, and a great deal of respect for, our public safety officers. However, in the future, I would appreciate it if you would stay elsewhere."

First time in his life he had ever been 'banished' from a place. Two 'Strikes' and you're 'Out'. Literally. The room at the Casino was plush to the max. Jacuzzi tub, which he immediately took advantage of. A small kitchen with a fridge stocked with various beverages, water and snacks. A porch with a view of the city and the countryside. No wonder guys want to go to the top of the ladder. Minus the getting killed part, he still loved this job.

The phone rang in the wee hours. Jay was instantly wide awake.

"Hello".

"Leave town now, or you won't live long enough to do so later." A gruff voice.

"Listen, Chase, I am going to be in the audience at either the Lethal Injection viewing or at your funeral. Either way, I will see you again." Jay was angry.

"You are a dead man. You just don't know it."

"Then I'll see you in Hell."

(Click)

After that, there was no going back to sleep. Instead, he got back into the Jacuzzi with a cold beer. He was not a drinker, but he hoped it would help get his anger under control. It didn't. At breakfast, he told Britt about the call and his response. She mulled it over in her mind.

"Let's mention this to Chief Yellow Feather, but no one else. With an insider somewhere, It might help force their hand to see us just ignore them."

"O.K." He said.

He picked at his breakfast. He was just too angry to eat. They took the rental car to the station. Britt said his car might be a target. So what? He was starting to think that a face-to-face with Chase was inevitable. Maybe, the sooner the better.

CHAPTER FORTY SEVEN

In every deliberation, we must consider the impact of our decisions on the next seven generations.
(Iroquois maxim)

C hase's phone buzzed.

"Yes."

"Good mission, last night. The target wasn't correct, but the alternate target was not all that bad."

"Thank you."

"I will call that a 'clean mission'."

"Good."

"4 missions to go."

"4?"

"4 for now."

"Who?"

"In time. My friend, in time. For right now, it is our 'Collector'."

"The Bartender?"

"The Bartender was never our guy. He was a 'middle-man'. A Mailman, if you will. He only passed along the envelopes. Your mission is his wife. She lives in the cottage behind the bar."

"When?"

"Yesterday wouldn't be soon enough."

"Understood."

"You already know the address."

(Click)

"I'm not risking taking the giant", Chase thought. "Lonnie needs to stay put. It was hard enough sneaking him into this flea-bag motel, without trying to sneak him back out. 4 more jobs and I probably need to terminate his employment. I guess that will be the time to 'retire'. I hope Jay Nation is one of the other 3. If not, I may have to do my first 'Freebie'."

"Look, Lonnie, I have to run an errand for the big boss. I'll be back no later than tomorrow night and I will pick up plenty of food and drink for you. You need to stay put. No going outside now or tomorrow, till I get back. This is straight from the big boss, understand?"

"I guess. But hurry, I'm hungry now." Lonnie grumbled.

CHAPTER FORTY EIGHT

Don't let yesterday use up too much of today.
(Cherokee proverb)

When Jay and Britt got to the station, they noticed the Chief's car was not in his reserved space.

"Hope this isn't a bad sign." Said Britt. She had a concerned look.

"Probably just out catching a few crooks.' Jay said with a smile.

Inside, the front desk area was empty. Not a good sign.

"Hello. Jay Nation. Anybody home?"

The Desk Sergeant scurried up from the back. She was in tears. His first thought was about the Chief.

"What's happened? Where's the Chief?" He asked.

Crying, she managed, "He is over at the hospital with Ben's wife."

"What happened?" Asked Britt.

She overdosed last night on sleeping pills.

"Accidental?" Britt asked.

"I don't think so." She was crying real hard, now.

Britt went around the desk and put her arms around the Sergeant. After a few soothing words, the poor officer began to speak again.

"We knew she was taking it extremely hard. Wouldn't eat. Couldn't sleep. Couldn't stop crying. It was pitiful. The Chief's wife stayed with her all day and all night. Chief spent as much time as he could over there. He found her early this morning. The pill bottle was on the bed, empty. It was just too much for the poor lady. We don't know if she'll make it." She began crying again. Britt held her.

Jay's anger was almost beyond control. "Chalk another one up for Chase and his boss. When I catch him, I hope he's armed."

Later, when the Desk Sergeant was better, Britt and Jay discussed what they should do next. They didn't get to finish. Chief Yellow Feather stormed in the door. And headed for his office. They followed him.

"I'm deputizing the Pushmataha brothers, nephews and cousins." He said.

"Is that a good idea, Chief?" asked Britt.

"Yes." He said with a note of finality. "Britt, this ain't my first rodeo."

"Yes sir, just trying to make sure it's not your last."

"Yeah, I know." His voice sounded a little less angry, but you could see the veins popped out on his temples. His blood pressure must be on a rocket ride.

"Chief, we were very sorry to hear about Ben's wife. How is she doing?" asked Britt.

"She's alive. They won't have a report until she wakes up. They're hoping there's no brain damage."

"This is not the best time in the world to bring up the Bartender." Jay said.

"There is not a better time. The Pushmataha deputies will be here in a little while to go over the plan. We make our move tomorrow, mid-morning."

"Mid-morning? Jay asked.

"It's a Night Club/Ice House. Ice house for beer from about 10:30 am, on. Night Club cranks in for hard liquor about dark and goes till about 2:00 am. They should be gettin' to work there about 9:30 or 10:00 in the morning."

"Do you anticipate trouble?" Jay asked.

"Nowadays, I always anticipate trouble. The plan is pretty simple. We surround the place, use the bullhorn to tell everyone to come out with their hands up. We frisk them, cuff them, and then clear the premises. We know the bartender is the contact guy. We don't know if he has an alternate for his days off, or if the whole bunch of them is involved. We should have no trouble getting them to talk. Even if we have to introduce the Pushmataha Deputies and offer all of them the chance to be interviewed individually, by the Deputies."

Britt, looked at Jay. He could tell that this was not in keeping with FBI protocol.

"Britt, maybe you should sit this one out." Jay offered.

"Not on your life."

When the new Deputies arrived, the plan was discussed. Then Britt spoke.

"Guys, I know that feelings are running high, right now. But I have something I have to say before this action takes place. Anger, resentment, revenge, and much more is probably at the top of everyone's list. I get that. But I have to tell you, as an Agent of the FBI, it is my obligation and responsibility to advise you, no, ... actually to *warn* you, that you are bound by laws that do not take family anger into account. Just because you have a gun doesn't mean you have a right to use it, except to save your life or someone else's. We want an arrest, not a murder."

After the guys were gone, the Chief cleared his throat.

"Ahem. Britt, I want to thank you for what you said. Coming from you, it meant more than it would from me. They know I'm tore up over Ben and his wife. I don't want them to think that I would approve of them breaking the law. But I fully intend to use that threat on the Gang. I hope we are all O.K. with that."

Britt simply nodded.

Jay added, "Chief, threats normally are for TV cop shows, but in this case, I think it's just another tool in the toolbox for what we are about to contend with." He glanced at Britt.

Another minor hint of a suppressed smile. They returned to the Hotel. They met for breakfast at 6:00 am and were at the station before 7. The Chief was at the hospital, but would be on the way in a few minutes. They were anxious to hear about Ben's wife. He showed up in a few minutes and went straight to his office. They joined him. His back was turned as they walked in.

"Chief, how is Ben's wife". Jay asked. He turned around, his eyes were red.

"She didn't make it." He folded his hands on the desk and stared at them.

"Brain damage?"

He just nodded. Then he looked at them both. "Now, I'm between a rock and a hard place. I am going to need your help. I can't call off the raid, the Pushmataha family would take the law into their own hands. They would be Vigilantes going after Vigilantes. I can't tell them they can't come, for the same reason. Only by having them involved, can I keep them out of trouble. Having them involved, could be just as bad. I hate to put my problems on you, since I am the one responsible for the problem, to start with. About the only option I have, as I see it, is to divide my force, like we did at the barn and put you each in charge of 1/3 of the deputies. I would also take 1/3. Most of my own guys will be with me and they already know the law. I am not going to think bad of you if you treasure your career enough to not want to be involved in a family feud. The choice is absolutely yours."

"Chief, I wouldn't think of being anywhere else tomorrow." Jay said.

"That goes for me too." Britt said, immediately.

"I can't begin to tell you how much that means to me."

He looked like he was about to tear up again.

"Britt and I will see you in a few minutes, Chief, we both need to check in."

They walked out to the car. They did, both, check in. Britt talked with someone in her office and Jay tried to check in with Mac. He was out of the office according to John. He filled John in and all John said was, "Good luck."

By 7:45, all of the officers were in. By 8, the new Deputies were starting to arrive. All were carrying both pistols and hunting rifles. The Chief met us outside.

"O.K. officers, and you all *are* sworn officers of the law, as you know, we are hitting the Coyote Night Club & Ice House. I didn't prepare a map, because I know you all are familiar with it. We don't want the employees arriving for work to know ahead of time about the plan. So, there is a Walmart right up the road from their place. We will park in the Walmart lot. We will roll from there at 10 sharp. ETA at the Coyote, is 10:05. I want my officers and Ben's sons, with me. Nephews with Jay and the uncles and cousins with Agent Thorpe. Remember what she said, yesterday. If anyone violates those orders, I will personally arrest you. And I will hand you over to the State for prosecution. I am dead serious. If you don't believe me, you are in trouble already. No gunfire, except on my orders. Let's go in groups of 3 or 4 cars at a time. No reason why you newer deputies can't carpool and cut down on the number of cars that could attract unnecessary attention. I'll go first."

They all headed out for the parking lot rendezvous, where they parked near the truck unloading dock. By carpooling the new deputies, the number of vehicles was greatly reduced. Included were 7 vehicles with only Ben's relatives. That was still over 30 extra deputies. It resembled the group at the barn. They gathered, outside of their vehicles, in small groups. Britt looked worried. You could see that the Chief was too. Jay figured he must look the same. At 9:55 everyone loaded up and cranked their engines. Sounded like the Indy 500 race getting ready to take the green flag. At exactly 10:00 the Chief headed out with the caravan lined up behind him. For whatever reason, Britt had decided to drive and she and Jay were in the first car behind the Chief. The Chief was pushing it well past the speed limit.

CHAPTER FORTY NINE

**Live your life that the fear of death
can never enter your heart.**
(Chief Tecumseh   Shawnee)

Chase awoke at 5:00 am. He had picked up a mountain of snacks
and drinks for Lonnie, the night before. He got ready as quietly
as possible and slipped out the door. He was ready, he had two
automatic pistols, a sniper rifle with scope, a Seal knife and both a
smoke grenade and a regular hand grenade. His supplier could probably
get him a tank if he asked. RPG's were also a snap to get, but he didn't
think he would need them for this job. He would move in, shoot the
target and anyone else in the immediate vicinity, if needed, and then
move out. He had been to the Coyote many times. He knew that if
he went around 10:00, all of the employees would probably be inside,
leaving the contact, Rachel, in the little cottage out back. All alone.

He timed his arrival for about 9:55. He would be done by 10:00
unless there were complications. There would be no complications
that he couldn't handle. At a minute or two before 10:00, he rolled
through the parking area and around behind the Coyote. He got out
and knocked quietly on the cottage door. Rachel answered, still in her
Pajamas and robe and she only opened the door a few inches.

"My husband is at the Club at 10:00, you know that."

"You're right. I know that."

He fired one shot, right in the middle of her forehead. Then, he calmly walked to his car. He was pulling onto the highway, fronting the parking lot, when he was astonished at the convoy of cop cars and other vehicles turning into the lot. Both of the first two almost hit him. If he hadn't taken to the shoulder, they would have. There was no way that they could have gotten there that quick, even if someone had heard the shot and called 911 without checking to see who shot what. He hoped that whatever was going on would not involve the fact that two cars almost hit him, leaving. They probably got a good look at his car, if not his face. He pushed his car a little faster, and starting taking back roads, just to make sure he wasn't going to be followed. It was still a "clean" mission. 1 down, 3 to go.

He wouldn't mention the near collision upon leaving the parking lot. The Big Boss would only find something to criticize and ask a million questions. In Chase's mind, this little detail should not count in the "clean mission" calculation. Why muddy the water.

Lonnie was waiting in the room when he got back. It was a lot earlier than he had expected.

Lonnie said, "Glad you're back early. This room is like being in a jail cell. I have to get out for a few minutes. What do I need to do to get out for a few minutes, without making the big boss angry? I don't want the boss docking my pay. I'd have to hurt somebody."

CHAPTER FIFTY

A frog does not drink up the pond in which it lives.
(Native American saying)

The Chief's car had almost gone sideways. He went into the parking lot entrance, a little too fast and Britt followed suit. A black sedan was exiting the lot and was taking more than his fair share of the entranceway.

"Idiot." Britt exclaimed. "Probably drunk."

"Didn't look drunk. Looked scared, to me." Said Jay.

The cars fanned out near the Coyote's front door. Most of the employee cars were lining the left side of the lot, leaving more room for customers. The men quickly deployed. It only took a couple of minutes. The deputies circled the whole building. No mistakes this time, like they made at the Barn. The Chief took the bullhorn.

"This is Chief Yellow Feather. Everyone come out with your hands over your heads. Do it now. And I mean everyone".

People started coming out the front door, hands over their heads. When the group had gathered, he said,

"Who's in charge here?"

One man said loudly, "I am the owner. What's this all about, and who fired that shot?"

"I'm asking the questions here." Said the Chief. "Is this everyone? If not, there could, very well, be some shots in a few minutes."

The owner looked at the group and was mentally checking off his people.

"This is everyone. What is this all about? And who fired the shot?"

"Clear the building", the Chief said.

And his guys started into the building. In a short time, they came out and said all was clear.

"There is no one else, you are sure." He said, pointing at the owner.

"Yes, I told you. Well, except my wife. She is in our cottage out back. We live on premises."

"Jay, take someone with you and check it out."

Jay grabbed the nearest officer and headed for the cottage. The door was ajar. He drew his weapon and so did the other officer.

"State Police." He shouted and kicked the door.

The door only opened part-way. Something was blocking it. He crouched and shoved it hard. It only opened a few more inches, but it was enough. He could see a pool of blood on the floor and a leg. He sent the officer back to get the Chief. Britt came too. The officer had already reported to them about trying to kick-in the door, and what they saw. The Chief stopped everyone short, except some of his officers and Britt. He didn't want to take the chance of contaminating the crime scene. The employees out in front of the Coyote were cable-tied at the wrists and guarded by a bunch of the new Deputies. No one would survive trying to run. Two cruisers were parked to block the entranceway.

"It's the wife", Jay said. "This is either a gang warning, or she is deeply involved. Her husband will know."

The Chief said, "Rather than bringing the whole group to the station, let's set up an interview room in the Coyote. We'll start with the owner."

With all the help, it took only a few minutes to set up a table and some chairs in a quiet corner. After getting set up, Britt started.

"Sir, what is your name?"

"Jim Coyote. That's actually where the business got its name."

"Mr. Coyote, I am Agent Thorpe with the FBI. I regret to inform you that the shot you heard was from your cottage. Your wife was killed.

"No. No. No. No." He grabbed his head. Then he looked at Britt. "You guys shot her."

"No sir, she was dead before we even arrived. The shot you heard was probably from her killer. Someone has a grudge against you or your wife, or both. I 'm sure that you know who it is. We want your complete cooperation. Murder is a serious business and we know that you are involved with the Black Brick Gang. We have several independent witnesses that have identified you as the contact between the Gang and their customers.

"Can I see her?" he said.

"We can talk about you viewing her later. Right now, we need answers."

He was distraught. In shock was a better way to put it. He mumbled her name over and over. "Rachel. Rachel".

"Mr. Coyote, the quicker we can get our questions answered, the quicker we can start making arrangements for you to see your wife."

"I told her this was not going to end well. I told her. I said, when you lay down with dogs, you get up with fleas. These guys were worse than dogs. They were killers. And now they've killed my Rachel." He began sobbing.

She gave him a minute to compose himself, Then Britt began again.

"Mr. Coyote, our informants all say that they passed an envelope to you containing the name of someone they wanted killed and then you passed it on to the Gang. You then collected the money, on the Gang's behalf, and passed it on to them to perform the murder. That makes you an accomplice. It's as if you did the murder yourself. The only way you can help yourself is if …"

"No, you've got it all wrong. They left an envelope with my wife's name on the front. I passed it on to her. She passed it on to the Gang. I was just a mail handler. I never knew who or what or when, I just knew she was collecting a couple hundred bucks every time she handled the exchanges. I didn't suspect, for the longest, that it was this Black Brick Gang, until they hit Walt Washoe."

"Who was your Gang contact?"

"Some guy named Chase something or other."

"Chase Stormcloud?"

"Maybe, I don't know. She only mentioned it once or twice. I just don't know. This can't be happening. I run a clean business here. We don't have any trouble. A lot of cops are customers here. I told her. She wouldn't listen."

"When was the last time you handled an envelope for them?"

"A while back. I don't know. It was right before that Judge got killed. I thought, at first, that we might have helped set him up. Then, I heard it wasn't the Black Brick Gang that killed him. So it couldn't have been something that we were involved with. I can't believe I didn't put my foot down and stop it. We didn't need the money. We do well here. She just wouldn't listen."

"Are you usually the Bartender here?" Jay asked.

"Yeah, I don't trust anybody else to do it. Only way to keep out the stealing. They steal money, they steal liquor. I can't let that happen here. I work it six days a week, 16 hours a day. This business is my life."

The Chief had taken notes. Britt had it recorded. His cooperation will go a long way with the D.A. But for now, his business was closed. They interviewed a few of the other employees, but it appeared that only the Coyotes were involved. As they drove back to the station, Jay was thinking about how Chase had beaten them again. They had to hit him soon and hit him hard, before more people died.

"I kind of feel sorry for Jim Coyote. He actually didn't do anything except handle his wife's mail." Jay said.

"When he suspicioned it was the Gang, he didn't stop it. He crossed the line."

"I guess we are kind of at a fork-in-the-road. Would you rather stop by the station for more questioning, or head back to the office?"

He remembered his first call to his friend at FBI about Britt. So far she hasn't wrung him out. He wanted to keep it that way for as long as he could. He'd already broken a record.

"Tell you what, I need to think about this awhile. I think this will be counted as another screw-up, rather than a missed opportunity." Britt said.

"But, we have just taken down the main link in the chain."

"Get real, Jay. We still don't have an 'Al Capone', and people are still dying,"

"Yeah, I guess a death is a death, no matter which side of the fence they are on. I'm just glad it wasn't on our side, for a change."

"Let's head back to the office." She mumbled, deep in thought.

"Britt, There is no way that the shooter could be anybody but the guy in the car that you almost hit when we got to The Coyote. We probably were just getting there about the same time that Jim heard the shot. That's a huge coincidence. Did you get a look at him?"

"No. Only a glimpse. I was focused on avoiding the car. He looked Native American in a dark medium size sedan. Had to be Chase."

Nothing else was said on the way back to Oklahoma City. When they went in, he went straight toward John's office. He felt very uneasy about even saying "Howdy" to Mac's secretary. His anger and stress were too high to keep suspicion out of his eyes. If she is the one doing this, Mac is going to freak. Knowing Mac, he would confront her and probably end up with a bullet in his head. Jay had heard that she was a crack shot. If she isn't the one, since Mac is the kind of guy who cuts his folks a lot of slack, he would not think kindly of anyone even suggesting that she might be involved.

He needed John's help on this one, big time. He went in John's office and closed the door. Anytime he did that, John would immediately stop whatever he was doing, even if it was the middle of a phone call. That was just the kind of good guy he was. Jay respected him almost as much as he did Mac. Jay could tell him anything, in confidence. Even this kind of problem.

He took his time and went back and recapped for John each important point along the way. It had to be someone in the office. It had to be someone who had access to all the information. He couldn't think of any other possibility unless it was Mac himself, and that just wasn't possible. He knew Mac well enough to say that with complete confidence. That left only one possibility. It had to be Mac's secretary.

"Have you discussed this with Britt?" John said.

"A little hint, here and there, but not with any great confidence in my theory."

"Try her." He said. "Let me know."

He was right, of course. But, Jay couldn't help but wonder if it was just him wanting, badly, for it to be her, and would Britt think that he was just being over-protective of Mac? That, would look bad on his part. The most important thing for him, right now, was not to think about anything other than doing what was right. For some reason, he thought of what his Uncle Jay once said. "The failure of Justice may be more detrimental to society than crime itself." He said it was a quote from a very famous lawyer named Clarence Darrow. Jay didn't know anything about him, but what he said made an awful lot of sense. "Justice is my job, all the other stuff is just noise." Jay said to himself.

Britt was at her desk. They had converted an old interview room, which was always a little too small and had become a storage room for files, into an office of convenience for Britt. Jay closed the door. She looked up, puzzled.

"I hope you don't mind me closing the door, but I want to discuss something with you that I could not let anyone in the office overhear, even by accident. Is that O.K. with you?"

"Sure, Jay." She replied with that usual poker face.

"I am going to shoot straight from the hip on this. It's been bothering me for more than a few days. I can't seem to shake it from my mind that there are only two persons in the building who could be involved in this. And until Johnnie Wolf can bring himself to give us more information, I have almost convinced myself that Johnnie's contact here was Mac's secretary. I know that sounds crazy, and probably sounds like I am being over-protective of Mac. And I may be. But I can't help how I feel. Barring any evidence to the contrary, I have to go with my gut feeling. I don't know exactly how to resolve the dilemma and hoped that by bouncing it off of you, there may be something you could suggest that would resolve the issue for me. There, I've said it and I feel better for having done so. If my head is screwed on wrong, I have every confidence that you will be totally honest with me about it."

"You never have to worry about two things, Jay. First, that I will always be honest with you, and second, that I will never criticize you for expressing your thoughts concerning this, or any other issue, as long as it is cop to cop and you are doing your job."

"Thank you, Britt."

"And for your information, I have been struggling with some of those same thoughts. I wish we had talked sooner.

The reason is that, yes, I think I might have a solution. It is underhanded, but under the circumstances, I would be willing to take the risk. I would not have involved you, before, because it is actually more than underhanded and given the fact that I am a visitor here, there are a lot of precedents that would make my solution a very bad career move, if it went haywire.

Had you not said what you just said, I was ready to go for it, alone. And once I have explained it, if you prefer not to be involved, I will understand and will not hold you accountable. If you agree, and it does go haywire, I will do all that I can to protect you and take full personal responsibility."

"It's like my Uncle used to say, 'in for a penny, in for a buck'." I will take equal responsibility. Let's just get it done."

"O.K., here's the plan, and we will have to involve Johnnie Wolf to make it work. How do you feel about that?

I know you have not felt very good about his involvement in all of this."

"As far as I am concerned, he's a 'dirty cop'. I know his daughter's sickness was an extenuating circumstance, but just the same, he did cross the line."

"If this works, his help will have a great deal to do with how a judge would treat his bad behavior. With that said, I don't think we will have any problem getting him to do his part. Let's call him in."

"Do you think it is a good idea to have John in on this, too?"

"Absolutely. And the timing is perfect, the Chief is out of the office."

"Let's make it quick", he said as he headed toward John's office.

John was on his phone. "O.K., I'll call you back." He hung up. John was one of only a few on the staff that still used his land line phone as much as his cell phone. Maybe more.

"John, can you get hold of Johnnie Wolf and ask him to come in so that Britt and I can have a planning meeting with the four of us?"

"Sure."

Jay returned to Britt's office. "John is making the call."

"Did he say how long?"

"Knowing John, he will have him here in less than 10 minutes. John is definitely a 'Do-It-Now kind of guy."

Jay checked his watch. It actually took about 6 minutes for both of them to be closing the office door and sitting down.

Britt kicked it off. "Sergeant Wolf, are you still unwilling to let us know the name of your contact for the gang?"

"I won't say 'unwilling', I prefer 'unable'. My wife is dead and I am the only parent that my daughter has left. I won't put her in the position of losing me or possibly jeopardizing herself or maybe even the both of us. The Gang is ruthless and sociopathic. My daughter can't leave the hospital with the Leukemia issue she has. Otherwise, I would move her into hiding and tell you in a heartbeat. All I can do right now is offer my help in catching them, if I can do so without them knowing it. I hope you understand that."

"Just wanted to make sure that we are all on the same page." Said Britt.

"So what are you suggesting, Britt?" Asked Jay.

"Here is what I have in mind. Since I first arrived, I have had my office in Washington monitoring cell phone transmissions from this site. By doing so, we were able to eliminate two key people as suspects, Lt. John Two Feathers and Officer Jay Nation. But, no one else, so far. The phones being used are throwaway types, so getting the actual user or getting the words that were said, is just not possible without Federal Wire-Tap warrants. Even then it would be difficult. It would take more time than we have available, and there is always the chance that it would not be approved.

So this, in my opinion, is a case of being more likely to get 'forgiveness', than 'approval'. The only solution that I can come up with, is to plant an actual small listening device, in the offices of Major Mac McCall, his secretary and the conference room. These would be on 24/7 recordings that would need to be reviewed by someone. There are ways to fast forward through blank spaces and stop and slightly rewind if we hear something that sounds like Donald Duck. Still, it will be time consuming. There is always the chance that it will produce nothing."

John said nothing, Johnnie said only "Ugh". They knew that Johnnie spends virtually every hour off-duty at the hospital with his daughter.

"John, your thoughts?" Jay said.

"Can we do both?" John asked.

Britt thought for a moment, then said "I think so".

"Both what? Jay's mind was spinning through what he had heard but he thought he might have missed something.

"John is asking if we can plant the devices, but also file for the warrants in case the devices don't do the job. I think that would cover all of our bases. But please understand two things. First, both could fail. Second, even if Johnnie gave us his statement in writing right now, it is only his word against the other person. We have no hard evidence that would stand up in court. A taped call would be that proof."

"O.K., It's settled then." Jay said. "Britt, I assume you have a source for the devices we need?"

"Yes. I can get 3 Micro-mics from Washington that are pretty unique and highly advanced. They are so tiny that even if you see them they appear to look like small, screw heads. I will make that call right now."

"How do you download them?" Johnnie asked.

"They are similar to transponders, except they have atomic batteries and have a range of some 30 miles. If you poll them for info, they automatically download to your Micro-mic app. I can put all 4 of us on that app. I am probably the closest to the office. Jay, you are about 39 miles away and it's not likely that you would be able to tap into the data unless you find a place closer-in to park and poll. Johnnie, you are way out-of-range", she explained. "So, I guess that means the monitoring will be done by John and myself."

"O.K." John said.

They all went back to their separate desks and Britt closed her door. After she got off her phone, she walked by Jay's desk and gave him a 'thumbs-up'. Nothing to do now, but just wait. Jay thought. He was wrong again. His phone buzzed. It was Chief Yellow Feather from Durant.

"Hi Chief. Everything O.K.?"

"Just picked up a bit of information that I thought might be of some help. One of the nurses watching over the Nashoba brothers told me that she had overheard them talking about one of their buddies. The name was 'Lonnie'. She thought that might be important."

"Very important Chief. Thank you, and be sure to thank her for me."

"Everything else good?" Jay asked.

"Well, any word yet on when Myra will be moved?"

"Chief, with Eddie killed, I don't think anyone is pushing it right now. I don't even know if he has been replaced yet. I'll ask Britt to check. Meanwhile, you might remind her that she can leave right now if she thinks the Gang will cut her some slack for her working with us. That should buy us a little more time before she decides to get herself a lawyer."

"Will do, let me know, Jay."

Jay went to Britt's desk. "Britt, I just heard from Chief Yellow Feather. The last gang name we need has just surfaced. His name or nickname, is 'Lonnie'. Probably ex-military. Can your Fed folks run that one to ground?"

"Absolutely. That's one of the things they can do without it taking forever, and do it well. They have instant access to all military data bases."

"How quick?"

"Maybe 10 minutes."

"Do we tell the Team?"

"No. Not until we get the devices in place. They are being overnighted. Should have them by first thing tomorrow morning."

"I'll get a cup of coffee and come right back. O.K.?"

"Sure. And can you bring me a cup? Black."

"Now, ain't that something?" He thought. "Britt has left the building, again."

He ran into Sarah at the coffee machine. He started to turn around but he was too late.

"Well, hello stranger." She said. "How are things going?"

"Hi Sarah, I guess, about as good as can be expected." He said guardedly.

"That's good to hear. I expect Mac to be calling me in a few minutes. Anything you want me to pass along?"

(Shields Up.) "No, I think he has all that I know, as of right now. But thanks for asking."

"No problem, Jay." She took her coffee and left.

He wondered about whether he may have given something away. He had a tendency to wear his feelings on his face. Well, what's done is done. Tomorrow, they would take control of their destiny. He hoped. He went back to Britt's office and along with their coffee, came a quick lesson from her on the technical aspects and uses for the Micro-mics. She was right about the quick response. The information had already come back from Washington. "Ex-Navy. Leonard (Lonnie) Justice. Sociopath, Murderer, Escapee from a prison transport van, Full file enroute."

"I'll print the file when it comes in. Take a copy home with you. Leave it there." She said.

Once that was done, he asked her about Myra's release and whether they had appointed a replacement for Eddie. She immediately had a troubled look.

"No problems, I hope." Said Jay

"Well, scuttlebutt has it that the opening has been filled but not yet announced. The new guy will be the one to push the Witness Protection issue. He may want to take a few days to review the case before he proceeds." Still scowling.

"I suppose you know the guy?" He had to be careful here.

"He and I go way back. He tried to get me banished at one point, because he couldn't accept working with a woman. It backfired on him and he was bypassed, for a while, on promotions and good assignments. He was on somebody's list. Now I guess I'll be on his list."

"Politics. I'm glad we don't have to worry with that here. Makes me wonder why anyone would want to work in Washington."

"Sometimes, I wonder too." She went back to her computer and printed two copies of the Lonnie Justice file.

It was late. Jay took his copy and headed out.

CHAPTER FIFTY ONE

Tell me and I will forget.
Show me and I may not remember.
Involve me and I will understand.
(Native American Proverb)

J ay was at work around 5:30am. Britt was already there.

"Morning. Spend the night?"

"Just an early riser. I don't require much sleep." She got a peculiar look. "Actually, it's none of your business."

"Those were the exact words I was going to say. You beat me to it." He said with a rendition of the Britt Poker Face. "When does the package arrive?"

"I already have it. It went to the FBI office in town, they delivered it about 4:30 this morning." She pulled out a padded envelope.

"4:30?" He thought. "That's it, I'm done, no more contest. She wins. Another point on her side. Not that I am keeping score or anything."

She took out and unwrapped 3 things that looked like screw heads. Dark brown, about the size of hearing aid batteries. Peel off backs.

"Are both of them here?" He asked.

"She is. He's not. She usually visits the ladies room at 10:00 sharp. She is very punctual. I'll do his desk first. Then hers. Then the conference room."

"You'll have enough time?"

"I won't even have to stop walking. I'll slip them under the edge of the desk as I pass by. They are sensitive enough to put them anywhere."

"Will you give me a "thumbs-up" when it's done?"

"Sure."

Nothing to do now but just sit and wait. Didn't happen. Jay got a call from the Chief again. "What now?" He thought.

"Hi Chief, everything alright?"

"Actually, yes and no. We had an issue at one of our Casinos last night. It was in Atoka, the same one the Judge was after. A small place, almost a mom and pop truck stop casino. One prostitute in custody, two security personnel in custody, a patron is in the hospital and we are about to talk to the guy they call their Operations Manager. The place does a huge business for a small casino. The motel rooms are attached and also do a big business. Suspiciously big. Mostly renting rooms by the hour. I wouldn't call you on this, but I got a threatening call about turning them loose and making no record of the incident. Sounded too much like a Black Brick type deal, so I thought I'd just give you a 'heads up' in case you thought it might lead someplace. Especially after the Judge's death. The Sheriff seems to be in favor of just letting it slide. 'Boys will be boys', and all that garbage. Not on my watch."

"I'm glad you called. I will get with Britt and call you back."

Jay filled Britt in. "Jay, I would be interested in what we can learn from them and see if it has ties to the Big Boss. The problem is that tonight is my first night to monitor recordings. I want to have John there so I can show him how to work it. Can you grab someone to go with you?"

"As a matter of fact, I have a young fellow, Jack Grant, here from Sac & Fox, who Chief Grey Eyes asked if I would give him some training on how we interface with the various Nations. It might be good training for him to join me. I understand he did well on his Police Academy training."

"O.K., but you know who we are dealing with and the fact that you have a great big target on your back. You need to make sure he doesn't become another Chase or Lonnie victim."

"I know that's right. I'll keep you posted. We are heading out for

Atoka. With the devices in place, are you letting the Team know about the Lonnie file?"

"You can bet your boots I am, and your horse if you have one. Stay in touch"

"Whoa." Jay thought. "Was that humor I just heard, or was she needling me? Had to be a needle. There is not an ounce of humor in her whole body that I have found. I bet she doesn't even have a 'funny bone' in her elbow. Next she'll be bringing up deer meat."

Jay gathered up the recruit and filled him in. He thought he would give the recruit an option about going.

"O.K., look. I just got a call from Durant. The Chief there asked for my help on a situation they had last night at a local small casino. I want you to have the option of going with me or staying and training with another person."

"No, I would rather stick with you and see you in action, if that's alright."

"I hope there won't be any action." Jay tried to sound calm.

They loaded up and headed out for Atoka. Jay didn't mention about the "target on my back" stuff. The last thing he wanted was a "newbie'" with a gun, sitting by his side, who has just been told that someone out there is going to try to shoot him. He would fill him in, on the possible connection between this casino and a sophisticated group of criminals who they had been tracking for several weeks. That's it.

On the trip down, he filled the trainee in on what they did to take 3 of the Gang members down. He was quiet and only asked a few intelligent questions. Turns out he was in the Academy when the Walking Eagle matter happened and already knew most of the details on that incident. They were soon in front of the Casino.

"O.K., this is it. Looks like the parking lot is full. We'll park on the shoulder. A little exercise will do us both good. We are here to meet Chief Bill Yellow Feather from Durant and Sheriff Parker, the local County Sheriff. He's related to Chief Quanah Parker, the last Chief of the Comanche's back in the late 1800's and early 1900's."

"Who will we be questioning?"

"I'm not sure. We're really here to help in any way we can, but my interest is seeing if there is any connection between the Gang and this Casino, or anyone else."

They walked to the Casino and noticed two police cruisers near the front door. This was not a small operation.

Maybe small in physical size, but when they walked in the door, it was crowded. Loud music, even louder talk. Semi-dark inside, no smoke. Probably, smoking was restricted to outside. Poker tables, one roulette wheel and a myriad of slot machines. No craps tables. He thought that was a little strange. Maybe because they took up so much floor space. They stopped at a long bar and flagged down the busy bartender.

"Can you direct us to the Operations Manager's office?"

"You a cop?"

"Isn't the uniform a dead giveaway?"

He eyed Jay up and down, scowling. "That way." He pointed to the far corner.

"Friendly guy." Said the trainee.

Jay saw an open door and caught a glimpse of Chief Yellow Feather inside.

They went into the small office. "Hi Chief. … Sheriff."

There was a large man behind the desk who stood up as they came in. Sheriff Parker made the introductions. Big smile.

"Rick, I want you to meet Officer Jay Nation with the Crime Task Force in Oklahoma City. And I'm sorry, I don't think I know the other officer."

Jay said, "This is Officer Jack Grant III. You can call him 'Tres'. Tres, this is Rick Blackhorse the Casino's Operations Manager, Chief Bill Yellow Feather, Chief of the Choctaw Nation and Superintendent of the tribal police and this is Sheriff Paul Parker of Atoka County."

Hands were shaken all around. Tres and Jay remained standing, there were no chairs.

"Sorry about the cramped quarters". Said Sheriff Parker.

"That's O.K. we just had a long ride from Headquarters, so standing is good." Jay said.

He wondered why the apology came from the Sheriff and not Rick Blackhorse. Makes one wonder who's in charge here.

"Rick was just filling us in on the little incident that kind of got out of hand last night. Looks like there was a little too much liquor and maybe a little too much testosterone. Jay, I'm sure you've run into that before." Said the Sheriff. Big smile.

"Paul, a guy fighting with a prostitute is one thing. Getting a beating that put him in the hospital is more than a little too much testosterone. Your bouncers didn't have a mark on them, except, their knuckles", said the Chief.

"Now, we don't want to blow this thing all out of proportion. If the guy wants a cash settlement, that's no problem. We'll do that and take care of his hospital bill." Said Rick. "Besides, he was part of the problem too."

"Cash settlements don't absolve criminal behavior." The Chief fired back.

Rick had stopped smiling. "Look Chief, we treat you guys pretty good here. We handle all of our own problems and cops never have to pay a dime for drinks."

"Or anything else, I assume." Jay said, looking straight at the Sheriff.

"What's that supposed to mean?" The Sheriff said.

"Don't act dumb Paul, you know exactly what I mean." Jay said.

"If you are accusing my men of something, spit it out." He was now red faced.

"Do you really want this to be an official state inquiry, complete with interviewing all of your deputies? And all of Rick's employees? Say the word." He said.

"O.K. look, let's tone things down a little." Said the Chief. "We are here to find out what happened last night. Just the facts, that's all."

"I am good with that." Jay said.

Rick was looking like a deer in the headlights.

"Rick, I know you've covered this with me and Sheriff Parker, but I would like you to go over it again for Jay and Tres." Said the Chief.

"O.K., This guy comes in, plays some machines, got in a poker game and apparently attracted some doll's attention. She apparently wanted to get to know him better. She invited him to her room for a drink. Somehow they got in an argument and they started slapping each other. She called my security team and they responded. He was belligerent and they had to use force to subdue him and get him out of the room. In the process, he got banged up a little." Paul had a hint of a smile as he stared at the Sheriff.

"And according to the hospital, the victim had a broken nose, missing teeth, lacerations to his face, two cracked ribs, bruising to the stomach and ribs and is listed in serious condition. And they suspect a slight concussion. Did they also accidentally run over him with a truck?" Said the Chief. He was now getting a little red faced himself.

"Look, if there is a fine or something, for them using maybe a little too much force, the Casino is willing to pay it and compensate the guy for his pain and suffering. I'll bet if we offered him a hundred thou', he'd be willing to forget the whole thing." Said Rick smugly.

"Maybe he would" Jay said, "but maybe I won't."

"Look, this is not a State issue. Remember, this is my area and my responsibility." Said the Sheriff.

"And violence or suspected gang type activities are my responsibility, so if you don't have any *meaningful* objections, which I would duly consider, I would like to interview all parties to the incident. I also would like to see the guest register from your Motel." He said. "And I don't want you to send it over someday, I want to see it right now."

Sheriff Parker and Rick looked at each other, more deer in the headlights.

"I'll go get it." Rick said and stood up quickly.

"Tres, you go with him and see that it comes back intact." Jay said.

As they left, the Sheriff said, "that's insulting, there's no call for that."

"Insulting to who Sheriff, you or Rick." He said, still wondering who's in charge.

They came back with the register. A quick check confirmed Jay's suspicion.

"Looks like the lady was not registered until the two of them went to the room. Although, she was registered a couple of other times that day. Each time was for an hour. Sheriff, in spite of your minimizing this and Rick's false information, it seems we have enough here for a charge of prostitution. Chief do you agree?" Jay showed him the register.

"Absolutely. And if the Sheriff doesn't want the county involved, I will be more than glad to do it on behalf of the Choctaw Nation." The Chief added.

"Rick, you may want to start a new register, we are taking this one as evidence." Said Jay.

"I am calling an attorney." Said Rick.

"You'd better call one for your prostitute and bouncers as well." Jay said.

If a hateful stare could kill, he'd be a walking dead man. Again.

"Chief, we need to go to the Atoka County Jail and do some quick interviews. I want to start with the prostitute."

They drove to the jail and arranged for her to be brought to an interview room. When she was brought up, she was actually quite attractive. And young. Very young. She was wearing an orange prison jump suit. Long blonde ponytail. Scared. They had pulled her criminal record. It was clean. Her claimed name, 'Candy Bar'.

"Candy, if that's your real name, my name ..."

"That's my real name."

"Good. We'll talk about that. My name is Jay Nation, I am an officer with the State Crime Task Force. This is Officer Tres Grant who is in training with me today. I would like to know your real name. And let me advise you that giving false information to a State Officer is a State crime that would be prosecuted in a State court, not a County court." That seemed to shake her.

"We are running your prints, as we speak. I would advise you to give us your real name, right now."

"My real name is Jane Barr, B A R R. But my friends have always called me 'Candy'."

"Thank you. I hope we have started off on the right foot. I will be completely honest with you Candy and I want you to be completely honest with me. O.K.?"

"Yes sir."

"What is your age? Not the one you gave the deputies, I want your real age."

"15"

"Have you been in trouble before?"

She paused, then hesitantly, "Yes sir."

"Recently?"

"Yes sir."

"You weren't prosecuted?"

"No sir."

"Why?"

"I don't know. Somebody from somewhere calls, and they let us go."

"Us? Are there other girls that have been in trouble here?"

"Yes sir."

"Young, like you?"

"Probably, but nobody talks about their age. It's a Casino rule."

"Here is a piece of paper, I want you to write their names for me. Their real names if you know them." She wrote a few names.

"How many gentlemen do you 'entertain' per day?"

"During the week it's slow, mostly just the cops, but on the weekends it's busy."

"How long have you been with the Casino?"

"Maybe 3 months."

"Have you ever entertained the Sheriff?"

"Look, I don't want him on my case. That could get me hurt."

"I want the truth, Candy. The Sheriff?"

"A few times, maybe 3 or 4. He said if I ever told, he would make me disappear."

"Here is another piece of paper. I want you to write all that down. What he did and what he said. Also the names of the cops you entertained, if you know them." She began writing.

After a few minutes, she finished. Jay read it and thanked her.

"Can I go now? Rick will have a fit if I don't get right back."

"Sorry, Candy, there have been laws broken here. We are going to have to keep you for a little while. But don't worry, you'll be safe. I promise. And don't mention our conversation or your notes to anyone. Especially not the Sheriff. If asked, just say you don't remember."

"Yes sir."

Next, they interviewed the two Bouncers. They pretty much confirmed what Rick had said. They admitted that they kind of went overboard on the guy. The victim was not in very good shape right now. But Jay still had one fact to verify. They went to the hospital and were allowed to see him, but only for a few minutes. He was still in serious condition. He verified that he had hired a prostitute and had been offered a very low price. When they were done, she asked for considerably more money. He refused, she slapped him. He slapped her back. They struggled. The body guards showed up and almost killed him. All of his money was stolen from his wallet. Tres wrote it down and had him sign it.

They reported all of this to the Chief. He made copies of the notes from the victim and from Candy Barr. Then he arrested Sheriff Parker and transported him to the Jail in Durant. Tres and Jay headed back to H.Q. When they got back, Britt said she had a lot of information that she had gathered from her contacts in Washington. She said they needed to talk, but somewhere away from the office. It was getting late in the day, so they decided to meet at her place around 7pm. There would be 4 of them. She said she would order in some food. Jay spent the rest of the day making notes and picking Tres's brain to get his take on the happenings of the day. Tres had picked up several interesting tidbits that Jay added to his notes. One was the unwillingness of the motel clerk to give up the Register. Tres said Rick had to threaten to fire him to get him to turn it over. The guy had mumbled something about being more scared of the big boss than of Rick. There it was, *Confirmation!*

CHAPTER FIFTY TWO

Find your dream.
It's the pursuit of the dream that heals you.
(Billy Mills Olympic athlete   Lakota)

Jay was curious to see how and where Britt lived. He was pleasantly surprised. It was an "upscale" condo in an upscale part of Oklahoma City. Top floor. It was fairly spacious. When she invited them in, the ambience was pleasing. She had a great view from a huge picture window. It was an open space treatment with no walls between the kitchen, dining room and living room. There was a door open in the back which was obviously her office. A closed door which Jay assumed was her bedroom. And a smaller open door that was the bathroom. The walls and ceiling were stark white but there were pictures of rolling hills, mountains, streams and horses, a few plants here and there, and one big pot on the floor that held an 8 foot schefflera tree.

The furniture was beige and ample with a few tables including a monstrous coffee table in front of the sofa and chairs. Nothing on the table, no books in sight, anywhere. Nice. Not exactly 'Spartan', but neat and efficient. Very nice. Jay loved the pictures so he went close to look. They weren't pictures, they were paintings. And in the bottom right corner was a signature, "B.Thorpe". No way would he ask. Not now. Maybe not ever. That was personal.

The food arrived before they could even get settled in. They all helped spread it out on the dining room table. Basic American. Roast beef, mashed potatoes, gravy, several vegetables, yeast rolls and chocolate cake. Britt had several different beverages in her fridge.

"Jay, I have to apologize, I tried everywhere and just couldn't find any venison. I know how much you love it. But the roast beef will have to suffice." She said poker faced.

John, turned his back and pretended to be studying the view from the big picture window. Johnnie crammed his drink into his mouth, but with eye squint, you knew he was trying to keep from laughing out loud. So there it was. Another point for her side. Not that he was keeping score or anything.

The meal was a feast. And feast they did. There was light casual conversation around the table. Jay asked John for an update on his daughter. No change. Britt asked Jay about his ranch and he got some laughs when he told them about a fight between Butch and Hank. With Butch coming out the victor after chasing Hank around the field until she finally gave up. Hank will probably need some doctoring from being bitten on the neck. Next, when they were done and the mess was cleaned up and put away, it was time to get down to business.

"We were able to gather enough information on prostitution, to have the Sheriff indicted and there will be, no doubt, a shakeup in the Sheriff's office. We have names of some of the officers that were involved and there could be more. The 2 bouncers will be tried for assault. The young prostitute will be turned over to Juvenile Court. And the motel clerk and Casino Manager are being indicted for robbery and prostitution. In essence, the Casino is shut down. But my trainee, Tres Grant, overheard the Motel clerk tell the Casino Manager that he was more scared of the big boss than him. There's your link."

"That's some good intelligence for us on the Casino involvement. You can bet that it could be the same with some of the other Casinos." Said Britt.

"Did we get any hits from the recordings?" Jay asked.

"I haven't listened to today's yet, but from yesterday afternoon, nothing."

They spent the next couple of hours going over the recordings from all three Micro-mics and still nothing.

"There is one very interesting thing, however", Said Britt, "There were several calls made around 10 am, from our building area to various prepaid throw-away cells in Durant and Atoka. As well as to here in Oklahoma City."

"How can that be?" Jay said.

"Easy." John said. "Parking lot or ladies room."

"Exactly." Said Britt.

"O.K. then, we'll have to put another one in the ladies room."

"Hold on. I don't mind bending a few rules in case of an emergency, but there is no way I am going to put one in the ladies room. We'll have to figure another way." Britt said with absolute certainty.

"So where does that leave us?" Jay asked.

"The Cell Tower records." She said. "I released the memo on finding Lonnie's name and who he was, at about 10:05 yesterday. At about the same time, a cell call was made from our general area to the cell phone that we now assume belongs to Chase Stormcloud. It had to have been made from either the parking lot or the ladies room."

"10:00 am on the button, every day like clockwork, Sarah goes into the ladies room. I think that is evidence." Jay said.

"Maybe not" said John.

"John's right." Said Britt. "Lately the Chief has been out of the office a lot, in the mornings. He could just wait till 10:00 to go out and call. He could also call from anywhere and we might not have him on the Cell Tower or the recordings. I feel pretty confident in saying it is one or the other. Or here's an interesting option. What if it's not one or the other but both. Sarah stopped by my desk yesterday and asked me why Johnnie Wolf was spending so much time working with Lt. Two Feathers. I told her that I was sure John needed the help and that Johnnie and John had been friends for a long time. If she was curious, you can bet she and the Chief had discussed it."

"You think it's time for Johnnie to take a little personal leave time, to be with his daughter?" Jay asked.

"Maybe", said Britt. "John, what do you think?"

John thought for a minute, then said.

"Johnnie, what do you think?"

"I've been out of touch with my contact for quite some time. For my daughter's sake, I think it's a good idea. But what about the ankle monitor?"

"I think I can trust you, Johnnie", said Britt. She unlocked and removed it.

"Thanks. If you don't mind, I need to drop in on my daughter before she goes to sleep. She'll be worried." He said.

They decided they had done all they could do tonight. They wished Johnnie the best for him and his daughter, but reminded him that the business between him and the Gang was still to be addressed. He nodded.

"One thing more." Jay added. "Let's not forget that the Casino Operator, Rick Blackhorse, is Sarah's nephew."

They thanked Britt and headed home.

CHAPTER FIFTY THREE

Even a small mouse has anger.
(Native American saying)

Chase's phone buzzed.

"Yes."

"I have another mission for you."

"Good, I'm ready."

"In case you forget, this will be a second mission. You haven't completed the other one yet. So now you have two."

"Yes, I know. I have been thinking about the other one. He moves around a lot. But I will get him. Who is the new one?"

"An officer with the Creek Nation Lighthorse Tribal Police. Muskogee."

"O.K."

"Get it done right away. This one is urgent. With luck and planning, you may be able to get both of your missions resolved at once. I will text you a name and a possible schedule that would put them in close proximity. But either one would be a good option."

"Very good. No problem."

(Click)

Chase thought to himself. "Best to find a room nearer Oklahoma City. I will need Lonnie's help on this one. Got to find a ground floor room with outside entry."

"Lonnie, let's get packed. Your dream has come true, we are clearing out and headed for Oklahoma City."

"Bout time." Lonnie grumbled.

On the way to Oklahoma City, the text message arrived. At first glance, Chase's spirits soared. Jay Nation and Johnnie Wolf were scheduled for a meeting and then take lunch at a local restaurant. This would be his first "double header". Two kills. Two bonuses for two clean kills.

The only problem was that they would be have to use handguns rather that the Black Brick. Of course, this would not be identified as a gang hit if they used guns. Sure, the advertising value would be lost, but these were not scumbags being flushed out of the system. These were just troublesome cops whose existence was problematical and a challenge to their continued success.

They would first need time to case the area around the station house. Then confirm an escape plan, which was going to involve a stolen vehicle, since this was a full daylight job, right in front of the police Headquarters. Best to get the vehicle from a large parking lot. Probably a movie theater parking lot would be best. Chase would check out movie show times and be in place before the start. That would give them plenty of time to do the job, return to the lot to get their own vehicle and escape. Perfect. This should be a "slam dunk".

CHAPTER FIFTY FOUR

**Remember that this land does not belong
to you, it is you who belongs to the land.**
(Native American belief)

J ay got to the office at 6:30 am. He considered the "get-there-early"
contest had outlived its usefulness.

"Glad to see you in so early." He said with a smile, "It is a goal I
think I will have to work harder on."

"The early bird catches the worm." Britt said, continuing to type.

"Yeah, but it's the second mouse who gets to eat the cheese."

He saw that hint of a smile tugging at the corners of her mouth. She
kept typing. Finally looking up.

"We have some bad news this morning."

"That is getting to be the benchmark for this case." He said.

"I got a report this morning from my guys in Washington. Seems
like Myra was right. They have now identified a few other murders in
various parts of the country and all are confirmed except one. That one
they can't absolutely confirm that it was the Gang, but the M.O. is so
similar that they are convinced it was."

"How so?"

"That is the worst news. There was a Judge murdered in Florida
who was known to have ties to the Mafia in New Jersey. It went down
like this, according to my guys. A group of men made an appointment
to talk to the Judge about what has turned out to be a fake problem.

The secretary led them into the Judge's office and then closed the door. Only a few minutes later, they walked out and shut his door. She said the Judge liked to work with the door closed.

His next appointment was 30 minutes later, when 3 of his law clerks showed up for a scheduled meeting. She led them into the Judge's office, but he wasn't there. There is no other door. She walked up to the desk and that's when she saw him lying behind the desk and when she saw blood, she fainted.

When she woke up, there was only one law clerk there and he had her laying on the Judge's couch with a cold rag on her head. She woke up confused. Then she remembered and asked what happened. The law clerk said that the Judge had been killed and that he had just called 911. The police were on the way.

Upon their arrival, there was no evidence of a black brick. So, it was not mentioned in the police report. There were no red flags, until the local media sprung the story about a serial killer gang that was using a black brick as a murder weapon in Oklahoma. The police report mentioned the description of the killers that the secretary had given. It was 4 guys who looked like they were either Spanish or some other darker skin race and that two of them were unusual in their appearance. She described one as a 'scarecrow' and the other as a 'Giant'. Our guys began putting 2 and 2 together and with the descriptions we gave them, they were certain.

They decided that the missing brick was probably carried off by one of the law clerks, destination unknown. That's when the matter took a really bad turn.

We have several low-level plants inside the N.Y. and N.J. 'mob' operations. One reported, that sometime back, he heard some guys laughing about how some 'Oklahoma cowboys' were fixing to meet their maker. Our best guess is that the brick was delivered to the mob in N.J. and a 'hit' was ordered. My guy said that we may have competition for who gets the Black Brick Gang first. They said we now had two gangs to be on the lookout for. They wished us luck." She finished still wearing her poker face.

"Sounds like they might save the taxpayers a chunk of money."

"Sure, Jay. That may sound like a good thing, but it is still against the law. Not to mention the fact that my new boss would love it, since it shows that the Mafia is smarter and better at their jobs than yours truly." She was staring at her keyboard.

"We're not going to let that happen. *I'm* not going to let that happen." Jay said, "We can't afford to lose any time. Whatever we are going to do, we have to do, now."

Jay visited Lizard to ask further questions about the Mafia Judge killed in Florida. Lizard was asleep. He asked the guard on duty how Lizard was doing.

The guard said "Lizard seems fine and he could 'talk the horns off a Billy Goat'. He had a nice visit from his Catholic priest. Of course, that was a religious deal, so I let him in. No other visitors are permitted."

"Why'd you let *him* in? NO ONE is permitted." Fired back Jay. "Who was this priest?"

"Father Justin or Julias or something like that. ... No, now I remember, Father Julian from St. Joseph's." He said meekly.

"Did he stay long?"

"Well, 15 or 20 minutes I guess, till a nurse came in and ran him off."

"Did the priest show any credentials?"

"No, but he was dressed in black with one of those little white strips on his collar, you know, like all priests wear."

"Can you describe him?"

"Yeah. But you probably have him on the security cameras."

"Describe him."

"I don't know, maybe mid to late 50's. Balding on top. Obviously a yankee. Sounded like maybe from New York or up in there. Had a little sing song way of talking like you see in movies where Eye-talians are talking."

Jay called St. Joseph's Catholic Church in Muscogee. No priest by the name of Julian or Julias or anything similar. He decided it was time to wake Lizard up.

"You again?" He said groggily. "Howdy Officer."

"I understand your priest dropped in for a visit?"

229

"He's not my priest. I'm not Catholic. Used to be a Baptist when I was a kid. Let me tell you the story about why I stopped goin'."

"Not right now Lizard, maybe later. Right now I need to know what he said."

"DIdn't say much of nothin'. Just asked a bunch of questions. Asked about the Mission we did in Florida. I told him it was some judge who was crooked as a dog's hind leg. Was gettin' Mafia guys out of jail. A real skunk if you ask me."

"Did Lonnie leave his black brick at the scene or take it with him after the mission?"

"He never takes a brick back. That's our signature. It lets the bad boys know that there's somebody out there ready to make things right."

"What were some of the questions?"

"Who was our team leader, who did he report to, where was the Big Boss stayin'? That kinda thing. I told him all about how our team operated and that I didn't know nuthin about the big boss. Chase was our leader and was currently listed as 'Missing -in-Action'. I thought I'd get a laugh on that one. Nope, he didn't seem to see the humor in that or maybe he wasn't familiar with M.I.A.s." Lizard laughed. "Hey, you want to hear one about this guy I knew who was a M.I.A.?"

"Not right now Lizard, But I'll get back to you on that."

Jay called Britt. John was in her office. He gave them a recap of what had happened. He told them that there was no question about it, now. The Mafia was on the hunt too. He asked Britt to check flights for last few days from N.Y. or N.J. direct to Oklahoma City. He got a copy of the hospital security cameras, but the guy kept his face out of view, even in the parking lot. This guy knew his stuff.

Jay drove quickly back to the office. Britt had gotten the information on flights. There were six names. She found that two were residents. Four were non-residents. Data checks found info on two of the non-residents who were employed by big international companies and a further check showed them attending business meetings in Oklahoma City. On the two remaining, one was a very young female, leaving only the male as a possible. There were no records on him. They ran the name against criminal records and other records, social security info and more. The male's name didn't exist anywhere. The ID he had used with the airline was obviously phony. That could be their guy.

A trip to review the Airport Security cameras was more productive. At the time the flight arrived, a man fitting the description was seen boarding a city Cab # 303 and then by checking with the cab company, trip records showed him being delivered to the Casino hotel in Oklahoma City.

Britt and Jay next visited the hotel and the front desk remembered checking in a man fitting that description. The name on the hotel register was different than the name registered by the airline. Probably another phony. The clerk said that it looked like the man was still checked in. They got the room number from the desk clerk, then went to the room and knocked. No answer.

Britt called for a warrant from a local judge, to enter and search. Once that was approved, Hotel security unlocked the door. They went in with guns drawn. No one was there. Britt called for a "rush" forensics tech. When he arrived, he found that there were no good, clear prints. Some smudges and one partial. The guy must have wiped everything down. He didn't wear gloves because the tech was able to collect the one possible partial print and took it back to the lab to see if they could get a match. There was nothing in the room but a few changes of clothes.

Forensics ran the one, partial print and they got a 90% positive hit. It belonged to Vito Palmisano, a member of a prominent Mafia family in N.J. He had a long rap sheet. A mug shot was emailed to the hotel. The desk clerk recognized it. Vito had been tried for murder, no conviction. Notes on his profile described him as smart, tough, and real trouble. Possibly armed and dangerous.

They left everything in the room undisturbed and posted a man in the lobby with the file picture of Vito.

As if Jay's day wasn't bad enough, he got another phone call from Chase. Same old "walking dead-man" stuff as before. Jay told Chase to go *"chase"* himself and laughed. Chase was so angry, he made a mistake. In his rage, he said,

"You may think you are the apotheosis of intelligence, but I am going to show you what that gets you".

"Whoa", Jay thought. "He used the word *Apotheosis* before hanging up ... Proof?"

A quick call to Britt put a damper on his excitement. She said that if Chase picked up on that word, he could just as easily have gotten it from Sarah, who probably had heard it from Mac on numerous occasions. So, still, no proof one way or the other.

At least they now knew who this new adversary was and they had his picture. That hopefully would help them in either stopping or catching this "Vito" guy. Still, they weren't a lot closer on their case than they were before.

CHAPTER FIFTY FIVE

**Speak truth in humility to all people.
Only then can you be a true man.**
(Sioux proverb)

Vito was prepared. His computer research had given him the address of the State and Indian Nation Liaison Force. He found a large Walmart with a very clean restroom where he donned his priest outfit from his briefcase, including a small beard and mustache. He grinned in the mirror as a young man passed behind him and said, "Good Morning, Father". He chuckled and then drove to the address he had found.

When Vito entered the building, he quickly scanned the office and spotted what looked like an executive secretary at a desk in front of a large office door. This was a new and probably state-of-the-art facility. He had been in enough police stations to be able to spot any cameras and where he was most likely to find the guy in charge. The lady at the desk was nicely dressed and had gray hair. Another standard for police stations, the boss's secretary nearly always had gray hair, as did the boss. He approached the desk. Her desk name plate said "Sarah Blackhorse".

"I hope I am not imposing", he said, "but I was just walking around the neighborhood and something told me I should stop in. I am inviting people to our Friday evening fish fry, at the local City Park. It is open to non-Catholics as well as Catholics. We would love to have you come."

"How very thoughtful of you." She said. "Actually, I'm afraid I'm no great lover of fried fish or any other kind of fish, so I guess I won't be able to come. But thank you for the thought."

"Oh, that's O.K. Say, is there a good lunch place around here? I am not real familiar with this particular part of town."

"Yes", she said, in fact I eat there often. Right down the block on the left side of the street. The Burger Shack. Great food."

"Thank you, so much." He said and he departed.

He was doubtful that she would check under the front edge of her desk for the listening device he had pressed there. He waited in his car until she left for lunch. He watched as she headed down the block and crossed the street. When he verified that she was going in the Burger Shack, he parked across the street and went in.

He spotted her looking over a menu. He took a seat at the counter, near the front and ordered a hamburger, no cheese. No fries. Coke. He watched from the corner of his eye and tried to be as unnoticeable as possible. Hard to do when you are dressed like a priest. She didn't dawdle. She ate and began gathering up to leave. As she neared him, he took the waitress's check and almost bumped into Sarah as they were right by the cash register.

"Excuse me. Oh, hello again", he said.

"Hello, I see you took my advice."

"I did, fortunately, I did. It was as good as you said. I will probably come back here from time to time. Oh, by the way, as a priest, I get the chance to talk to a lot of people from time to time, about problems or whatever is on their minds. It's not just part of my job, I really care about people. I want to give you my name and phone number in case you ever want to just chat. I would be honored."

"Well, O.K., but I am pretty happy with my life right now."

"That's wonderful. I am glad to hear it. But should the occasion ever occur, I would feel like I was just paying you back for the wonderful food you just pointed me to. Please have a blessed day."

"Thank you, father. I guess I can call you that. What was your name?"

"Father Julian. Here, I'll write my name and number on your

receipt. And your name? I forgot to ask when I was in your office, I apologize for that."

"Sarah Blackhorse."

"What a lovely name. Thanks again Sarah. Here. Call anytime." He handed her the receipt.

She slipped it in her purse and left.

He would call her if he found that his other methods of tracking his target failed. She might be a valuable source of info. Or even a hostage, if it came that. He wanted all his bases covered. Failure was not an option. He was good at what he did.

CHAPTER FIFTY SIX

**It is less of a problem to be poor,
than to be dishonest.**
(Anishinabe proverb)

An old lady shuffled up the sidewalk from the parking area and turned to enter the big automated doors of the hotel. Fortunately, the floor was carpeted so her steps were sure, though short in stride. Her cane assured that her balance would not be a problem as it is for some elderly guests. Her humped back only exaggerated the rotund belly that was filling the old cotton print blouse and skirt she was wearing. Her medium length, bluish gray hair left no question about her advancing age. The small hat pinned to her head was a style of long, long ago. She toddled up to the elevator and punched the button. There were no other passengers on the elevator, so she punched her floor as the doors closed. The chime soon sounded, announcing that she had reached her floor.

When the doors opened, she toddled out slowly and moved to the first door in the hallway, on her left. She raised her glasses and peeked under them to see the room number up close. Her nose almost touching the door. She then went to the next door which was on the right and repeated the process of peeking under her frames at the number. She continued to toddle up the hall, inspecting each number in turn. As she reached the room, formerly occupied by the Mafia thug, she did the same process and looked at the "Do Not Disturb" tag on the knob.

Then moved on. She continued until she had checked every door. Then she turned, shook her head and toddled back to the elevator and pushed the button.

Anyone viewing her on the hotel's security camera would probably assume that she could not find the room she was looking for, and then lose any interest in her. What they would not notice, was when her quick look at the "Do Not Disturb" tag hanging on the door knob, discovered that the two grey hairs that she had left lodged between the tag and the knob shaft, when she last departed the room, were now missing. Someone had been in the room. When the elevator arrived, she proceeded to the lobby floor. Then she continued toddling through the big front entranceway and retraced her steps down the sidewalk.

When she reached her car, parked in the front lot, she got in and removed her gray wig and tossed it into the back seat next to a wig with long red hair and a complete cowgirl getup, another disguise. Embroidered western shirt, blue jeans and pink cowboy boots, a bandana with a turquoise clasp, the works. She unbuttoned the front of her faded blouse and pulled the bra she was wearing around to the front where she could unhook its fastener. She shed her padded bra and tossed it and her cane in the back next to the priest shirt and the Cowgirl outfit. The blouse came right off exposing a blue golf shirt she had worn underneath. She slipped out of the old shoes with the short platform heels and exchanged them for Nike black tennis slip-ons. The skirt slid right down past the black Bermuda shorts and She/He sighed and then grumbled, "O.K., Vito is back in town."

His next stop was to a Walmart where he paid cash for some socks and underclothes. He thought to himself,

"These country bumpkins didn't even check to see if I had marked the door to show a security breach".

He grinned, feeling very satisfied with himself. Even though it was a small inconvenience losing the extra clothes he had brought, it was worth it for the success of his time spent in arranging some surveillance details. He drove to a nearby shoddy motel. One of those where you can pay by the night or by the hour. It smelled bad, but he had been in worse in New Jersey. He listened to his Micro-mic for a little while, then switched to his second planted device. The one he had planted after his lunchtime visit to Sarah. He hoped that this one would be more enlightening. It turned out that it was. Four names were mentioned. Major Mac McCall the Unit head, Sarah Blackhorse his secretary, his second in command Lt. John Two Feathers and his lead investigator Jay Nation.

On the internet, it was easy enough to get home addresses on all four. But he had to pick one to follow. Everything seemed to flow through John Two Feathers. So Vito picked him to follow, first. He hoped it wouldn't take too many days. The Motel was almost unlivable.

CHAPTER FIFTY SEVEN

Lose your temper and you lose a friend.
Lie and lose yourself.
(Hopi proverb)

John stepped into Britt's office. Jay was there. "We have a problem. Johnnie Wolf has been shot."

"Details?" Asked Jay as he rose.

"Drive-by. Out in front of the Creek H.Q. No witnesses. John took one in the chest. Went clear through. Serious but not critical. He saw one of the shooters. He's sure it was Lonnie."

"Let's go". Britt said.

With lights and siren, the drive to Muskogee only took about 50 minutes. The Security officer in the lobby escorted them to Johnnie's room. Johnnie was in pain, but was able to talk. There were several cops in the room. They were discussing the Black Brick Gang. They now had 8 officers who had been hurt by the gang. They wanted blood. The Chief was there and Britt asked him if she and Jay could speak to Johnnie alone for a minute. The Chief didn't like it, but he agreed.

Jay saw a doctor coming past Johnnie's room. He stopped him.

"How is he Doc?"

"There's wasn't a lot of bleeding. No internal injuries that we can see. No organ damage. Those are all good things. The bullet broke one rib which deflected it out of his body. If he takes it easy, he should be doing well in a couple of weeks. The bone will take another month to completely heal."

"How long before he can leave?" Jay asked, thinking about whether the Gang would make another try right away.

"Maybe two or three days. Other than the rib it was a clean puncture in and puncture out. We only had to do a few stiches. Still, he will need to be careful", the Doc said as he left.

"I was supposed to meet with Johnnie today. Wish I hadn't cancelled it." Said Jay. "I might have been able to help."

"And you might have become a second target." Britt said.

After the room was cleared, Britt took over.

"Johnnie, I know what reasons you had for not telling us about who your contact was. I don't know what it is like, to be a parent with all the things you are dealing with. But you can see now, that either someone has figured out that you are helping us, or they have decided to silence all past connections. Either way, neither you nor your daughter are safe. I want three things, I want first, to move your daughter to an Oklahoma City hospital where we can provide the protection she needs. Second, as soon as you can be turned loose, I want you to move to a safe house. Third, I want the name of your contact. If you can't do all of those things, we can't help you."

Johnnie thought for only a second, then said,

"I can't tell you for sure, whether it is Mac or Sarah who heads up the Gang. They kind of walk in the same shadow.

It could be both of them. But it is Mac who I call. I still have this gut feeling that it's Sarah who is the big boss. On the other two items, yes, I would feel much better about my daughter being in Oklahoma City. The sooner the better. As for the safe house ..."

"Johnnie", Jay said, "I think the safest place for you to be, and the place they are least likely to look, is at my place. I have plenty of room and I would like you to stay there. That way we can also work out ways to get you to see your daughter without having to worry."

"Jay, are you sure that isn't putting you in even more danger?" He asked.

"Johnnie, I already have a target on my back."

"O.K. Thank you. Both."

They headed back. Jay was so disappointed that it was difficult to talk. Mac was his mentor. He was like another Uncle. Jay was having real trouble believing Johnnie. Finally Britt broke the silence.

"Jay, do you think he was telling the truth?"

"I don't know. I am torn between, 'I hope so' and 'I hope not'." He said.

"I can understand. I can't get into his head," she said, "but he has more reason to lie, than to tell the truth. Basically, what he gave us was wishy-washy and still doesn't give us enough information, or proof, to arrest anybody. I think it may be time to confront Mac."

"How?" Johnnie asked.

"I don't think it should be you." She said. "I think I could tell him that we are pretty sure that Sarah is in tight with the gang and see what his reaction would be. What do you think?"

"It might help *make* things happen instead *waiting* for it to happen." He said.

"I can tell him that she had your schedules, your information on the leaks and all the things we were questioning the other night, which made her a suspect. I think he'd buy it. He may even dump the whole thing on her. At least it would be a start." She said.

"We should probably give it a few days to make sure he doesn't tie it to our visit to Johnnie. Then, I think you should probably break it to him in confidence." Jay said, thinking out loud. "Tell him that you and I have not discussed it. That way he may be more open. We have to get with John as soon as we get back.

From here forward, he needs to know as much as we do about what is going on."

"I agree." She said.

The ride back was used to discuss the logistics of moving Johnnie and his daughter. Jay headed straight for John's office when they arrived. Mac was in John's office.

"I heard about Johnnie Wolf, will he be alright?" Mac said with a believable show on concern.

"It was a chest shot. Jay said, "He is in serious, but not critical, condition. He was on his way to visit his daughter. He's got to be the unluckiest person I know."

"You've got that right. I am going to have Sarah send him some flowers."

Jay thought to himself that maybe they would need to get the flowers checked for a bomb.

"Mac, I think that would be nice and I know his fellow officers would appreciate it. So would Johnnie." Jay said.

He would have to catch John after Mac left the office.

Mac left early. Jay got with John and discussed the plan to have Britt cover their suspicion about Sarah. John agreed and it was settled. After a few days, Jay loaned his horse trailer to one of the Creek officers. The following day, he returned it and Jay had him leave it in the barn. After the officer left, he opened the horse trailer and helped Johnnie out.

"How was the ride?"

"I felt every bump in the road, but I'm not complaining. It may have saved my life."

"I think you can bet on it. I can't promise that my ranch isn't under surveillance. So, stay here and when it gets dark, we'll get you in the house. I have a place fixed up for you. I kind of dismantled the little room I use for my office. Until you get better, I will bed down in there and you will take my bedroom."

"No, Jay. That's ..."

"You want to start an argument on your first day here? Remember, in your condition I could probably whip your butt."

"Jay, you probably could even if I wasn't in this condition."

"It's only for a few days, until you get more stable on your feet. Right now, you can't take any chances. So, don't give me any argument. That's an order."

"Yes sir." Johnnie saluted and smiled.

After dark, Jay showed him in and fixed supper for both of them. And after that, he showed him around the house. Later, Jay got him settled into a recliner.

"Jay, I don't even know how to begin to thank you. I just hope that

I haven't set you up for the Gang's vengeance. In your own home." He shook his head.

"Like I said before, Johnnie, They already have a target on my back. So, it doesn't change anything for me. I don't think anything is going to happen, but while we are on the subject of Gang vengeance, I have a little surprise for you. Nobody knows this, not even my Mom. Not long after I joined the department, I put in a safety feature, 'just in case'. What's the old saying, 'better to have it and not need it, than to need it and not have it'? I want to show it to you."

He opened the closet door in the bedroom, pulled up the rug and lifted the trap door in the floor.

"I don't think you are in any shape to try it out right now, unless there was a 'real' life-threatening emergency, of course. I have tried it several times and it is a snap. The only difficulty is getting the trap closed almost all the way and snaking your hand out to pull the rug back down. That takes a little practice. The crawl space under the house is big enough to travel on your hands and knees. The foundation flashing around my house covers up the crawl space, except right beside the back steps. Later, I will show that to you. Meanwhile, get your rest. I get up early, so I will fix us some breakfast and leave yours in the microwave. See you tomorrow. Call me anytime if you need me."

The next morning, Jay was surprised. As he was fixing breakfast, Johnnie came into the kitchen. They sat and ate, looking out the back door at the farm.

"This is nice, Jay. When it's safe, I would love to go out and see it all. It's the kind of place I dreamed about having someday for me and my daughter. 'Blossom' is what I call her. That's the English translation of her Creek name. I know that with what I've done, I can forget about that dream."

"Don't give up hope, Johnnie. The circumstances that got you there and the help that you have given us since, buys a lot of forgiveness with a Judge."

"Yeah, but can I ever forgive myself?"

Jay called in to say he would be taking a day off to attend to some inescapable duties around the farm and ranch. He needed this day to learn more about what Johnnie and his contact had discussed. He wanted to have a better understanding about how it started, how long it lasted and what all was passed on. Both to his "contact" as well as to Dutch. He still wasn't sure that there wasn't some deeper, hidden connection between Dutch and the Gang. Johnnie said that if there was, he was not aware of it. Jay spent the rest of the day doing exactly what he had said he needed to do. Before long it got too dark to do any more chores. He was exhausted and preparing for bed when she called.

"Jay. We have a problem."

"We have lots of problems." He said.

"This one is new and serious. I have, as a habit, for years checked any place I stay for 'Bugs'. I got lax. Haven't checked for a few days. I found my very first one a little while ago. I don't know when it got there, who did it, or what might have been compromised."

"Anything unique about it, make, model, that sort of thing?"

"No. It is a new design. Small, efficient, I've seen some of them before."

"Any sign of forced entry?

"No. But these days there are plenty of electronic lock openers available."

"Anything disturbed or missing?"

"No. A professional job. If it hadn't come up on my hand scanner, I'd have never known. What are your thoughts? Would Mac or Sarah have done this or ordered it done?"

"No, I'd be more inclined to think it was our Mafia guy."

"The complex has security cameras for the foyer and parking lot. I am going to check those next. If we can pin it down to a date and time, we can then review to see what could have been heard on the bug."

"I'm on my way."

When Jay arrived, Britt was watching his arrival on the live parking lot camera. She stepped out the door and called him over.

"Hi Britt, found anything yet?"

"Yes. There was a middle-aged Catholic priest who arrived a few days ago, spent about 10 minutes and left. We are trying to get a better image of his face. Looks like he spotted the cameras and kept his face turned or was covering it by pretending to scratch his head. We're not going to get much."

"Had to be father Julian. Was it before or after our dinner meeting?"

"Before. We have to assume he knows our plans. Worse, he knows we have two suspects. Sarah or Mac, or both."

"Britt, trying to think like the Mafia might think, and knowing the way the Mafia works, their best option is to try to take out both."

"I don't know how we can warn them without tipping our hand."

"We can't. We'll have to make our move sooner rather than later."

After a brief talk, it was decided that they should launch their plan tomorrow. Jay returned to the ranch and filled Johnnie in on the problem. The next day went quietly, when the time seemed right, Jay left work early. He didn't want to be there when Britt had her private conversation with Mac about Sarah being her top suspect. Her story to Mac would indicate that she had not discussed it with anyone. She had promised to call Jay and let him know how it went. He stopped at a truck stop, a few miles away and waited. He wanted to be close in case something didn't go right.

Britt was ready for her discussion with Mac. John and Sarah had both left, as well as the rest of the office. She knocked lightly on his open door. He was gathering up some files to take home.

"Come on in, Britt, what's up?"

"Mac, I have something that I need to discuss with you, in strict confidence."

"Sounds serious."

"I'm afraid it is."

"Well then, you have my undivided attention." Mac sat down.

Britt settled into a chair in front of his desk.

"First, let me say that I hope you don't take this the wrong way, or take it as any kind of personal criticism of you or the job you do. I have come to have a great respect for your knowledge, honesty and the way you handle your job. I have learned a lot since I've been here."

"Thank you Britt. I have nothing but the greatest respect for you also. And I assure you that whatever you want to say will be between you and me and I will listen with an open mind. Whatever it is, I know that you are just doing your job, and doing it conscientiously."

"Thank you, I was confident that you would say that. I would appreciate it if you will let me go through it completely, and then we can discuss it. When I first arrived, I had everyone on my suspect list. You, included."

Mac shifted uncomfortably in his chair.

"As I narrowed it down, it became obvious that we had a leak internally. In fact, I began to suspicion that it had to be coming from someone near the top. This was confirmed by Myra who said that some incidents at the Durant Casino were being covered up or influenced by someone in this department. I think I have gotten to know you well enough that it could not have been you. For one thing, your reputation is impeccable, and for another, you are nearing retirement. It just didn't fit. Sarah, on the other hand, was my only other suspect. She had access to everything we were doing, she knew Jay's schedule. Also, she is nearing retirement age and the chances of her staying off food-stamps is not good.

Another more damning clue, is the fact that the Bureau approved the tracking of cell phone calls originating from this building and some of the phone calls we tracked were occurring at a few minutes after 10 am. As you well know, Sarah visits the Ladies room promptly as 10 am, every day, come Hell or high water. It all fits. I have decided that the investigation should focus on her. We may need your help, even though we know that it would be very hard for you, considering your habit of defending your people. Don't get me wrong, that is an admirable trait for a leader. Sarah is not your ordinary employee, she is and has been, a huge part of your life. I can appreciate that. I am sure this is as hard for you to absorb as it is for me to say it. But, it is what it is. There, I'm done."

"Britt, you are only doing your job. Yes, it is difficult for me to even imagine such a thing. Seems like she has been with me forever. She isn't so much an employee as she is a close friend. Like the relationship between cops and their partners. You would lay down your life for them. This is a shock. I'm not sure you are right, but as head of this department, I have to take it seriously. I would be lying if I didn't say that I hope you are wrong. I don't know. I want to think about this overnight. We can discuss it in the morning if that's O.K.?"

"Absolutely, Mac. I wouldn't expect anything less. Thanks, so much, for letting me get it all out in the open. And I am so sorry that it couldn't have turned out different."

"Who all have you discussed this with?" Mac quickly inquired.

"Only you. After you have thought it over, I would like to have a meeting of the Task Force tomorrow and let them know what is going on and develop a path forward. If that's alright with you?"

"Fine. We will talk in the morning. I probably won't sleep tonight."

Britt called Jay after she left. "O.K., it's done. It went well, I asked for a Task Force meeting, first thing in the morning."

"That ought to shake things up," said Jay. "We'll have to wait and see. It's still early, I have to see to Johnnie and then I have to give the horses a shot and look after the cows and chickens. You know how that goes."

Britt chuckled. "You'd make a good mother, Jay."

"Sometimes I feel like one. Give me a call later if you hear anything."

"Will do."

It didn't take long. Britt had just finished her supper when the call came. It was Mac.

"You'll probably think I jumped the gun. I couldn't get this off my mind. I'm not a 'sit and stew' kind of guy. I called Sarah and had her come in."

"O.K."

"I told her I had an emergency that I needed her help on. After all these years of loyalty and mutual trust, I felt like I had to confront her. When I went over some of the coincidences that seemed to add up, she simply shrugged her shoulders and began to admit the whole thing. This has apparently been going on for quite some time. When I asked her 'why' she simply said, 'Money'. I know she doesn't make a lot of money in her position. I don't make a lot of money in my position, either. But she lives alone and the idea of trying to live off Social Security and a small retirement from the State just didn't let her see any light at the end of the tunnel.

She is a very bright woman. She figured this scam out, all by herself. She had access to files and criminal records. In my curiosity about this whole mess, I may have unwittingly contributed to the problem by getting info from Johnnie Wolf and having Sarah file it away for historical reasons. I am a little embarrassed to admit that I am considering writing a book. A lot of people in unique jobs are doing that these days.

Sarah was with me for a long time before I got this assignment. She has been my right hand. When she first suggested that I consider writing about my experiences, I told her that I was no writer. She said she would help me write it. I've never had much of an ego problem, but I think her constant encouragement may have stimulated a little ego situation. She was constantly pushing me to build a file of crooks and their activities. She said it would be critical for the writing of the book.

I'm still having a hard time accepting this. The thing that was most disappointing, was when she said that no one would be able to prove it. Not even me. She said she would retire and I would never see her again. She also suggested that for the good of all concerned, I should just drop the whole thing and that trying to prosecute her would only make me and the whole department look bad. Maybe even destroy it. She was right in most of that, except for one small detail that she was totally unaware of. I had taped the whole thing. And I told her so, which may have been a mistake.

She left in a rage. I began thinking about what I should do with the tape. Then it came to me that, with or without the tape, I might be the Gang's next target. I would feel better if you would come get the tape and then go straight-away and arrest her. It would be hard for me to do it and maybe even unhealthy. I haven't told anyone, but I've been having some tests done during the day. You guys may have noticed my absence lately. I have degenerative heart failure. I have to try to avoid stress or it could kill me."

"Sure, say no more, I am on my way." She said.

"Thanks, Britt. Just hurry please. I don't know what she will do, or when she will do it."

CHAPTER FIFTY EIGHT

A good soldier is a poor scout.
(Cheyenne proverb)

C hase's phone buzzed.
"Yes."
"Get Lonnie and get to this address, as soon as possible. I'll text you the address."

The boss had used Lonnie's name over the phone. That is a big No, No. Something big must be going down.

"Who is the target?"

"I'll tell you in person when you get here. Just hurry."

(Click)

Chase was confused. "In person"? Something was wrong. Dead wrong. Is the big boss shutting down the team? Am I fixing to get "fired?" Both me and Lonnie?

Chase began to pack some gear. In addition to his service weapon and hidden ankle derringer, he placed a holster with a small pistol in the small of his back. That was about as "armed" as he could get without creating suspicion. Meet with the big boss in person, right now? He thought, that this was beginning to stink to high heaven. His stomach was in a knot. Self-preservation over loyalty. That was his main thought. If I have to, I'll kill Lonnie and the big boss as well. And I am not turning my back on either one of them until this is over.

In less than 5 minutes, they piled into the car and hurried out of their Oklahoma City sleeze-bag motel. Even before the address text showed up.

"What's up?" Asked Lonnie. "Where we goin'."

"Actually, we are going to meet with the Big Boss, in person, just you and me."

"Why?"

"Just consider it a promotion."

CHAPTER FIFTY NINE

**How smooth must be the language of the whites
when they can make right look like wrong and
wrong look like right.**
(Chief Black Hawk   Sauk)

Britt had tried to call Jay. She got a recording. She left a note simply saying "Call me, I'm on my way to Mac's house."

He had been really busy with the animals and forgot to keep his cell phone with him. When he got back inside, he saw the missed call, collected the message and tried calling her back. He got a recording. This was puzzling. His phone buzzed in his hand. It was Mac.

"Hi, Mac. What's up?"

"Have you talked to Britt?"

"No, not since I left the office."

"Jay, Britt told me about a suspicion she had that Sarah may be involved somehow with the Gang. I had Sarah come back to the office and confronted her with it. She openly admitted it and made an unbelievably unapologetic confession. Her attitude was belligerent and she said that I would never be able to prove it. I was totally blown away. You know how close we were, for so many years. It was the money, Jay. More money than she could refuse. I told her that I had our whole conversation on tape. She was livid.

After she left, I realized that I had just made myself a target. I called Britt and she is on her way. I want to meet with you both right away.

We all three are in danger and we should make the arrest tonight before she has time to retaliate. Please hurry."

"On the way."

Before he left, he covered the call with Johnnie and told him to be alert. He knew now why Britt had called. She was on her way to get the proof they needed to prove what he had hoped all along. Mac was innocent. Jay knew it. Now everyone would know it. His heart was racing. He kept trying her phone, but it continued to go to a recording. She was probably checking in with her people.

This was the final vindication for Britt's problem in Washington. And it was a vindication for all concerned who had worked so hard and put their lives on the line to solve the puzzle.

He was not very far from Mac's place now. When he pulled in, he saw Mac's big sedan in his driveway. The house lights were mostly off. The barn lights both inside and outside were all on. He saw Britt's rental car parked at the barn and he parked beside her. Britt was not in sight.

He found Mac coming out of the barn and after 'hello', he said "where's Britt?"

"She went to the house. Had to make a 'Pit Stop'. Should be back in a minute."

"I understand you have some good news."

"Yes, in a way. Bad news for Sarah, to be sure. I am still struggling with it."

"Why didn't you arrest her on the spot?"

"I don't exactly know why, Jay. I guess all the years. I just couldn't bring myself to do it. If you will, I would rather you and Britt make the 'collar'."

"Sure, no problem."

"This whole mess is getting to my attitude." He said a little gruffly.

That struck Jay as peculiar. The Major was the calmest, least emotional person he had ever known, even in the worst of situations.

"Take a look, Jay, while we are waiting on Britt. Britt has a wire loose under her dash somewhere. She and I couldn't figure out why the dash lights were flickering. You know more about this stuff than me. I'll see if I can find a flashlight." Mac walked into the barn.

Jay looked and couldn't find anything wrong. He crawled out and went into the barn. Mac was stooped over a toolbox. As Jay kneeled down, he heard a muffled noise from one of the four horse stalls.

"What was that?" He said.

He started to pull his service weapon when a momentary pain shot through his head and the lights went out. When he awoke, he was laying in the straw in a horse stall. Lying beside him was Britt, gagged and tied. He was also gagged and tied. The two voices he heard were easily identifiable. One was Major McCall and the other was the voice of Chase Stormcloud. He remembered that voice from the calls saying that he was "a walking dead man".

Then he heard another gruff voice, almost a growl. That had to be Lonnie Justice, the Gang's "Do-er".

"Look, I ain't never killed nobody with a gun. I don't want to do that. Why don't I just twist his head off? He'll be just as dead." Lonnie growled.

Then Mac spoke up. "Look, Lonnie, One word from me and the Feds will have you in prison for the rest of your life. If you are lucky. A lethal injection if you're not. It has to be done and it has to look like they shot each other. Besides, when this is done, I can make arrangements for you to go to wherever in the world you want to go. You pick a place of your choice, where life will be easy."

"O.K., I'll do the cop. I might enjoy doing a cop. But I ain't never killed a lady, cop or not. Almost killed my cousin, but she was an accident. You gotta do her."

"O.K., Deal. And may I remind you again, that there is a huge bonus in it for you. I am talking 6 figures huge. That should help you get whatever you want in life."

"How you want me to do it? Bullets leave evidence, so do powder burns." He growled again.

Chase added, "The Feds will be all over this. Lots of questions. Shouldn't we do this somewhere else, like maybe his ranch?"

"I can set that up." Mac said. "I can say she called me with her suspicions and I told her to drop by his place and see if she could get any more information from him. I'll need to place a call from her phone to mine. And then from her phone to his. It can only work this way. She discovers that he is a dirty cop, she confronts him and he thinks she is going to arrest him. They get in a gun fight and they kill each other. His gun is in his hand and his bullet is in her heart.

Her gun is in her hand and her bullet is in his brain.

We leave no fingerprints or DNA. We will have to fire several shots around his house that miss.

We will get them in the cars. My car stays here. Chase, you drive her in her car to Jay's place. I will drive Jay in his cruiser. Lonnie, you drive Chase's car to Jay's. You can drop me back here when the mission is complete.

Take their gags off. We can't chance them choking to death before we kill them. It would mess up the forensics. And we will keep under the speed limit.

Tonight we have to think of any situation that could interfere with the plan, and control it.

Best we leave right away, the crime scene set up will take time. We have to be perfect from here on out. Everything rides on it."

They began loading the hostages.

"Check your vehicles for gas. We won't be risking a stop to buy more gas", said Mac.

All the cars had adequate gas. They were good to go.

Mac led the cars as they left.

CHAPTER SIXTY

**Misfortune will happen to the wisest and best of men.
What is past and what cannot be prevented should not be
grieved, for misfortunes do not flourish only in our lives.
They grow everywhere.**
(Chief Big Elk   Omaha)

S arah was confused about what she should do. She knew she had
to do something. She remembered the note the priest had given
her. She called the number but it went to a recording. She left
a message about her concerns and that she was going to one of her
boss's house for help and please call. John and his family lived only
a few minutes from Sarah's house. She drove there quickly. His kids
had already been put to bed and when John answered the door, he was
surprised to see her. Sarah had never been there before. She was crying.
John took her into his kitchen and told his wife that he needed a few
minutes alone with Sarah. Sarah was bitterly distraught. She was crying
and wringing her hands. John had never seen her this way.

"John, I don't know what to do. You know how devoted I am to
Mac. I have been with him for more years than I care to count. He is my
most beloved friend." She was having difficulty talking as she sobbed.

"As I was leaving work, I heard Mac mention a meeting, so I tried to
hear what it was about. I didn't hear it all, but I did hear him mention
something about meeting Britt at his place to give her something or other
that was apparently very important to the investigation. At least it seemed

so to me. I began having this unshakeable foreboding that Mac was going to do something unthinkable. I was torn between calling Mac and trying to talk him out of what I feared he was about to do and save him from destroying his career or else call you and try to save Britt from getting hurt or maybe killed." She began sobbing again. She was shaking uncontrollably.

"Please try to go on, Sarah." John said.

"I have always treasured the loyalty and trust between Mac and me. But, I am at the point where I can no longer let it continue. I have a strong religious conviction about things and when I know something is seriously wrong, I can't tolerate just sitting and doing nothing. I respect you John and I admire your honesty and hard work. I felt like you would know the right thing to do."

"Thank you. Go on."

"I don't know when I began to think it, but I began to feel like Mac was somehow involved with that horrible Gang. I've suspected it for a long time, but my feelings for Mac were such that I just turned a blind eye and hoped it would just all go away. I am sure that Mac is perhaps the head man and is going to try to stop Britt from discovering his involvement. John, you have to do something. You have to save him from himself." She began sobbing again.

John had his wife come in and try to comfort Sarah and told her that he would be back later, he was going to meet with Mac and Britt. He put on his service revolver and donned his Police Jacket. He tried to call both Britt and Jay.

No answer. He drove to Mac's place. His big sedan was in the driveway. The house was mostly dark, as was the small barn. He knocked hard, then banged. No response. He thought it best not to call Mac, since he was obviously planning something that John had to stop. In person.

Whatever was happening probably involved both Britt and Jay and was most likely going to happen at Jay's ranch. He turned onto the highway with siren and lights going. He was still quite a distance from Jay's place.

CHAPTER SIXTY ONE

The heart never knows the color of the skin.
(Chief Dan George   Salish)

On the ride from Mac's to the ranch, Jay had to ask.

"Mac. I guess I'm not just naïve, but also too dumb to understand this. You have a spotless record. A solid reputation. You were my mentor. Almost a father to me. My mind can't grasp the 'Why' in all of this."

"Not that it matters now, but it's easy. As a rookie, I took bullets on two different occasions. One still causes me problems after all these years. Late and long nights, very little compensation or appreciation. All I ever heard was that it was my job. Sometimes a pat on the back. While crooks took in thousands of dollars, all I took in was bullets and lumps. No one really cared. My salary was less than what a waiter makes in an up-scale restaurant. Retirement income was a joke. A pittance. I am not going to go on food stamps. I finally had enough. I was not going to continue to take it, 'for the system of justice'. Where was my justice? We arrest them, smart lawyers and corrupt judges turn them loose. There's your 'Why'."

"All the time, we thought it was Sarah. Couldn't be you. You're too smart and too good a person." Jay said.

"That's why I'll get away with it. I think Sarah knew it was me. She never said anything but I can read her like a book."

"So she never made any attempt to confront you or discuss it?"

"No. I haven't talked to her about it. She is clean. Always has been. She treasured loyalty over everything else. I guess we will have to let Lonnie or Chase 'Do' her as well."

"Why did you work so hard to make me a good cop?"

"To be above scrutiny, we had to be the best. I wanted everyone to help make that happen. Why do you think I had you head up the Task Force on the Gang? I needed you to keep me informed. To be on my side no matter what. That was even more important after Britt Thorpe and her Bureaucratic Bunglers showed up."

"Why Walt Washoe? That's what started this whole investigation."

"The whole Washoe thing was a little mistake on the part of Chase. He set it up without getting my prior approval. I could have handled that part of it. Then Britt shows up unannounced and things started getting sticky.

That was my mistake, I should have made her have an accident early on. I will take care of that tonight."

"You had them kill two judges, and tried to kill Johnnie?"

"Johnnie was a trouble maker and he had some information that I could not afford to have exposed. The two judges made me more money than I will ever need. After tonight, I will have to make a show of remorse for not getting it stopped and I will retire in disgrace and blame it on my failure to stop them. I will laugh all the way to the bank. I am a wealthy man. A very wealthy man. I have more in the bank right now than I have made totally during my career as a cop. I have an offshore account that runs in the millions. That's what leaders do. I was a good leader."

"You were the Casino's inside man, too."

"When you started looking into the Casino's, I knew you were getting too close. Jay, you just wouldn't let things go. My mistake. I underestimated you. That, too, we will take care of tonight."

The rest of the ride was quiet while Jay explored his options. The convoy swung into Jay's property. They parked out front and began unloading the hostages. They assumed the house was empty. Jay stumbled and fell, trying to buy all the time he could for Johnnie to get out the trap door. He stumbled again on the porch. The giant picked him up and threw him through the doorway that Chase had, thankfully opened.

"Easy Lonnie, he has to die of a gunshot wound with no other damage." Said Mac.

They began setting up the crime scene. Mac was calling the shots. He said placement was everything. The giant was to hold Britt and Chase was to hold Jay. They would shoot almost simultaneously and then wipe the guns clean and put them in the cop's hands.

CHAPTER SIXTY TWO

**Certain things catch your eye,
but pursue only those that capture your heart.**
(Sioux proverb)

Vito had 4 names on his list and 3 were in and around Oklahoma City. But John was his focus right now. He had a gut feeling. He had followed John home and was parked just up the street, when he got Sarah's message. Then Sarah showed up. And after a few minutes John went tearing off, with siren and lights. Vito followed. He hung back but tried to keep up, lights off. In a few minutes, John pulled into Major McCall's place. Then only a couple of minutes later, he was on his way again. Lights and sirens again. After they had traveled several miles, Vito recognized that he was headed in the direction of Officer Jay Nation's place. When the cruiser turned off its flashers and killed the siren, they were only a couple of miles from Jay's ranch. Vito slowed when he saw John's lights all go off and his car turn into the narrow dirt road at the edge of Jay's property. He also noticed several cars parked at Jay's house. This looked like a big meeting of his principle persons-of-interest list. He knew from his "bug" that the primary suspects were either Mac or Sarah and according to Lizard, the big boss was probably a man. So it had to be Mac. Sarah's phone message confirmed it.

He parked just past the property, got his sniper rifle and binoculars out of the trunk and crept up to the entrance way. He saw nothing of John's car. There was a grove of pecan trees between the highway and the house. It was closer to the house than the roadway. He continued creeping forward until he reached the trees. He found a perfect spot in the grove where he could rest his rifle on a low limb with a good view of all of the front windows. With his binoculars, he could see that there was a giant, another big man and a medium size Native American in the living room. The Giant and the smaller guy were holding two people who were handcuffed. One was a woman. John was nowhere in sight. The big guy was giving orders. That was his target. Mac.

He sighted-in with his scope. The big guy was standing fairly still, and very near the window.

"A piece of cake", he thought as his finger settled on the trigger. "Now if he will just stand still for just another few seconds.

CHAPTER SIXTY THREE

May the stars carry your sadness away.
May the flowers fill your heart with beauty.
May hope forever wipe away your tears, and above all,
May silence make you strong.
(Chief Dan George   Salish)

John arrived with no lights and no siren. He turned into the
easement that was the border just outside of Jay's fence. It circled
the whole property. He immediately noticed three cars and
movement of people. It was a bright moonlit night. He was able to
make out Britt's car and Jay's. The third car was a dark sedan fitting
the description of the one used by the Gang. He parked behind some of
Jay's border trees, which blocked the view from the house. He climbed
over the pasture fence and crept noiselessly, as only Indians can do,
toward the rear porch.

Johnnie Wolf had seen the motorcade arrive. He knew that it was
trouble. He made his way to the trap door, threw back the rug and lifted
the trap door. It was difficult getting down and through the hole, the
pain was significant. He had even more difficulty getting the trap door
down due to the pain in trying to raise his arms over his head from a
crouched position. He managed to get it down without it slamming,
but he had to wait a few minutes to catch his breath and let the pain
subside a little. He began a slow and painful crawl toward the back
of the house. The pain from putting all that weight on his arms was

mind numbing. Finally, he was able to reach the back opening in the flashing. As he stuck his head out, he saw John approaching the house. He risked calling softly.

"John, over here, its Johnnie."

"You O.K.?" John whispered.

"I don't know. Jay has a trap door in his closet floor. I almost didn't make it. I think my wounds may be bleeding again. My back feels sticky. They have Britt and Jay in there, handcuffed. Mac has two guys with him. Black Brick Gang members. I don't know how we can help."

"Can you help me any at all? Maybe create a distraction?"

"I'll do what I can." Johnnie said

"I know about where his closet is. I'm going under and come up in his closet. Give me 3 minutes, then come in the back door and see if you can help cover me or at least create a distraction. Watch yourself Johnnie and try not to be a target."

"Let's do it." Johnnie checked his watch.

John checked his watch and went under the house. Johnnie crept slowly and silently up the steps and crouched behind the door. He was feeling weak and dizzy. But that was not going to keep him from doing what he had to do.

John had no trouble finding the trap door. Johnnie had left a trail that he could see with the light from his cell phone. He entered the closet silently and peeking out, saw nothing beyond the bedroom door, but could hear their voices. He inched to the side of the bedroom door and checked his watch. One minute to go. Johnnie stood up and was ready to kick the door open when he heard a loud rifle shot from somewhere on the other side of the house. He kicked the door open and went in.

John heard the shot and saw a cloud of blood spatter explode from Mac's head and he dropped to the floor. The shot had alerted the other two who were focused now on the front and back doors. As the back door was kicked in, Chase fired and Johnnie dropped. John shot Chase, knocking him out the open front door. Lonnie looked confused. Then he roared and started toward John. John's first three shots didn't slow him up. Backing up, he fired three more shots and Lonnie dropped to his hands and knees. Then he began crawling toward John, cursing and roaring. John put one more bullet through the top of his head and Lonnie fell flat as blood began pooling under his head.

John quickly checked Johnnie. It was bad. The bullet entry was in his forehead right at the hairline. There was no exit wound. Then he checked Mac. No pulse, he was dead, from a head wound. John went and untied Jay and Britt. Jay darted out the front to check on Chase. There was blood on the porch, but Chase was gone. Britt gathered up the weapons and John did what he could for Johnnie while calling 911. Both the Creek police and the Sac & Fox police were notified. Britt tagged each weapon with names while being careful not to smudge fingerprints. She included John's and Johnnies along with hers and Jay's.

Within minutes, cruisers and ambulances began showing up. They immediately triaged Johnnie and loaded him to transport him to the hospital in Oklahoma City. He was still alive. The officers began combing the area around the farm. Even with the full moon, there was no sign of a trail or of blood. They knew he was injured and on foot. They also knew he was skilled in survival methods. The officers would spend the night searching. Jay left about midnight and headed for the hospital in the city.

The original report said Johnnie was in very critical condition. He had lost a lot of blood and his brain was starting to swell. He had lapsed into a coma. His body was shutting down. A team of doctors began working on him. Jay stayed. In the early morning hours, a doctor approached the group in the waiting room. It included Jay, John, Britt and the Chiefs from Sac & Fox in Stroud, Creek in Muscogee and Even Choctaw Chief Yellow Feather from Durant. The doctor gave them the grave news.

"I'll tell you the facts as we know them. They apply for right now only and could change." He began. "Your officer is currently in a coma. He has lost a lot of blood. Most of it was in his skull cavity. The bullet entered the skull on his frontal, left side. It skidded and tumbled all the way around the inside of the rear of his skull, finally lodging just above his right eye. Its location made it very easy to remove. However, as it traveled, it took some small and some not so small chunks out of his brain. Our immediate problem other than numerous bleeders, was swelling. We had to remove a large portion of the top of his skull to both do our work, as well as to allow the brain to swell. Such swelling is a natural body reaction to any type of brain trauma.

If he recovers, the section we removed can be replace in a follow-up operation. Meanwhile we are freezing it to keep it viable. The principle word is 'IF'. My experience has been that we have lost patients who had damage even less than his. It may be several days before we can give any more information. The next 24 hours are the most critical. We have to deal with blood loss, shock, potential infection, coma, and then if all goes well, we have to assess any physical or mental capacities impacted by the reduced blood flow, causing a reduced oxygen flow to the brain."

"What does that mean in layman's terms?" asked Jay.

"There could be significant brain damage. How much, we will have to wait and see. There undoubtedly will be some." The doctor left.

The group began to slowly leave, after making sure that they would be notified of any new information about Johnnie. Conversation about the Gang or this evening's action was not appropriate at this time. Jay and Britt continued to wait.

In the wee hours, they were told that he was still in a coma, still extremely critical and they would not even discuss the percent chance of him making it through the next 24 hours.

"Look", Britt said, "I'll stay here and keep you informed. You have to notify the Task Force and deal with telling Sarah. I will report the results to my new boss. I expect he will quietly and politely, frcak out."

"Thanks, keep me posted even if there is no change."

"Will do. And by the way, your little delay tumbles at the house, probably saved both our lives."

"Nah. Just clumsy."

It took quite some time to notify all of the Task Force members. Jay did this with phone calls rather than by text message. All had questions. When that task was complete he turned his attention to Sarah. She had no clue what had just happened, but she was so overwrought, that she did not show up for work. She spent the night at John's with the comforting care of John's wife. Jay had earlier talked to John and asked him to delay any conversation about the night's action until he was there. He drove to John's house. He did not elaborate on the gory details of blood and wounds. Just the basic overview. He credited her with saving a lot of people's lives by her conversation with John.

"And what about Mac?" She asked, trembling at the probable answer.

"Sarah, I am sorry to say that he was armed, as were the other Gang members. There were shots fired and Mac died. Johnnie Wolf is in the hospital and may not make it."

Jay had heard tales of people turning white, but this is the first time he had actually seen it. It was as if all the blood had drained out of her head. Apparently, it had for a moment. She fainted. John and his wife helped her into a bed. She was to remain there for a couple of days. She barely ate or drank. Britt called regularly, but the report on Johnnie was always the same.

Britt had suggested that a schedule of some kind be set up to visit with Johnnie's daughter, "Blossom". Jay was first on the schedule. It was his job to let her know why her father was unable to visit right now. He dreaded this more than the visit to Sarah. He drove to the hospital. He had no idea what to expect whenever he was shown into her room. Or what to expect when he told her about her father, or what her current physical condition might be. He had never had a chance to meet her. He stopped at the gift shop and picked up a small plant with several small flowers. Blossoms. Also a small teddy bear dressed in an Indian costume. When he walked in, there was the usual assortment of hospital equipment. Hanging bags with tubes, but the person in the bed was not usual. A little frail, but absolutely beautiful.

"Hi Blossom". He said quietly.

"Hi Mr. Nation. Well, I am glad to finally meet you. My dad talks about you all the time."

"All good, I hope." He said. "How did you know it was me?"

"Are you kidding me, I expected you to fly in with a red cape streaming behind you. You are about the most special person, I think I have ever known. And now I know you in person. Dad has shown me many pictures of you and him doing stuff together. Please have a seat and tell me all about how you're doing. I do hope you are quite well."

"Actually, I am. And a lot of it is because of your dad. If anyone needs a red cape, it's him." He said, beginning to enjoy this conversation.

What a bright, energetic and totally captivating young lady.

"Well, I know he would say that he's just an ordinary person, but he'd be wrong. Which he rarely is, mind you. He is my hero." She said.

"Actually Blossom, that's why I am here. I came to verify that he is a hero. In fact, last night he saved me and an FBI agent's life. Now, that is about as heroic as you can get."

"No way. Really?"

"Yes. Cross my heart."

"When can I see him? I want to know all about it." She was squirming with excitement.

"First, let me introduce you to a new friend. Now he may look like an ordinary stuffed bear, but he is not. I have officially deputized him in the State Of Oklahoma special police, with all the rights and privileges, except for the right to carry a pistol. It might be too heavy for him."

"Will he have a badge?" She asked.

Jay thought to himself," Oh. Oh. My bad."

"Of course he will." Jay said. "Maybe I can have another officer drop it by and pin it on him either this afternoon or tomorrow. O.K.?"

"Yes. That would be special. Can Dad bring it?"

"Well, I know when you save someone's life, it creates a whole lot of extra paperwork. And with two lives saved, you just can't imagine the stacks of forms you have to fill out."

"My Dad hates paperwork. I tell him all the time. 'Now Dad, I hate schoolwork, but sometimes you just have to do what you have to do. Like it or not.'"

"I can tell you are a great positive influence on your Dad. He is the nicest person I know. And we have been friends for a long, long time." Jay said. "If it's O.K., let's cut him a little slack so that he can get it all taken care of. Meanwhile, I'll make sure that someone checks on you every day and reports back to him on how you are doing. That would make him very happy. And they can also report to him whatever you want him to know. Does that work for you?" He asked.

"Sure. Can we start right now?" She had a bright smiling look on her face.

"Absolutely. What would you like for me to report today?"

"Two things. I have a neat new friend, whose name I have not yet decided, but it has to be a Creek name, since he is an Indian bear. Second, That I love him more today than yesterday, and less than I will tomorrow. And therefore, I am totally in favor of him getting his paperwork done, even if it means that I will have to miss seeing him for a little while. And also I want you to give him my hug."

With that, she threw her little arms around his neck and gave Jay a big hug.

"Now, I am a big, tough, rough, guy." Jay argued to himself. "So the moisture in my eyes is obviously some kind of allergy floating around in this hospital."

He thanked her and made his exit before the allergy got any worse. He understood now, that Johnnie was the richest man he knew.

The media circus, which had been bad up to now, had become even more so, now that the reports started to go out. The department had to contend with National TV News, newspaper reporters, media from foreign countries, Radio stations, Tabloids (who, of course, got it all wrong), even people wanting to buy book and movie rights.

Britt, John and Jay did what they could to paint Johnnie as the real hero. They attributed the relationship he had with Mac, only as gathering information to be used for Mac's desire to write a book. His slate was wiped clean. The Governor called about giving him a Citizenship Award. They explained that Johnnie was still in critical condition in the hospital and was having no visitors. But that he would gladly accept it when he was more fully recovered. That drove the media nuts. Security even had to arrest a reporter who had donned a doctor's outfit to try to sneak into Johnnie's room. The guy was lucky the guard posted there, didn't shoot him.

Through it all, Johnnie remained in a coma. It took a week for the doctors to begin saying he 'might' pull through and in another week he began to come out of his coma. The big question on everyone's mind, but not discussed, was the issue of brain damage. Even the doctors didn't know. It boiled down to "Time will tell".

CHAPTER SIXTY FOUR

I see a time of seven generations
when all the colors of mankind
will gather under the sacred tree of life
and the whole earth will become one circle again.
(Chief Crazy Horse   Lakota)

Brit was smiling.

"Jay, I thought it might be appropriate to celebrate the case closure, by letting me cook a nice German/American meal for us. What do you think?"

"I think that would be great. When?"

"How about tomorrow night?"

"Fine, what can I bring?"

"Two things."

"O.K. Shoot. Not literally, of course."

"Just bring an empty stomach and your most gentlemanly manners. For a cop, that is."

"I accept and will bring both. I can be a virtual Saint when I choose to be so."

"Right. That'll be the day. Tomorrow at 7:00."

"O.K. It's a D … a great opportunity. Thank you."

"No big deal", He thought to himself. "I've eaten there before."

There were still some things about her that he didn't like. Sure, she is a great cop, 100% focused, outspoken and plain spoken. (Providing you own a dictionary). At least you always know where she stands on things and she doesn't hold back anything, just for the purpose of being polite. Of course, she is, without a doubt, the most hard-headed cop, or woman, he thought he have ever met. And someday, he intended to tell her that. Maybe. She also is very attractive, whether she likes it or not. After all, "plain spoken", works both ways.

Jay showed up at exactly 7:00. One thing he had learned from her was about being prompt. For him that was a pretty good improvement, he had to admit. He was not in uniform. He decided to wear his Sunday-best. Not to impress her. No-way. It just made him feel good to wear it to supper sometimes. Although he couldn't quite remember when the last time was.

He knocked, she opened the door and he couldn't even mumble anything intelligible. She was wearing a very attractive long dress and her hair, which he had thought was permanently cemented in a knot, was loose and lying on her bare shoulders. Instead of mumbling something stupid, he just stood there.

"Would you like to come in, or do you prefer eating in the hallway?"

There is no possible answer to that kind of question without totally sounding like a dork.

He walked in. There was a delicious smell drifting from the kitchen.

"Cat got you tongue, '*Indian*'?"

"No, '*Brittini*', um hello. I just was surprised to see that you actually have hair and shoulders. I mean… Wait. That didn't come out right."

"Linebackers have hair and shoulders Officer Nation. Have a seat at the table, supper is ready."

After his disastrous start, supper actually went rather well. They both agreed that although it took considerable effort, they had managed to work out a partner-like relationship that worked well for both of them.

"Of course, it was probably harder for you than me." He said as a courteous gesture, fishing for a similar compliment in return.

"You're right." That was all she said.

Apparently Britt was "back in the building". One more point for her. Not that he was keeping score, or anything. When you get past 100 it becomes meaningless.

"I guess you will be heading back to the marble halls of D.C. soon."

Then she dropped her bomb.

"No, actually that is not true. I have been asked to consider being the replacement for Major Mac McCall. If I decide to accept, I will be moving to Oklahoma City and you, Officer Nation, will be working directly for me."

He was dumbfounded. "What is my happy little world coming to?" He almost said out loud.

"Britt, you know of course, that you will be working closely with not only the Chiefs of the various nations and various mayors, but you will also be working much more closely with Butthead."

"But I won't be working '*for*' him." She smiled sweetly. "Besides, it would be a refreshing and welcome change from my current boss, who is 10% law enforcement and 90% politician. Maybe I could presume upon you to help me find a place and teach me a little about farming and ranching?"

That did it. He now knew that this was only a nightmare and he would soon wake up. She laid her hand on his arm and said,

"Jay, I have decided that since we are probably going to be working together, I guess we need to at least be civil to each other. And you did help save my life, although I was already working on my own plan to get loose."

He was only hearing parts of what she said. His arm hair was standing at attention. This was the first time she had ever touched him. Never even a firm handshake. He didn't know what to say or do. He coughed and mustered up what he thought John Two Feathers would say.

"Yup!"

After supper, he helped with the kitchen scullery duties, which were much easier than at the ranch. He didn't even own a dishwasher. *He was* the dishwasher. When they moved to the living room for coffee and cake, he stood for a long while, studying her paintings. She used strong, bold brush strokes where strength was a desired effect, exactly what one would expect if they knew her. Yet everywhere were the small, light strokes where exactness and detail were expected. She painted like she was. An enigma.

"You into paintings?" she asked quietly.

"No, not really. I never really thought about it. For some reason, these are relaxing to look at. They are beautiful."

"I know you want to ask, so go ahead."

"I see the signatures. A relative?"

"No, me."

"I can almost see my ranch in them. When I sit on my porch and look out over my spread, it relaxes me."

"That's why I paint. In our line of work, it's needed."

"Well, if you ever want to paint a little bit of heaven on earth, feel free to come paint my place."

"I'll think about that." she said."

"Britt, you asked me once if my unusual name had a story behind it. It does, and I promised you I would tell it to you, before you went back to your Washington halls of justice. I would be glad to share that little bit of me with you now, if you'd like."

"O.K."

"But it has to be a swap. You must first tell me something about yourself."

Her face clouded. "Jay, I am sure, by now, you know I am a very private person."

"I know that, and I admire that in you. It doesn't have to be something all that personal. Tell me something about your job."

"Can I tell you about why I am considering leaving the FBI? In confidence?"

"Absolutely."

"My new boss told me that I had not done my job with this investigation.

I told him that he was just still angry about our disagreement years ago.

He said I should think seriously about whether I was cut out for the job.

I told him I thought he was carrying his grudge, years beyond what any reasonable, intelligent and professional person would.

He said 'Britt, it's like what the old saying says. All things come to he who waits'. I knew at that second, what I would do."

"Now it's your turn." She said.

They settled-in on the big couch while Jay told his story.

CHAPTER SIXTY FIVE

**I am no more proud of my career as an athlete
than I am of the fact that I am a direct descendant of
that noble warrior Chief Blackhawk.**
(Jim Thorpe, 2 Gold Medal Olympian, First President of NFL   Sac & Fox)

The official installation ceremony was very well attended. Surprisingly, both the Governor and Andy Jernigan, the Governor's Liaison Assistant on Crime and Indian Affairs, were there. Chief Yellow Feather, Chief Mary Gray Eyes, the Little Bird cousins who were now permanently assigned to them, and a whole "gaggle" of other chiefs and Law Enforcement personnel, were also there. Jay was heartened to see Johnnie Wolf there. He was done with his wheelchair and was on crutches and a skull protection helmet, since his skull had not yet been made whole again. There were numerous photographers, news people and TV cameras. The kinds of things you would expect when the Governor was involved. The Governor made a short congratulatory speech with pointed appreciation for the job she had recently done. When Andy took the podium, for the benefit of the media, he pulled out a tablet page and began to read.

"Without regard for her personal safety, she, with the help of many of you here, managed to do the following: The Gang broken up and either killed or incarcerated. Their headquarters demolished. Their weapons confiscated. A Casino criminal conspiracy stopped and its operators jailed. A murderer caught and prosecuted. Three other murderers on

Death Row. Sadly, the arrest of an internal illegal conspiracy among our own law enforcement family. She is truly, in my mind and the Governor's, an equal to the famed Elliot Ness, who to the uninformed was the person who put away Murder Incorporated's Al Capone. Britt is our assurance that never again will Oklahoma be faced with a home-grown Murder-for-Hire operation. All told, 25 criminals taken off our streets. We are honored and gratified that she has agreed to take the position of 'Director, of the State & Indian Nation Liaison Force'. Let's give her a round of well-deserved applause."

There was thunderous applause. The Governor stepped up and put his arm around her for the cameras. Jay noticed her stiffen. After pictures, there was cake and snacks, and a steady stream of well-wishers, which Britt handled, bravely, by clutching a plate in one hand and a drink in the other. Apparently, her own version of a shield. When they were finally alone in her new office, Jay began.

"Britt, I have to say, you handled the Ceremony and Reception very well. One point I thought was interesting, was how well you …"

"Officer Nation, if you say one word about the Governor's hug, I will put you in the hospital. And don't think for a minute I can't do it."

Jay laughed a huge roaring laugh. Then, so did Britt. A "real" laugh.

CHAPTER SIXTY SIX

**We must Protect the forests for our children,
grandchildren, and children yet to be born.
We must protect the forests for those who can't speak
for themselves such as the birds, animals, fish and trees.**
(Chief Qwatsinas   Nuxalt)

J
ay swung smoothly from the saddle and let the reins just drop.
He knew that Hank would not wander away but would just stay
and graze there by the stream side while Jay enjoyed the beautiful
day. Fall was Jay's favorite time on the ranch. Blue sky, tree leaves in
yellows, reds and golds, painted as if from God's own palette. A light
breeze creating the white noise that reminded him of the important
things in life and washed away the negatives and distractions. The hot
summer days were only a distant memory that the fresh scent of nature
helped to hide or at least made to seem insignificant. This was the time
and place where he wanted to be.

He was laying on a gentle grassy slope that continued to rise to the
tops of the hills bordering the back of his property. He felt at peace. He
began to take a mental inventory of the events of the past year.

Blossom Wolf had become a virtual family member of three separate
Native American Nations. She named her bear, Little Nokose, which
means "Bear" in the Muscogee/Creek language.

John Two Feathers was given the Federal reward of $100,000 for
the capture of the leader of the FBI's most wanted gang leader. He sent

½ to Sarah Blackhorse who had now retired, sold her home and moved to Colorado to be closer to some of her family.

The Media's coverage of Johnnie Wolf's injuries and his daughter's Leukemia went viral and donations began pouring in. Primarily from various Law Enforcement groups and individual officers around the U.S. There was talk of movie and book deals as well. Johnnie will never be able to work again and won't have to. He is O.K. with just walking and talking and taking care of his beautiful daughter Blossom and her new best friend Little Nokose.

Mr. A. Butler Hedstrom, Mayor of Oklahoma City, had adopted a manner of dress appropriate to his high station. Western-Cut suits and custom boots. Although, the Garbage-can lid cowboy hat remained. Fortunately, he only wears it outdoors now.

They had found a record of the rental car used by Vito. In it was a gray wig and some old lady clothes. There was no record of a priest or little old lady flying out of Oklahoma to New Jersey and the only passenger that they couldn't find was a red-headed cowgirl who they felt could not be their suspect. Jay had his doubts.

Dutch was convicted of several charges and The Beer Shack was bulldozed.

Honey went to jail, also, for parole violations. Perhaps her dependency on drugs can be fixed.

Jim Coyote moved to Texas and rumor had it that he opened a new bar called "Rachel's". Jay would maybe visit him someday. Jim was a good man.

His new boss was making progress, Britt will always be Britt, but that was OK with Jay. He liked the way she did her job. They had worked out a good working relationship and she had expressed an interest in using his farm and animals as painting subjects when time permitted. They had made some forays together into finding her some property for a homestead.

He had not had much time to ride Hank the past few months. But that was probably going to change now that he had offered and she had accepted, happily, his offer to go riding on Sundays. Britt on Butch and Jay on Hank.

He had even been able to put the thought of Chase Stormcloud in its proper place in the grand scheme of things. Not forgotten, but probably never again a reason for concern.

Life was good again.

EPILOGUE

Brick Storm saved the national newspaper article so that he could pull it out occasionally and read it, in order to maintain his focus. It was one of the small pleasures in life that he treasured. He built many dreams around it. As he finished reading it again, he folded it and put it in its little plastic envelope and slipped it into his billfold. The words that he wanted to remember explicitly, were the words the article had published from State Liaison Officer Jay Nation, way across the country in Oklahoma. Officer Nation had stated,

"There are 3 on death row, one dead, and unfortunately one escaped and is still at large, their leader, Chase Stormcloud. We should remember the old saying. 'Leopards don't change their spots'. We'll see him again."

The mail clerk stepped in to deliver some mail.

"Here you go Mr. Storm. Looks like mostly junk mail."

"Thanks friend."

"Say, I mentioned you to my friend the other day about how nice you were to everybody and a pleasure to work with. And he said 'where did that name Brick come from?

Is it a nickname?' I told him I'd never thought about it. How did you get that name, is it one of those family names that gets passed down?"

Brick laughed, "Probably will be someday, but no, I got it the simple way. It's a nickname that my folks gave me when I was still a tadpole. They say it suits me. Head hard as a brick. Brick sounds better than stubborn mule."

They both laughed.

Brick had been on his job for a little over 2 months now. He was liked by all. His boss told him that his good points included "Considerate, Smart, Flexible and Helpful." He would be getting a raise in his next paycheck. He wanted to live up to his recommendations from 2 previous employers.

One said he was "Hardworking, Friendly and very impressive." The other one was also complimentary, saying he was "Clean, Orderly, almost Military-like and will go far."

Unfortunately, both companies were now out of business, but he was able to get the letters anyway, somehow. They were Xerox copies. One letter was in block letters, one in script. Both, interestingly, were done by left handed persons. "I guess the world is full of lefties like me", he chuckled to himself. Both were barely readable.

He kept a Spartan office with no desk or wall decorations. The only exception was the odd paperweight for his inbox. They would sometimes kid him about it and he said it was heavy and squashed paperwork down so that he didn't appear so far behind.

When asked about where it came from, he simply told whoever was asking, that it was a gift from a friend who was a Native American cop, who had been in on that big bust in Oklahoma. Brick said he had done some private investigation for the cop, Pro-Bono, and this was his thank-you gift. Brick Storm, picked up the brick and turned it over and smiled. On the bottom in tiny white letters on the black brick, almost too small to read were the two words that he, himself, had written.

"Indian Nation"

"Soon, Jay". He thought. "Soon"